FOREVER AFTER

"Davan, it's Jova. Can I come up?"

Jova? He pushed the button, buzzing her inside the building. He tossed his baseball cap on the hook beside the door and ruffled his hair to life. No time to change out of the overalls. He opened the door and stood in the hallway, waiting for Jova to come off the elevator.

Jova walked to him like a vision in a dream. She wore burgundy shorts with a matching blouse, the V cut giving a modest hint of her cleavage. Snappy sandals completed the outfit. Her silky black hair was parted down the middle and two long braids hung to her shoulders. She carried a large straw bag on her shoulder, another in her hand. She waltzed up to him and dropped the bags on the floor. "This is my second visit today. You weren't home earlier."

Sassy, he thought.

"Davan, I did the wrong thing."

He crossed his arms over his chest and leaned against the doorjamb.

"I don't want you to be mad at me."

He liked where this was going. "Why?"

"Why?" Jova shifted her weight from one foot to the other. "Why? Because we have a good friendship and I need all the friends I can get right now."

"Friendship?"

"Well, yeah." She couldn't hold his gaze.

"I want to be more than your friend." He stepped forward, wrapped his arm around her waist, and pulled her against his body. He pressed her close, erasing her resistance. He lifted her chin in his palm, lowered his head, and kissed the corner of her mouth.

BOOK YOUR PLACE ON OUR WEBSITE AND MAKE THE ARABESQUE ROMANCE CONNECTION!

We've created a customized website just for our very special Arabesque readers, where you can get the inside scoop on everything that's going on with Arabesque romance novels.

When you come online, you'll have the exciting opportunity to:

- View covers of upcoming books

- Learn about our future publishing schedule (listed by publication month and author)

- Find out when your favorite authors will be visiting a city near you

- Search for and order backlist books

- Check out author bios and background information

- Send e-mail to your favorite authors

- Join us in weekly chats with authors, readers and other guests

- Get writing guidelines

- AND MUCH MORE!

Visit our website at
http://www.arabesquebooks.com

Forever After

KIMBERLEY WHITE

BET Publications, LLC
http://www.bet.com
http://www.arabesquebooks.com

ARABESQUE BOOKS are published by

BET Publications, LLC
c/o BET BOOKS
One BET Plaza
1900 W Plaza NE
Washington, DC 20018-1211

All Kensington Titles, Imprints, and Distributed Lines are available at special quantity discounts for bulk purchases for sales promotions, premiums, fund-raising, and educational or institutional use. Special book excerpts or customized printings can also be created to fit specific needs. For details, write or phone the office of the Kensington special sales manager: Kensington Publishing Corp., 850 Third Avenue, New York, NY 10022, attn: Special Sales Department, Phone: 1-800-221-2647.

First Printing: May 2004
10 9 8 7 6 5 4 3 2 1

Printed in the United States of America

This book is dedicated to my son,
Christopher Charles Judson,
who knows more about cars than I ever will.

ACKNOWLEDGMENTS

Wow! Who would ever have thought I'd have gotten this far in the publishing business? Don't tell the folks at BET, but I would have been happy with one novel to sit on my mantel and marvel at. I know I would never have been able to do this without the support of my readers, and I thank you. Keep those e-mails and letters coming! You inspire me.

The best fans ever: Leon and Geneva White (my parents), Eleanor Lewis (my grandmother), Leonette, Regina, Leon Jr. (the siblings); my sister-in-law, Christina; my entourage: Stephanie Williams and David White; my niece/daughter: Tasha Williams; shout-out to: Tiffany and Elijah, and the second generation of nieces and nephews; to all my aunts, uncles, and cousins: they keep track of me and never let me forget where I come from.

The usual suspects (writers who take time from their craft to help me with mine): The Three Wise Men; Karen White-Owens; Angela Wynn; Natalie Dunbar; and Rainelle Burton.

To the one who has taken it upon himself to teach me the true meaning of passion, you're in my heart always. (You'll thank him too when you read the next book!)

This book would not have been written if not for Eric Jerome Dickey. It's very simple, without him I would never have even considered writing professionally. He has supported me at every turn, never becoming annoyed because I was asking another question, or seeking more advice. Support this brother not only because he is a dynamic writer, but because he is a good person with a big heart.

Chapter 1

"Your Honor, this is a frivolous lawsuit. I let Herman borrow my car to go to work—"

"What was the nature of your relationship with Mr. Norman?" The judge peered at Jova Parker over gold-rimmed glasses. She looked overworked and downright tired of wasting her time presiding over trivial legal arguments. Jova had hoped having her case heard by a woman would be to her advantage, the sisters-who-have-been-done-wrong bond at work. But with the stern expression marring the judge's face, Jova realized she was in big trouble.

Embarrassed, she cleared her throat. "We were involved."

Herman felt the need to jump in and clarify. "I was her man."

Jova threw him a look. He resembled Taye Diggs having one of his better days, tall, dark, and handsome, with a cool swagger and a commanding voice. Jova had fallen for him faster than Kmart stock. There had been a time he could control her with the edgy authority of his voice.

Jova rolled her eyes, sending a look of disdain his way. Those days were over. "Like I was saying, I let him borrow my *new* Lincoln to go to work. Next thing I know, I'm getting a call from Herman saying he's in the ER. He's in the ER, and my car is totaled. I can't see why he would think it's my responsibility to pay his medical bills."

The judge turned her stern gaze on Herman. "Maybe he can explain it to us both."

Herman shifted his weight, straightening his tie and going into schmooze mode. "Your Honor." Oh, he was using *the voice*, too? "Your Honor, Ms. Parker lent me her car to go to work."

"We've established that, Mr. Norman. Explain to me why I should order her to cover your medical bills."

He smiled, refocusing. Jova knew from experience Herman could make an argument in his favor with the tiniest thread of evidence. "The accident was not my fault. The other driver slammed into me."

"It wasn't my fault!" Jova interjected. "I wasn't even in the car."

The judge slammed her gavel. "Ms. Parker."

The burly bailiff shifted his attention away from the computer screen, and onto her.

Jova's lips snapped shut.

"Continue, Mr. Norman."

Satisfaction with this small victory made Herman more confident with his argument. "The accident wasn't my fault. The other driver was uninsured with a suspended license. Ms. Parker's insurance won't cover my expenses because I'm not on her policy. With all those facts, Your Honor, I feel Ms. Parker should be responsible." He smiled, as if saying, *Nah, nah, nah, nah, nah.*

The judge peered at him for a long moment, as if actually considering his logic. It had to be the Taye Diggs thing. It was all so ridiculous. The judge looked at her bailiff; then she looked at Jova. She was staring at Herman when she said, "You've got to be kidding me."

Jova left the courtroom thankful the judge had not been as easily charmed as she had been. Herman ran after her, trying to mend their relationship. What a nerve. He had totaled her car, never offered to help pay the outstanding balance, and actually sued her to pay his medical bills. She'd seen the bills. They were inflated. Five thousand dollars for casting a broken leg? Pain and suffering? She was the one in pain from a broken heart, and suffering the embarrassment of her stupidity.

I should have sued him! Jova thought. *Well, enough is enough. After this little incident, I'll never date again.* The last string of men she'd been involved with were "Hermans" in one way or the other.

A couple sprinted past Jova up the stairs into the courthouse, hand in hand. The man turned to see if his girlfriend was keeping up with his long strides. The woman smiled, revealing a strong bond between them. Just the sight of a man showing the slightest bit of caring sent Jova over the edge. She was tired of the *what can you do for me?* mentality of the men she'd dated lately. Whatever happened to chivalry? Were there any men left in the world who believed they should be the breadwinners? Had the word *housewife* been removed from the dictionary? She'd never been the helpless female who had to depend on a man, but nothing beat a good-hearted, strong black man. Despite her brave declaration to never date again, she still longed for a loving relationship with a righteous man. Her chest tightened as she watched the couple go through the courthouse doors. She blew out a puff of air. "Better get used to being alone. I don't think my heart can take one more crack."

Jova cursed Herman again when she slid behind the wheel of her 1986 Ford Mustang. Fully loaded, it couldn't compare with the luxury of the Lincoln she'd sacrificed in the name of infatuation. And to beat it all, her finances were so tight she had to make a payment plan with Ben, the neighborhood used car salesman. Five hundred dollars up front, fifty dollars a month, and a free salon visit for his mom every two weeks until the car was paid off. "I bought a used car on layaway," Jova grumbled.

Negotiating away her salon services was a definite no-no, the beauty shop being her only source of income. She'd taken every cent of her mother's life insurance money and sunk it into Tresses & Locks. She had a steady stream of customers, but she was nowhere near financial stability. Lingerie sales in the salon helped to boost profits. Women in Detroit wanted their hair tight, and their bodies dressed just right. Rich or poor, skimping on getting your hair coiffed was never an option.

Jova started out of the parking lot. Herman appeared in her rearview, waving his arms frantically. Proud his looks no longer affected her, she flipped on the radio. He did know how to wear a suit though. She began singing along with Macy Gray, trying her best to ignore him. She knew what lay beneath the nice suit and debonair appearance—a user. The lawsuit had been the turning point, her wake-up call. Herman Norman was no longer her concern. She glanced in the rearview. "All that gone to waste." She pulled away and left him standing at the curb with his fists digging in his waist, staring after her.

She eased onto the freeway, trying to soothe her nerves as she hurried to the shop. It was a little windy, but a sunny August day. The temperature hovered around eighty degrees. The shop would be packed with women wanting to look good for possibly the last nice weekend of the summer. You never could predict Detroit weather. People said, "If you don't like the weather, wait a minute. It'll change." She maneuvered a pothole, reciting another local sentiment, "There are only two seasons in Michigan: winter and construction."

Jova checked the time as she exited the freeway. She hated running late. All day long she would feel off-kilter. She could still make her two o'clock perm and cut if she stepped on it. The shop would someday make her a bundle, but right now she had to build her clientele one person at a time.

She and Dawn were licensed cosmetologists. They'd met briefly in school; Dawn graduated the semester she began. Their paths crossed later at a trade show. Jova told her about the new salon she was opening and gave her a card. A few months afterward, Dawn contacted her for a job. Spending long hours together in the salon, they'd become friends. Dawn was a master with short hairstyles. She'd invented a curl-patterning technique that stylists across the city were trying to mimic, but were having little luck.

Lisa held the only manicurist spot at Tresses & Locks. A single parent of a darling three-year-old boy, she supported her family with a devoted clientele. She worked hard to fight the single mother stereotypes. Maintaining her sense of humor through all her personal crises, Lisa was the one you wanted around in an emergency. She knew things about burns and cuts only a mother could know. When discussions in the salon became heated debates, Lisa stepped in to reestablish the peace.

Mimi earned extra money as part-time shampoo girl, working for tips. Having come from Nigeria, she attended the University of Michigan, dividing her courses between the Ann Arbor and Dearborn campuses. She kept the salon informed of new trends with the young up-and-coming. She firmly supported affirmative action, using her time at the law school to make a difference in the world of politics. Lisa often joked Mimi was the salon's mascot.

Finding, and keeping, a man to fill the barber position was proving to be difficult. Three had come and gone in the past six months. With the strong personalities of the females working in the salon, finding a man secure enough to muscle his way into the inner circle would take some doing. No, the men didn't stick around Tresses & Locks, but the sign was still hanging in the window.

Jova pulled into her personal parking space at Tresses & Locks. There were several cars, but since the lot was positioned on the east side of the building, she couldn't see how many customers were inside.

The personal parking space was necessary because she lived in the studio apartment above the three-chair salon. A flight of stairs made of fifteen steps—she'd counted them the first day she had to haul groceries up—led to the tiny landing at her front door. The studio was small, but cozy. Working and living in the neighborhood she'd grown up in made her feel secure. Especially since her mother was deceased and she had no family to speak of. She checked the time again; a few minutes to spare. If she hurried, she could change out of the suit she'd worn to court before her two o'clock arrived.

* * *

Davan Underwood's eyes zoomed in on a heavenly sight standing in the parking lot across the street. In a hurry, she dropped her papers and the brisk August wind took them swirling around the lot. She dropped to the ground next to a gray Mustang. Her round behind saluted the air. The most beautiful woman he had seen since moving to Detroit groped at the pavement, gathering up the papers.

Davan snatched the rag from his back pocket, wiping grease from his hands. The woman had retrieved the last sheet of paper, but was still groping the pavement. He watched her a moment longer before calling out, "I'll be right back." One of the mechanics grunted his acknowledgment over the buzzing of power tools.

He jogged across the street, keeping his eyes on the seductive movements of her bottom. "Hi. Do you need some help?"

The woman looked up at him from down on her hands and knees. A position he'd like to explore under more intimate circumstances. Her brown eyes were as large as quarters with Asian exotica. "I kicked my keys underneath the car."

"Let me help you." Davan knelt next to the Mustang and fished for the keys. The woman stood up, brushing her hands together. His eyes went to her shapely legs and red-painted toes. The black skirt ended well before her knees, giving him a pleasurable peek at her thighs.

"Here you go." Davan stood and dropped the keys into her palm.

Long, shiny jet-black hair curled in loose wisps danced on her shoulders. "Thank you." Her top lip was full, the bottom thin. Both were painted dark red. The only mark on her picture-perfect face was a mole next to the bridge of her nose.

"I'm Davan Underwood. I work at the auto shop across the street."

"Jova Parker, this is my shop, Tresses & Locks."

Davan had trouble taking his eyes away from hers. The building's exterior fit in well with the other businesses scattered on the small block. The two-story brick building had been painted stark white, and a sign announcing its name was spelled out in pink neon lights above the door. He'd noticed earlier that windowpanes monopolized the front and allowed him a clear view inside from the garage. "Looks nice. Have you been there long?"

"The salon's been open six months. I've owned the building almost a year." She grabbed the stack of file folders from the roof of the car. "I've never seen you at the garage before. I thought I knew everyone in this neighborhood."

"Moved to Detroit not long ago."

"I'm sure you'll like it here. I don't mean to be rude, but I'm late."

"Oh, I understand."

She tossed her keys in the air. "I owe you one." She turned and hurried away.

Davan called after her, "Maybe you could help me get acquainted with the city."

Jova walked backward as she spoke to him. "Where are you from?"

"Utah."

She smiled and Davan felt sure he would hit the pavement headfirst.

"I don't know anyone from Utah. I'd be happy to show you around Detroit."

He eagerly accepted her offer. "Maybe I can stop in at closing sometime?"

"Please do." She gave him the killer smile again. "Gotta go."

In town three months and already he'd met the woman of his dreams. Man, she was beautiful. Gracious and feminine, too. Davan liked women who pampered themselves, dressed in beautiful clothes, and fussed over their hair. Walking into the bathroom and finding a counter stocked full of creams and lotions turned him on. In his experience, high-maintenance women usually weren't attracted to blue-collar men who worked with their hands.

He watched Jova hurry inside the shop. She could be an exception. Remembering her on hands and knees, he knew he'd definitely be knocking at Jova Parker's door soon.

Chapter 2

Jova wrapped the plastic cape around her two o'clock's shoulders, fastening it at the neck. "Sorry to keep you waiting, Marie. I had to change out of my suit."

"Don't worry about it, darling." She flipped through the pages of a magazine. "I don't have anywhere to go but home."

Jova used a tongue blade to stir the permanent mixture to a creamy white.

"Dawn," Marie said, "today's lottery day."

"That's right!" Turning away from the customer in her chair, Dawn retrieved the old Ragu spaghetti sauce jar. "Who's in?" She walked the small shop, holding the jar out for each of the ladies to place her dollar inside. "Lisa?"

"Count me in. I feel lucky again this month." Lisa stopped rearranging her nail polish tray long enough to dig a dollar out of her tip jar.

Dawn crossed the room and held the jar out to Jova.

"I'm out."

The women in the salon groaned collectively. They prodded and encouraged until Jova agreed to drop her dollar into the lottery jar.

"You know this is crazy, don't you?" Jova moaned.

"A man lottery. Who came up with this bright idea anyway?"

Marie closed her magazine with a snap. "My great-grandmother, that's who. And it's worked through all the generations for the women in my family. With that attitude, you might need to stuff twenty dollars in the jar."

"Ladies, ladies," Lisa said from her corner of the shop. "I'll start it off."

Dawn grabbed a sheet of paper and a pen. "Go 'head."

"Employed."

"You always start off with that," Dawn said, scribbling the word. She ripped off the corner of the paper, folded it, and tossed it into the jar. "Next."

The women in the room called out one-word descriptions of the man of their dreams as Dawn added them to the lottery jar. According to Marie's great-grandmother, verbalizing and recording the qualities would bring the man into their lives. Tresses & Locks had put a different spin on it, adding monetary gain to the lottery for the woman whose dream man did come. They would reevaluate their dating status in a month, and the woman having found the man closest to resembling the man described would take the cash. No winner, the lottery would roll into the next month.

"Gawd, don't you people have any imagination?" Dawn griped after writing down qualities that dealt with physical attributes and income. "Go, Jova."

She blew out a puff of air, smoothing the perm into Marie's hair. "Well, *if* I were looking, I'd want a protective, caring man who worshipped me."

Dawn scribbled the words and placed them in the Ragu jar. "Protective. Caring. Whipped."

The women laughed.

"I didn't say whipped," Jova defended.

"What would Mr. Perfect look like?" Lisa asked.

"Handsome."

"Be more specific."

"Hmmm." Jova felt herself being sucked into the silly game. "Dark and clean shaven with good teeth. A nice body with killer thighs and muscular arms."

"With veins running up and down them?" Lisa asked.

"Yes." Jova laughed.

"I hear ya, girl!"

Marie broke in. "Did you get all that, Dawn?"

"Every word."

"Good. Jova, I'm burning something fierce. Wash this perm out, now!"

Hours later, Jova and Dawn sat side by side in their chairs at the empty salon. Jova had chosen the soft pinks and greens to decorate the shop because of their calming effect. Green swirly wallpaper bordered the ceilings. The walls were pale pink, picked up by the three burgundy shop chairs and the capes with *Tresses & Locks* etched across the front. Ceiling fans countered the heat from the dryers. Aqua carpeting covered the floor where the lingerie racks were displayed. Lately, she'd been considering adding an aquarium with huge exotic fish.

"I had a good day today," Dawn said. "Here's your fifty percent. Three hundred dollars."

Absently, Jova rearranged the presidents' faces in the same direction.

"So, tell me what happened at court," Dawn said.

"The judge agreed the lawsuit was frivolous, and she dismissed it."

Dawn examined her hair in the mirror spanning the wall of the salon. She plucked at her short curls, as she often did when in deep thought. After a while she asked, "Did Herman wear a suit?"

"Uh-huh."

This got her attention. She stopped fiddling with her curls and turned her chair to face Jova. "Did he look good?"

"Fine."

Dawn shook her head, making a sound of disgust. She jumped down from her chair and started cleaning her workstation. "You won. Why do you look so down?"

"Herman followed me out of the courthouse *pleading* with me to get back with him. I couldn't believe it." She picked up a brush and whipped it through her hair. Maybe all stylists did their best thinking while fussing with their hair. "My track record with choosing men hasn't been all that great. I'm going to take a dating break until I get the salon off the ground."

"Now you know the minute you say that, Mr. Right will walk into your life. You're just feeling down because Herman looked so good today."

"He did look good. The Taye Diggs mojo was working. I thought he had snagged the judge for a minute."

"Forget Herman." She faced Jova, smile blooming. "I've got the cure."

"No!" Jova laughed.

"I know what you need." Dawn used the remote to turn the stereo on. She rotated the CDs until Motown's favorites started to croon. Smokey, The Temptations, and the Jackson 5 helped wash Jova's blues away. When their shared Motown favorite, "Sexual Healing," started to play, Jova and Dawn jumped up. They performed their background singer routine, howling at the top of their lungs, giggling more than singing.

"Bravo."

The women turned at the distinctly male voice. Near the door, but not far enough to keep his masculine heat from overwhelming Jova, Davan stood with his feet apart, clapping. An erotic dream in tan Dickies, matching jacket, and cap, Davan grinned salaciously at Jova as he approached. "Bravo. I like the routine. Lots of bump and grind."

Jova's face flushed with embarrassment, but she answered with a saucy comeback. "Glad you liked the show, Mr. Underwood."

"Davan, please. And I *loved* the show. All praises to the late, great Marvin Gaye." He stepped closer. "Hi." He extended a hand to Dawn, keeping his eyes on Jova.

After introductions, Jova asked, "Is there something I can do for you?"

"I saw your shop lights on, and thought I'd offer to walk you ladies to your car. It's pretty late."

"I live upstairs, but you could walk Dawn out."

"Yeah." Dawn's voice dropped an octave. "You can walk me out. I'll grab my jacket and purse."

Jova shook her head as she watched Dawn prance to the back. Dawn could go from screaming banshee to slinky seductress in ten seconds flat when a handsome man walked through the door. It would take her a minute to return. If she knew Dawn, she was in the rest room combing her hair and applying lipstick. She'd never made it a secret that she wanted to be married before she turned twenty-five. At Jova's twenty-seven, Dawn must view her as an old maid.

When Jova turned back to Davan he was watching her with intense obsidian eyes and a crooked smile.

"You live upstairs?" he asked.

Jova crossed her arms over her chest, shielding herself from his scrutiny. "It's convenient because it takes a lot of hours to run the shop. Economical, too." Owning the entire building, she didn't think it wise to use the upstairs studio apartment for storage when she could save a bundle on rent. Although Tresses & Locks wasn't in the most exclusive of neighborhoods, the rent on a one-bedroom apartment nearby was still hefty.

Awkward silence stretched between them. Jova pulled her eyes away, wishing Dawn would hurry back.

"Your shop looked pretty busy today."

"Were you watching?"

"Couldn't keep my eyes off . . . of the place."

Jova had been flustered when she dropped her keys and she had to crawl around on the ground in a skirt. She hadn't heard him approaching until she looked up, and Mr. Davan Underwood was towering over her. When she'd looked up into the grinning face of the dark god, she'd wanted to remove his baseball cap to get a better view. She'd watched the muscles of his back flex and move as he fished for the keys underneath the car. She didn't miss his eyes wandering to her legs. She had even hoped he would flirt a little bit.

Hadn't she promised herself she was finished with men? All men. It didn't matter if they were dark brown with thick eyelashes and obsidian eyes like Davan. The fact that his body was tall, lean, and muscular did not give Davan permission to make her want to break her vow. She'd have to stay away from the handsome new mechanic working across the street.

Jova moved the conversation onto safe ground. "So you're working at David's garage? Motor City Repair Shop has been there for as long as I can remember."

"David's my uncle. His health has been bothering him, so he's taking an early retirement. I'll be taking over for him."

"Admirable."

"How so?"

"You moved from Utah to help your sick uncle. You must have made a lot of sacrifices."

"You do that for family . . . and the ones you care about." Davan had a way of making benign words sound like X-rated propositions. Sexy, but very hard to carry on a conversation with a man who keeps erotic thoughts dancing in your head.

"What's this?" Davan stepped over to the portion of the shop reserved for lingerie sales. He glanced in the display case, and then stepped to a rack of lacy PJs. He boldly fingered one of the gowns. Most men entering the salon never let their feet come near the aqua carpeting.

What a contrast, Jova thought. *Raw masculinity with a smudge of grease on his chin, intimately caressing dainty sleepwear.*

"This is part of your shop?" Davan asked, caressing a lacy red teddy.

Jova nodded, not trusting her voice.

"I bet your closets are full of these." He turned quickly, his gaze burning her.

"I'm ready." Dawn bounced from the back, holding out her jacket to Davan. He held it up and she slithered into it using her best hip action. She winked at Jova and pressed her freshly painted lips into a seductive smile. "See ya bright and early tomorrow."

Davan followed Dawn out the front door. Jova waited for the heat to dissipate before she stepped forward to lock up. She couldn't keep herself from sticking her head out the door. She wanted to see the body language between Davan and Dawn. She peeked out. No obvious connection between them; they were walking side by side, a friendly distance apart.

Well, Davan sure could wear a pair of overalls. He walked with a comfortable sway that naturally centered all attention to the high haunches of his behind. Naturally. His arms swung loosely at his sides, accentuating the sinewy muscle. Did he singlehandedly lift car engines at the garage? Suddenly, Davan turned as if he'd sensed her watching him. He scalded her with a blazing smile.

Chapter 3

Davan tossed his keys on the table and lunged for the sofa, grabbing the phone on the sixth ring. "Yeah?"

"'Yeah'? Who taught you how to answer the phone?"

"Hello, Uncle David." Davan settled on the sofa and switched on the lamp, shedding light on the boxes still waiting to be unpacked.

"Listen, I think I'm going to take tomorrow off. Spend the weekend catching up on my rest."

"You okay? Do you need me to stop by?"

"I don't need a baby-sitter. I need a weekend off. That's why you came, isn't it? To help me out?"

"I could help you out a lot more if you'd let me move into the house with you."

"I don't need a baby-sitter," Uncle David repeated.

His gruff attitude didn't fool Davan. His uncle had raised him. He knew the crotchety-old-man routine was his uncle's way of hiding his fear.

"Can you watch the garage or not?"

"Of course, but—"

"I'll see you Monday morning." David hung up.

Davan could hear the mild distress in the catch of his uncle's breathing. He held the phone to his ear, gripping the receiver and wishing he could tell his uncle how much he loved him.

The defect in Uncle David's heart had been detected earlier in the year. Being Uncle David, he hadn't notified the family until his testing was completed and he'd been released from the hospital. He didn't want his people flying in from Utah for a minor "spell." He didn't tell his sister, Davan's mother, about the seriousness of the heart defect for another month.

The family still didn't have the details of his illness. David told them something was wrong with his heart, and it couldn't be repaired. Months, maybe, the doctors gave him. Inoperable. The chances of dying on the table were too high for any of the cardiac surgeons to recommend operating. Instead, they offered medications and advice. "Take it easy," they'd told Uncle David. "Get your affairs in order."

Uncle David came out to Utah soon after learning his prognosis. For two weeks, he never spoke of his illness, or let anyone cry over him. One morning Davan's mother woke up and Uncle David had gone back home to Detroit. When they'd asked why he didn't stay with his family, he said, "I want to go home to what I know. I feel more comfortable in my own house. At the garage. Working at the shop makes me feel alive." No one argued.

But Davan David Underwood was his uncle's namesake. He gave his boss notice, broke the lease on his apartment, transferred his savings, and drove his truck to Michigan. His mother didn't want to see him go, but she didn't want David to be alone. She would have their extended family to lean on. Having never married, David had no one.

Uncle David had shared a home with his mother

from the time he was ten, until he turned eighteen. His mother recognized he needed a strong black man in his life, spoke to David about her concerns, and two weeks later he moved in.

Uncle David could be a father figure, or a cool big brother. He dished out discipline when Davan stepped out of line. When Davan had his first sexual encounter, David took him to the pharmacy and made him buy condoms. Davan laughed remembering that day. Once he had the condoms he had no idea what to do with them. David picked up on his puzzlement and demonstrated proper use with a banana. It was all very medicinal until David took him out for a beer and a man-to-man talk, when he'd turned eighteen. Then he shared the secrets of the dating game. David taught him being a man had nothing to do with sex and drugs. A man was defined by the way he cared for his family, and his involvement in the community.

Melancholy filled the room, choking Davan like a lethal smoke. He had no idea how he would survive his uncle's death. Good, he had time to spend with Uncle David, but how did he use it? It made a man think. Reflect on his life.

Davan had made foolish mistakes, but he didn't want to die without having had a loving wife and children. He'd tried marriage once, when he was too young to know he wasn't ready. After that, he settled into being alone. Sure, he'd dated back in Utah, but he'd never had that clubbed-over-the-head love that made everything wrong in the world right. David often said he'd get married and have a bunch of kids, if he could do it all again.

Davan pushed himself up from the sofa before his mood turned dark and depressing. His day had gone really well, in retrospect. Ms. Jova Parker had been a welcome respite from the male boasting in the shop. He stepped into the bathroom and began to peel away his oily overalls. *What did Jova think when she saw me in this getup?* Not exactly clothing to impress a woman, but maybe she'd respect him, viewing the monkey suit as evidence of a hard-working man.

He'd been told Detroit was the place to be for African-Americans seeking economic prosperity. He wasn't ashamed of being an auto mechanic. It was good, honest work that paid well, but Jova Parker was a real woman. Regal in her walk, intelligent when she talked. High maintenance. He felt like the toad waiting to be kissed when he stood next to her. And thinking about lying on the bed with her stretched out in one of those frilly things from her shop—it made him shudder.

Davan opened the glass shower door and stepped under the spray. He'd been impressed by the spacious layout of the one-bedroom apartment. The living room joined with a small dining room. Plush gray carpeting softened his steps, and the gas fireplace would help him adjust to the harsh Michigan winters he'd heard so much about from Uncle David. An average cook, he found the kitchen appliances suitable to his needs.

Davan stepped from the shower and wrapped a towel around his waist. He padded across the carpet into his bedroom. More boxes waited to be unpacked. After three months, he hadn't unpacked all his belongings because he didn't know what to do with them. He didn't know where to place the knickknacks or paintings. Which curtains went with which bedspread? The melancholy fog threatened. A woman would know about these things. *His* woman would know his tastes, and how to make his apartment a real home. Davan dropped the towel and stepped into his boxers. He had a lot of work ahead of him, but when he was finished unloading, assembling, and decorating, his apartment would be home.

Jova laughed along at a comedy video she had rented. Her fingers worked furiously at her latest project. Having learned to crochet from her mother in the third grade, she could weave spectacular projects from a skein of yarn. Crocheting relaxed her after a long day of standing on her feet, inhaling the fumes of beauty products. Much of her work decorated her apartment. She loved afghans, and even now she was adding the finishing touches to a marvelous burgundy and pink piece. She jumped at the rapid knock at her door. Setting the crocheting aside, she pressed *pause* on the VCR. She padded to the door after sliding her feet into her slippers.

"Jova, open up."

She didn't need the peephole to know Herman stood on the landing. She exhaled a deep breath, turned the locks, and opened the door. He was wearing baggy jeans and a white cable-knit sweater. He looked a little frazzled, but still temptingly handsome.

"I don't want to talk to you, Herman."

"I'm sorry about taking you to court. Hear me out."

Against her better judgment, she folded her arms over her chest and waited.

"I made a mistake. I needed the money so badly that I—"

Jova dropped her arms. "What do you mean you

needed the money?" Not only was Herman fine as wine, he made a bundle as a correctional officer at Jackson Prison.

He looked over his shoulder. "Can I come inside?"

"I don't know . . ."

"Do you think I'd hurt you? You know me, Jova. It didn't work out between us, but I still care about you."

"That's what I thought before you sued me."

"Jova." His voice cracked like a whip.

She winced.

His shoulders slumped, and his voice softened. "I can explain."

Big terry cloth robe and hideous slippers, no chance of tempting Herman. She tightened the belt on her robe before she unlocked the screen door and let him inside.

They sat together on the love seat. "What's going on, Herman?"

"I owe a man some money."

Jova stood up. "If you're going to play games—"

"No." Herman caught her wrist and pulled her back down on the sofa. He swiped a hand over his perfect face before he went on. "It started out as weekend trips to the casinos. Can't win no real money in those places, and if you do they ban you for life. You've seen the stories on the news."

Jova nodded, yes. The local news had reported for days on the casinos banning the big winners from their establishments.

Herman continued. "I fell into this back-alley poker game. The stakes were high, but I was winning big. The man who runs the poker games turned me on to craps. Next thing I know, my bank accounts are empty, I can't get any more advances at work, and I'm in to him big time."

"How big?"

Herman checked his watch. "Another twenty percent interest will be added at midnight, and that'll bring it up to six grand."

"Six grand!"

"Jova." Herman took her hands, trying to keep her calm. "This man doesn't play around. If I don't pay him something he's going to start having my bones broken."

"Herman." Jova watched his perfect face become marred with worry wrinkles. "This is bad, but what do you want me to do?"

"I thought, maybe, you could loan me the money to get this guy off my back. Then I can pay you back, a little at a time."

"I don't have that kind of money." If she did, she wouldn't loan it to an ex-boyfriend who tried to sue her. She'd take into consideration the fact a loan shark was threatening him, but she didn't have the money, so no use in playing the what-if game.

"Tresses & Locks does good business."

"Tresses & Locks does enough business to keep me afloat. I have expenses and employees. I've told you over and over owning the salon doesn't make me rich." Herman had never believed that, which was the reason he'd walked out on their relationship. He thought his ship had come in when he met her, but he soon found out she wasn't in the business of keeping a gigolo.

Herman dropped back against the sofa and covered his face with his forearm.

"I'm sorry, I can't help you."

Herman sat upright, eyeing her for a moment. "Can you take out a loan against the shop?"

"No!" Jova bolted out of her seat. "No! I bought the shop with money from my mother's life insurance. No way I'm jeopardizing it because you gambled yourself into a hole. I don't know why you came to *me* for the money. We aren't married. We aren't even dating. Try your friends or your mom."

Herman jumped up, panic making his eyes big and round. "Don't you think I've tried them? They won't help me anymore."

"Anymore? This has happened before?"

His gaze wavered, giving her the answer.

Jova marched over to the door and opened it wide. "I have to ask you to go. I'm sorry you're in trouble, but this really isn't my problem."

Herman hesitated. He opened his mouth, thought better of it, and dragged himself out the door.

"Please, don't come back," Jova said. She closed the door behind him.

Chapter 4

"I'm going to head home," Lisa said, joining Jova in the window of the shop. "Nobody's coming out in this storm."

Jova stood mesmerized by the gray sky and the rainy downpour. It matched her mood. After Herman's visit last night, she'd had a hard time falling asleep. Finally, she'd ended up calling Dawn and asking her advice. Dawn assured her she'd done the right thing.

Jova woke up to the pouring rain, soon accompanied by thunder and lightning. All but two of her customers canceled. Dawn's had done likewise. Not many people paid good money to get their hair done when they knew it would be ruined before they made it home. Dawn had gone home by noon, and now at three o'clock Lisa was heading out, too.

"Do we usually get thunderstorms in August?" Lisa asked, tying a rain scarf over her head.

"Doesn't seem like it."

Dawn peered up at the sky, jumping at the clap of thunder. "Unnatural. I'm going to pick up my son and have a warm, quiet evening at home." She turned to Jova. "You should lock up."

"I will. Drive safe," she added as Dawn left, running toward the parking lot.

Jova locked the door and went to set the answering machine. Next, she threw a load of towels in the washer for Tuesday. The shop was always closed on Sundays and Mondays. The only exceptions she ever made were for wedding parties. She was cleaning her workstation when a rapid knock on the door startled her. She turned to see Davan shifting from foot to foot, anxious for her to open the door.

"Is something wrong?" Jova asked. "You're soaked." She grabbed a towel from Dawn's station and handed it to him.

"The storm's pretty bad. We're closing up."

"Yeah, me too."

"I didn't know if you'd gotten a chance to stop for lunch." He held up a plastic bag and the aroma of delicious food reminded Jova she hadn't eaten since a bowl of breakfast cereal.

"You brought me lunch?"

Davan nodded. "From the deli on the corner. They say it's the best."

Jova took the bag, a shiver running through her when his fingers brushed hers. "Thank you." She surveyed the contents. "Where's yours?"

"I ate earlier. Thought you'd be hungry but might not feel like cooking. You sure can't go out in this mess."

Jova stood speechless.

"Well, I better head on home before this gets any worse." Davan made his way to the door. He handed her the towel, his fingers brushing hers again. "Don't forget to lock up."

Jova stood in the window and watched Davan run, through sheets of rain, back across the street to the garage.

"Hmmm." He'd been watching the salon, assumed she'd been too busy to grab lunch, so he delivered it in bad weather to her doorstep. "Thoughtful." He didn't call and ask if he should do it. He took the initiative and anticipated her needs. "Hmmm," she said again. The best part was he hadn't asked for anything in return. He hadn't hit on her. He didn't suggest she pay him in money or bodily currency.

Davan glanced over his shoulder before disappearing inside the garage. A real cutie with a masculine flare, he could do serious damage to her heart. The Dickies were splattered with car oil, a hat hid his hair, and he was soaked. How did he manage to look absolutely incredible so naturally? Feeling a scandalous tingle, Jova abandoned her place at the window, but visions of Davan continued to dance in her head.

Jova was holding the mirror up for her last client of the day when Davan stepped into the salon. "Hi, ladies."

Dawn spoke over mumbled greetings from the few customers remaining in the salon. "Davan, perfect. Jova needs a male model for the hair show this weekend. Are you game?"

"I don't know." He came closer. "What's a hair show?"

Jova concentrated on her client while Dawn explained. "It's like a fashion show, but for hair. One of the local radio stations is hosting it. The winner gets a prize package, and free publicity on the radio for a month."

"What would I have to do?"

Dawn was too enthusiastic. "Let Jova style your hair and take one—maybe two—walks down the runway. It's a blast. After the show the party goes on all night. Plenty of local celebrities will be there."

Davan slid his hands into the pockets of his overalls. "How come you need a model, Jova?"

"My barber had agreed to do it, but he quit recently." Jova didn't like Dawn using her to hit on Davan. They'd have to spend a lot of time together, and Davan was tempting enough without pushing togetherness.

"I see the sign in the window."

"Well?" Dawn pushed.

"I'll do it, sure."

"Good." Dawn beamed. "Hey, did you come to walk me to my car again?"

"I could do that, sure."

Dawn saddled her purse up on her shoulder, and gave Davan a heated glare. She finger-waved goodbye as she pranced to the door. Davan held the door open for her and they were gone.

Jova bit down on her bottom lip. After bringing her lunch the other day, she'd thought Davan might want to talk to her. Dangerous thoughts, she admonished herself. She remembered her staunch vow to lay off men and concentrate on running the salon. Obviously, Dawn had a thing for him. Maybe he had a thing for her too. Maybe bringing the boss lunch was his way of paving his way to Dawn—not her. Good thing she'd stopped dating. Good thing, right.

Worrying about what Davan and Dawn were doing in the parking lot, she'd missed her client's last comments. She envied her friend's luck in finding Davan. He seemed like a gentleman, not one to manipulate a relationship. For sure, he was a tremendous male specimen.

Jova accepted the fee with a smile, hoping her

client wouldn't ask any questions. She scheduled her next appointment, and prepared to close the shop. Another long day, but no one said being a business owner would be easy work. Tomorrow morning's schedule looked lighter, which would allow her time to manage the business and finances of her shop.

"Dawn is safely in her car," Davan announced upon his return. "When will you need me?"

As soon as he came into the room, Jova felt like butter melting under the sun on a hot day. His presence overwhelmed her, making her feel just a tiny bit *off*. Her thought processes became jumbled and she worried if she spoke, she'd sound like a rambling idiot. "Need you?"

"Dawn said you'd need to fix my hair for the show. This works out good for me. I turned thirty last week and I thought it might be time to do something about this." He pulled off his cap, revealing a bushel of wily hair. "Uncle David says I look like a cross between Ben Wallace and Sideshow Bob."

Jova didn't know who Ben Wallace was, but unless he was gorgeous, Uncle David was off his rocker. And as for Sideshow Bob from *The Simpsons*, no way.

"Who's Ben Wallace?"

Obviously amused, he grinned. "Only the defensive player of the year."

Huh?

"Have you ever heard of the Detroit Pistons?"

Sorta.

"Central division champions. Won the championship two years in a row in the 1980s. National Basketball Association."

"Oh, yeah. They play at the Palace where the Motown Review was held last year."

Davan shook his head, too polite to laugh at her. Twisting his cap, he approached. "Can you help me?"

Jova stood and signaled him to take a seat.

"I was thinking about cutting it off. Go with a fade."

She ran her fingers through the dark bush. "No. The weather's very unpredictable in Detroit. It could snow in September, and then you'll freeze."

After walking around the chair twice, Jova stood in front of Davan and gave her professional opinion. "It's not bad. I can definitely use you in the show."

"If you don't cut it, what?"

"A light relaxer to take some of the curl out."

He frowned. "A perm? Like Morris Day or Al Sharpton?"

Never, no matter what she did to his hair, would he look like Al Sharpton. On second thought, Morris Day would never be in his league either. She could shave him bald, and the competition wouldn't have a chance.

She ran her fingertips over the hair at his temple. "Cut and trim. Maybe lighten it up a little."

"A perm, cut, and trim? You do realize I'm a man, don't you?"

A shock wave ran through Jova's body. His manliness oozed, filling the room like a lethal vapor. It took a second to compose herself. She completed another lap around the chair before placing her hands on her hips studying his strong features. "I could see you with silky dreads."

"Dreads! I don't think so."

"Hold on. Let me show you." She waded through

a stack of magazines. Finding the one she wanted, she flipped the pages to find a picture of a male model wearing the style she had in mind. The shop was quiet without the chatter of customers, the radio or TV. She could feel Davan watching her. Something about the way he looked at her made her want to dim the lights and sip champagne. She glanced over her shoulder. He was watching, waiting for her to notice. She became momentarily rattled, thrusting the magazine at him out of nervousness.

Davan eyed the picture carefully. "How much?"

"Since you're modeling in the show: no charge."

"If I wasn't?"

"For the works? Perm, cut, dye, and lock—three hundred."

"Dollars!"

Jova smiled. "It's the first-time customer discount."

"With prices like that you should be driving a Mercedes."

"Hey." Jova smiled, swatting at him. "My car's a sore spot with me. When do you want to do this?"

"How about now? Before I lose my nerve. It took me a year to grow my hair out this long."

Jova would have wall-to-wall models in the salon come morning. Plus, she and Dawn had to style each other's hair. Tomorrow would be hectic. Now would be great, but she noticed the time. They wouldn't finish up before nine. Tying up his Saturday night probably wouldn't work. "It'll take several hours."

"Fine by me, if it's okay with you."

"Let's get started." Concentrating on work would keep her mind from wondering what Davan looked like in a suit. Every time they ran into each other, he was in the uniform overalls of David's shop. Not many men could look good in a pair of oily overalls, but he carried it off rather well. Probably had something to do with the way his behind stood proud and firm. Or maybe it was the bulge in the front always drawing her attention.

"You're quiet," Davan said.

"Sorry. Concentrating on my work." She wished. "Your hair's thick. The perm will help." She ventured carefully, "Looks like you and Dawn are hitting it off."

Davan laughed, a soft rumble rolled off his tongue, making a prickly feeling move over her skin. "I don't know about that. I actually come to see you."

"Really?"

Davan was draped and Jova was applying perm cream to his hair. "Your car has a knock."

"My car has a lot of problems." It suffered from used car layaway syndrome.

"You should bring it to the garage. Let me take a look at it."

"I will." *Focus on his hair. Don't get distracted.*

"Hmmm."

Concentrating on Davan's hair was a good idea, but Jova made that declaration forgetting how intimate doing hair could be. Every bump or brush held new meaning when Davan flashed his bright smile up at her. Good thing she was laying off men, forever. Because a man like Davan could do things to her, and make her do things to him.

"You seemed flustered the day we met," Davan said.

"Yeah. I had just come from court."

"Didn't go well?"

Jova rubbed her itchy nose with her forearm. "Actually, I won."

"Congratulations."

"Is it burning yet?"

"Like acid."

Jova giggled. "Why didn't you say something? Follow me. I'll rinse it out."

"I've never done this before. I thought it was supposed to feel this way."

By the time the perm, color rinse, and cut had been completed, Davan and Jova had dispensed with the small talk and were getting to know each other. They took a break to share a pizza dinner before starting the final phase of Davan's transformation.

"This shop must mean a lot to you then," Davan said between bites.

"It does. My mom was a single mother and she worked hard. I don't know how she was able to buy a life insurance policy, but I have to put it to good use."

"I think she would be proud."

Jova watched him. They shared an intimacy without words that was premature for their relationship. She'd only held three conversations with Davan, but felt as if they were old friends.

"You're easy to talk to."

Davan smiled and reached for another slice of pizza.

"David's your uncle and you're here to take over the shop?"

Davan nodded, washing down his food with a swig of soda. "If he'll let me. He's very stubborn and doesn't accept help easily. I figure I keep hanging around, learning the business, and eventually he'll be ready to turn it over."

"I'm sure you'll do him proud. I'm sorry to hear about him not feeling well."

Davan nodded. A sadness passed over his features that made Jova think David might be seriously ill. She didn't pry. They were getting along well. He would share it with her if he wanted to.

"What did you do in Utah?"

"Worked for other people, mostly. I have to admit I wasn't being very productive. Right after high school I went to a local college and became a certified mechanic. Started working and have been ever since. I love what I do, but like all young men, I squandered away my time when I should have been focused on my future."

"Looks like you turned out okay."

Davan smiled, his eyes following hers. After a moment of awkward silence, he continued. "I married young, and divorced too quickly, my mother would tell you."

"Any children?"

Davan shook his head no.

"Do you regret it?"

He thought before answering. "I don't regret anything I've done with my life. I've made a few bad choices, but I learned and grew from them. My ex-wife and I were too young to get married. We weren't mature enough to handle a serious relationship. We parted friends."

Jova started on another piece of pizza.

"What about you?"

"Never married. Never even close."

"I'm surprised."

Davan gazed at her with such intensity Jova knew not to ask what he meant by his statement. "Let's finish up."

Ninety minutes later, Jova stood behind Davan

at the wall mirror as he admired his new hairstyle.
Davan had been handsome when he walked into
the shop, but the silky dreads highlighted his dark
features and brought out his dazzling smile. All
she could think was, *Wow.*

"I wasn't sure," Davan said, turning to her, "but
this is nice." He ran his fingers over the dreads.
"Soft."

"It looks nice on you."

"Do I look nice enough to get that tour of the
city you promised me?"

Jova shifted. The words were innocent, but the
look in his eyes was lethal.

"You promised." He smiled, and she melted.

"Next week Sunday?"

"It's a date." To emphasize his meaning, he
stroked her chin. He transferred his heat with one
touch. "I wasn't sure about this hair show at first,
but spending the evening with you makes it worth
it."

Jova thought she would burst into flames.

Davan eased out of the chair. He stood inches
from her, studying her features and daring her to
look away. "I'll see you tomorrow?"

"You have all the information you need?"

He nodded. "I'd better go."

Jova walked him to the door.

"Lock up."

Jova locked the door after him, and watched as
he walked across the street. It was dark, the garage
long closed. A young man walked the street, his
pit bull pulling him along. It was after nine and
she was tired. A quick cleanup and then she would
head upstairs. When she returned to her chair
she found the cap Davan had worn into the shop.
She pressed it to her chest, remembering him be-

fore and then after his transformation. If possible, the after was better. Jova took the cap home, hanging it on her mirror before crawling into bed.

Chapter 5

Jova selected burgundy, her favorite color, for the models. She made a deal with a clothier in the neighborhood and he would provide the formal wear. The lingerie was Jova's gift for appearing in the show. Lisa manicured the women's nails with intricate designs that matched their gowns. With an evening wear, sleepwear double punch, Tresses & Locks would steal the show.

The radio station's DJ kicked off the annual hair show just as Jova stepped away from the registration table. By the volume of cheers, the show had sold out. After the DJ's opening, the salons would be announced in alphabetical order. When Tresses & Locks took the stage, Jova would introduce the models, describe their hairstyle, and say a few words about what they were wearing. All the models would come out at the end, and Jova would introduce Dawn and Lisa.

Local celebrities mingled behind the stage. The media accosted more famous stylists for interviews. Magazines specializing in African-American hair care snapped picture after picture. Jova remembered when the hair shows were considered a get-together for local stylists. With Detroit being named Hair Capital of the World over Atlanta and

New York last year, the city's reputation was on the line.

With the media buzzing all around, the owner of Tresses & Locks had to look good. Jova spent a month crocheting a soft knit dress with waves of burgundy, pink, and white. With thin straps and a deep neckline, the dress revealed her full cleavage. Sexy, three-inch heels emphasized the dress which showed a lot of leg. Risqué, but fabulous, Jova had wiggled into the dress ready to take on the catwalk.

Dawn found Jova in the thick crowd backstage. "I just checked on the models. The newcomers are a little nervous, but Lisa has it under control."

"What do you need me to do?"

Dawn shook her head. "Nothing. I have to run to my car and grab an extra pair of panty hose for one of the models. See you on the catwalk."

Jova greeted her colleagues as she made her way to the dressing room. She found Lisa inside weaving her motherly magic amongst the ladies. They were reviewing the order of appearance for the models when one of the show's organizers approached.

"Jova Parker?"

"Yes."

"Let's go over the procedure."

Jova checked all her models in, and received last-minute details.

"Has anyone seen Davan?" Lisa asked once the organizer stepped away. "Dawn would have mentioned him if she had."

Jova refused to panic. The show would not be ruined if Davan didn't show, but it would leave a model without an escort. She wanted to win this year! She needed the publicity to boost business.

"Why don't you go see if he's in the men's dressing room? I'll get the models lined up."

Jova went in search of the men's dressing rooms. Models had already started parading for the audience, which made it harder to maneuver backstage. By the time she reached the dressing room, she had no modesty about entering. She stopped at the doorway and shouted a warning. A couple of the men scrambled to privacy booths, pulling the curtain behind them.

"Does anyone know Davan Underwood?"

The men milling about didn't know him. A couple gave her assessing looks and she knew the dress was working to her advantage. She let her eyes wander the room, in search of Davan, of course. It looked like a Chippendales convention. Men of different heights and varied shades of brown adjusted their clothing. Several stylists hovered in front of the mirrors, fussing over their models' hair.

"Davan Underwood?" Jova called out as she searched the room.

"Check the booths in the adjoining room."

Sure enough, the beefcake had spilled over into another room. Jova called as she entered the dressing room. There were many fewer men milling around. It was much quieter. One man sat on the floor, his legs folded in a twisted yoga pose, meditating. Jova lowered her voice, calling out for Davan as she passed each privacy booth.

Davan's head poked out from one of the booths. "Wow," he said as she approached.

The heat from that one word made Jova falter on her three-inch heels. She recovered her composure quickly. "I wanted to be sure you'd made it."

"I made it, but I'm having a little trouble here."

He rolled his eyes around the room. "These guys are professionals. I'm out of my element here."

"Believe me, they've all had first show jitters. It's a lot of fun. The audience really gets into it with a lot of cheering. Afterward, there's a big party backstage."

"How big is this audience?"

Jova grinned. "What trouble are you having? Come out and let me help you."

"I'm not coming out half dressed. There was a guy out there eyeing me. You come in here." Davan opened the curtain and stepped back.

If not for the dark eyes and crooked smile, Jova wouldn't have recognized him. She stepped into the changing room, something she'd done plenty of times to help the models, but the rooms never seemed this small, or this hot, before. Davan was wearing a black tuxedo. Shiny black shoes and his burgundy cumberbund sat on a stool. A white dress shirt clung to the muscles of his arms. The shirt was unbuttoned, leading Jova's eyes on a scenic tour of smooth skin and rippled abs. One look at Davan's muscled chest and the heat hit her in waves.

"How does this go?" Davan asked, his voice husky with unasked questions.

"Huh?"

He grabbed the ends of his bow tie. "I don't know how this thing works."

"Oh, the tie. Well, first you have to, um, button your shirt."

"The buttons are too small for my hands." He held them up for her inspection. "Someone told me once that God gives a man hands the size he needs to . . . handle his business." He shrugged, smiling innocently. "Big . . . hands can be a curse."

"I'll find help." She needed help! If she didn't escape Davan's overwhelming presence soon, she'd spontaneously combust.

"No." He grabbed her arm. The skin-to-skin contact caused small sparks along her skin. "I want you to help me. Besides, you're here and it's almost time to go on."

Jova gave herself an abbreviated warning to keep her lust in check before turning to face him again. She approached Davan's hulking presence cautiously. She lifted the shirt away from his skin as she buttoned it. One more accidental touch would have her peeling off her dress.

He looked down at her, his chin grazing the top of her head. "Where'd you learn to tie a bow tie?"

"I've done many of these shows. It comes up."

"Hmmm." He buried his nose in her hair. "You smell good."

She jerked back a step.

"I shouldn't mess up your hair."

"You can put your jacket on now."

Davan locked eyes with her as he tucked in his shirt. The gesture became so intimate Jova turned her back. "You should find Lisa outside and line up with the other models. I'll see you onstage."

"Wait."

Her escape had been foiled again. She turned slowly, afraid of what he might need help with next.

"My hair got a little mussed while I was dressing. Don't you think you should fix it?" His crooked smile was anything but innocent, but he had a point.

"I'll meet you at the mirrors." She stepped out of the tiny dressing booth before he could stop her.

This meant she had to watch him approach. He was stunning in the black tux. He sauntered up to her, and paused looking down on her before sitting. She did a quick repair job on several of the silky dreads and made a hasty exit.

The women in the audience erupted when Davan took the stage wearing burgundy silk pajama bottoms. *Where is his shirt?* None of her male models wore shirts during the lingerie portion of her show, but Davan looked *obscene* without his. He strutted to the end of the catwalk and paused to play with the drawstring. Several women threw dollar bills onto the stage. He turned slowly and walked toward Jova, stopping midway on the catwalk. He caught her eye as he stood watching her with his hands on his waist. She'd stopped reading the description card when he stepped onto the stage. He turned and several women noted aloud Davan had brought a little something extra to the show. He was really bordering on obscene now. Jova thanked him, hurrying him off the stage before the Detroit police shut it down.

"Damn," Dawn and Lisa said together when Jova left the stage.

"I think Davan sealed it for us," Lisa added. "Did you see the size of his—"

"Do I have good taste, or what?" Dawn bragged.

Jova was saved from answering when the judges called out their scores. Tresses & Locks was in second place, but there were two salons left to go on.

Davan found Jova in the crowd of the after-show celebration. "You were robbed."

Jova shifted the third-place trophy to her left arm. "Third place for a salon open only six months is good. I'm not disappointed."

"Can I help you with that?"

"No. I'm beat. I'm heading home."

Davan took the trophy out of her arms. "I'll carry it to your car."

Dawn pranced up to them. "Davan, you were great."

"Thank you."

She wrapped her arm around his biceps. "Are you staying for the party?"

Davan shifted away from Dawn. A subtle movement, but Jova noticed; she'd been watching for his reaction to Dawn.

"I'm not much for large crowds or parties. I'm going to help Jova to her car, and then I'll call it a night."

Dawn gave him an assessing look that would have changed the mind of any man in the building. When Davan didn't take the bait, she said good night.

Outside, Jova pulled on her jacket. Her dress might be sexy, but she was freezing, even in moderate temperatures.

"Much quieter out here," Jova said, pulling out her keys.

"That was some show. I didn't realize hairstylists lived such a glamorous life."

"Glamorous, right." She pulled the back door open so Davan could put the trophy on the seat.

"I enjoyed it. Don't hesitate to call on me again."

"After the riot you almost caused?" Jealousy caused her to shove the door closed with more muster than she'd intended.

A satisfied smile moved over Davan's tantalizing lips. He held the door open for her, leaning inside while she fastened her seat belt. "Don't forget about Sunday."

"Sunday?" After seeing him in his PJs, boldly displaying his—assets—she couldn't go through with giving him a tour of the city.

"Yes, Sunday." He shook his finger at her. "Don't

even try to get out of it after I just made a spectacle of myself." He closed the door before she could answer. He waved and turned away.

Dawn bopped into the shop, grinning from ear to ear. "Do you think my new boyfriend will walk me to my car tonight?"

"New boyfriend?" Lisa joined her at the window.

"Yeah. Look."

Jova didn't need to join them to know Dawn was pointing at Davan bent under the hood of a car, his rear end stopping traffic.

"Wow. I guess you win the lottery."

"Yeah. Maybe I'll use it to buy my new friend dinner."

It only got worse from there. Dawn spent the entire morning reliving every moment of her brief encounters with Davan. She asked anyone who would listen what he could have meant when he said this or that.

"You should have seen it," Dawn said to her client. Still high from the hair show almost a week ago, she seemed to be doing more talking than hair today. "Davan walked out on the stage and every woman in the place went crazy."

Her client nodded, half listening.

"I thought I was going to have to beat them off with my curling iron."

From Jova's chair, Mary asked, "So where are you going to take him with the lottery money?"

"I could just kiss you for telling us about your great-grandmother's lottery." Dawn leaned against the counter, her palm supporting her chin. "I'll have to think about it. It'll be our first official date."

The salon began planning Dawn and Davan's

first date. People tossed out suggestions about where to go, what to wear, and how far Dawn should go the first time out. Jova listened without comment, reliving her own memories of encounters with Davan. His flirting hadn't been all that subtle at the hair show. He'd asked her to show him the city. He'd made it clear he came by the salon to see her. Whom did he bring lunch to?

By noon, Jova had convinced herself where Davan's interests lay. Regardless of her vow never to date again, she couldn't let Dawn be misled by Davan's kindness. Whether she wanted to admit it or not, she was attracted to Davan and she didn't like the way Dawn was going on about him. Deciding to intervene, Jova pulled her into the supply room.

"What's up?" Dawn asked.

There was no easy way to tell Dawn the truth. Beating around the bush would only make it more embarrassing for them both. "Davan hasn't been coming to the shop to see you."

Dawn glared, waiting.

"He's been coming to see me."

Dawn tried to laugh, but it came out as a grunt. "And why would you think that?"

"He told me."

Dawn glared, clearly not believing her.

"We sorta have a date this weekend."

"What? You asked him out on a date?"

"No, I didn't. He asked *me* out."

"Why didn't you tell him no? You know I like him, Jova. Tell him you can't make it."

"It's not that simple." She doubted Davan would let her cancel. For the first time, she realized she wanted to go out with Davan. He intrigued her. She wanted to learn more about Davan Underwood.

"I never thought you'd stab me in the back. You don't even want to date anymore. Why are you going after my man?"

"Your man? Davan walked you to your car twice. That's all." Jova never guessed Dawn would fall for Davan this hard, this fast.

"Oh, okay." Dawn crossed her arms over her chest. "Are we done here?"

"I thought I should be up front and tell you. You were talking about him so much. I didn't want you to get embarrassed."

"I am embarrassed. I'm embarrassed I was foolish enough to think you were my friend."

"I am your friend. Don't be mad at me because of this."

"I have customers."

"Dawn!"

She slammed the door behind her.

"Hey, Uncle David," Davan said. He stepped into the house and went to the kitchen.

"What's in the bags?"

"Groceries. I thought I'd make dinner over here. My apartment isn't quite unpacked, and besides, I don't like eating alone." Davan had really come because Uncle David hadn't been to work in two days. When Davan called to check up on him, he was short of breath and very tired.

"I don't have much appetite." Uncle David sucked in a deep breath, leaning against the counter to support his weight.

"That's okay. I do. Why don't you go watch television until I'm done?"

His uncle took a staggering step, and used a chair to gather his balance. He dropped down in the chair and planted his elbows on the kitchen table. "I'll stay in here and keep you company while you cook."

Davan pulled up a chair. "Uncle David, you don't look good. I should get you to the doctor's."

He shook his head no. "There's nothing they can do there. He was very clear about that. And I'm not ready to check into a hospital bed to lie around waiting to die." He took a minute to catch his breath before continuing. "I'm tired, Davan. I don't know how much longer I can come into the shop. You ready to take over for me?"

He didn't offer false hope or cardboard sentiment. His uncle would have resented it. "I can handle things."

Uncle David struggled for a few more breaths.

"Should I call Mom to come out and help?"

"Not yet. You'll know when, but not now. I can't deal with having her hovering over me, telling me everything will be all right when I know it won't. Or worse, calling my doctor and interfering. I want to get my shop in order. That's what I want to do."

"Whatever you say, Uncle David."

They shared a look that assured Uncle David that Davan would carry out all his wishes.

"Go on and get to dinner now."

Davan moved to the groceries and started placing the ingredients for spaghetti on the counter.

"The guys been giving you a hard time about that woman across the way," Uncle David said.

Davan smiled. "I guess I know I'm one of the guys now."

"She do your hair all up?" He'd encouraged Davan to cut it long ago.

"Jova Parker. She's beautiful. Sweet, determined.

Has a good spirit, too." Davan told him about the hair show and his upcoming date.

"You like her, huh?"

Davan nodded. "Mom would like her."

"Well, if you hit it off, you treat her right. Don't let her get away. You're getting older. It's time to think about settling down. You'll have the garage. It wouldn't hurt to have a wife and kids, too."

"I'm sure Jova would agree this conversation is premature. We haven't even gone out yet."

"Never too soon to start planning."

Davan labored painstakingly over chopping vegetables and blending tomatoes. Once the marinara started to boil, he helped Uncle David to his recliner in front of the television. Sitting at the table tired him out and he needed a quick nap. Returning to the kitchen, he dropped the spaghetti in water and popped bread into the oven. He shredded the salad and set the table, taking time to check on his uncle.

Uncle David looked fragile, sleeping in the recliner. Gone was the deep-voiced, loud-talking man who had raised him to be a man. Uncle David had always been his hero, and it hurt to see him weak and fighting to catch his breath.

Once dinner was complete, he woke his uncle and they sat down the dinner. Davan was quiet for a long while, brooding over his impending loss. He should be able to do something, to save his uncle's life.

"What are you moping about?"

Davan took a long drink before answering. "I should move in here with you."

"Ah, now you sound like your mother."

"You're not as strong as you used to be." Davan

worried about him, but saying this would make his uncle angry.

"I'm getting along just fine. I don't want anyone moving in here."

"Why not?" Davan pressed. "You took me in. Why won't you let me help you?"

"I don't have to explain myself to you. *I'm* the one who's dying. I should be able to live the way I want to until then. I promised your mother I'd call if I couldn't take care of myself, and I'll stick to our agreement, but that's it."

"But . . ." Davan halted his argument when he noticed his uncle's chest heaving with effort to breathe. Upsetting him only made things worse.

"I don't want to talk about this again, Davan. I know I'm dying, I don't need to talk about it every second of the day."

"I'm sorry, Uncle David. I won't bring it up again." As hard as it would be, Davan wouldn't mention his condition.

They ate awhile in silence, Davan not knowing how to change the subject.

"Why don't you bring your girl around on Sunday? I'd like that. Been a long time since a pretty girl was in this house."

"I'll see what I can do."

Chapter 6

After spending two hours flat-ironing her hair, and an hour in the bath, Jova picked up the phone and dialed Davan's number. Her fingers shook as she punched in the digits. A battle raged internally. She was attracted to Davan, but a little voice reminded her of past bad choices in men.

She wished she could be a vamp. Wildly flirt with him, quench her craving for his body, and drop him cold. She wished she could fight his pull on her and cancel their date, restoring her friendship with Dawn. She couldn't do those things because Davan never left her. She thought of him every minute. Before bed she would crush his cap to her chest, breathing deeply, trying to conjure up his scent. At night, visions of him at the hair show parading down the catwalk in silk pajama pants haunted her.

Davan possessed a magnetism that could not be explained with words. Always a gentleman, with a crooked smile that hinted at a hidden wild side. He dressed in overalls stained with motor oil, yet he wore them like a designer suit. The quiet rumble of his voice held magical authority. He reminded Jova of a wolf—so beautiful you wanted

to make it a house pet, but deadly once you
stepped into his territory.

"Hello?"

Jova jumped to attention at the sound of his
deep voice. "Are you ready?"

"I'm very close to being ready."

"Good, I'm on my way."

"I thought I would pick you up."

She had flustered him. "No, this is my tour. It'll
be easier if I drive. I'll pick you up. What's your
address?"

Davan lived in a quaint brick apartment building with a fence and flowers bordering the front
yard. The only apartments on the block, the four-
story building occupied most of the north corner.
Senior citizens owned most of the homes in this
neighborhood. A few young families just starting
out dotted the blocks, but the history of the neighborhood lay with its elderly. Rosa Parks had lived
in the area until recently.

Jova wondered how Davan had found this gem
from Utah. She had lived in Detroit all her life
and didn't know the building was tucked away
here. She made her way to the building, watching a man playing football on the front lawn with
three little boys. A warm breeze lifted the skirt of
her sundress, making it billow out around her
legs. Inside the lobby, she located Davan's apartment number and rang the intercom. He buzzed
her past the security door. She pulled out her compact and examined her face in the mirror. She
fought the jitters all the way down the hall.

Davan stood in his doorway, waiting. "Would
you like to come in?"

Jova answered in her head, but her mouth hung
open, unable to form words. A beige sleeveless T

and matching cargo shorts revealed the bulk of his muscular arms and legs. Chiseled, he was an exquisite hunk of carved mahogany marble. The brown streaks tangled in his silky dreads complemented his dark complexion. No chin stubble today, his skin was smooth. She fought the urge to reach out and caress him. He gifted her with a smile.

She shivered internally.

"Maybe later," Davan said. "I didn't mean to be pushy." He disappeared inside briefly, and returned with sunglasses and a jacket. Locking the door, he turned to her. "Ready for my tour."

Jova followed him through the lobby out into the mild August day. The weather would cooperate with their tour by providing sun and a warm breeze. He opened her door before getting into the passenger's seat. She watched him cross behind the car in her rearview. She gave a big sigh and tried to settle her stomach. She'd been around handsome men before, but none affected her like Davan did.

Davan waved as they passed the man playing football with the boys on the lawn. Jova helped him understand the network of boulevards and one-way streets enveloping his neighborhood.

"A map will never help you," Jova said. "Knowing your way around here is only learned from years of driving the streets."

"What is the speed limit around here?" Davan asked once they wore zooming down the freeway toward downtown.

"Speed limit?" She glanced over at him. "Detroiters consider speed limits *suggestions*. A *jumping-off point*, if you will."

He cringed.

"Are you turning green?" She laughed.

"No, no. I like fast cars as much as any man."
He gripped the dashboard.

Jova eased off the accelerator. "Better?"

Jova and Davan walked down Jefferson Avenue
with her pointing out all the sights. "Hart Plaza
is between the GM Building, Cobo Hall, and Joe
Louis Arena. The casino is across the street. Greek
Town is a couple of blocks over that way. Very easy
to find on your own."

"Joe Louis is where the Red Wings play," Davan
added.

"Very good." She teased him with a smile.

"What is Hart Plaza?"

"Hart Plaza is our version of Central Park in
New York. Except it sits on the Detroit River, and
instead of grass we have bricks."

The music of a live band could be heard before
they stepped into the plaza. Vendors lined the
walkway, selling various goods. High-quality,
unique products were peddled—everything from
paintings and books to jewelry and clothing could
be found there. After checking out the vendors,
they watched several men playing chess. They
stopped at the huge fountain in the middle of the
square, letting the mist cool them. The under-
ground food court was next, after which they
walked down to the river.

"What's bothering you?" Davan asked. He used
a broad finger to trace a circle on the condensa-
tion of Jova's lemon icee cup.

"Nothing." She stared out at the Detroit River,
watching a motorboat speed by.

"We spent three hours gabbing while you fixed
my hair, but you've hardly said a word since you
picked me up."

She watched the motorboat disappear near the Canadian side of the river.

"You insisted on driving today," Davan said. "You argued with me when I tried to pay the parking attendant. You wouldn't even let me buy your lemon icee. What's with the Ms. Independent routine?"

"I don't know what you're talking about."

Davan nudged her hip with his. "Lying isn't a good way to start a relationship." She cringed, but he ignored it. "I'm a hunt, kill, and provide type of man. You're seriously screwing with my head when you go into Ms. Independent mode. It's easy to see you're high maintenance, so don't tell me this is the real you."

"Are you insulting me?"

"No." He scanned her straight black hair, the yellow and red sundress, all the way down to the dainty sandals, and left her feeling naked in the middle of downtown Detroit. "I like women who fuss over themselves. Especially if they're doing it for me."

Her mouth dropped. She started to protest, but Davan interrupted.

"From the way you tensed a minute ago, I'm assuming this has something to do with relationships. Are you in one?"

"No." And she didn't want to be. No matter that her hormones were hopping around like Mexican jumping beans.

"Then what?" He leaned against the railing, watching the boats go by.

"Dawn has a thing for you."

"I have a thing for you."

Jova looked over at him, but he continued to watch the boats, sipping on his icee. "Dawn's very upset with me. She barely said two words to me all week."

He turned to her. "I'm sorry she's upset with you. I never gave her any reason to think I was attracted to her. I come to the shop to see you. Sure, I walked her to her car. It was the polite thing to do. Do you want me to talk to her?"

Jova shook her head. "I'll take care of it." It would only embarrass Dawn to know they'd discussed it. "Today is about giving you a tour of Detroit. Two friends hanging out together."

Davan nodded. His eyes narrowed into an *Ah, I get it* glare. "Today is about me getting to know you better." He lifted Jova's chin in his palm. "Today is our first date." He clinked their cups together. "Here's to many more."

"No. Today is not our first date."

"If I kiss you, it's a first date."

"You're not going to kiss me." *No, no, no!* This was not going as smoothly as she had hoped it would. "We're two friends spending Sunday afternoon together. I have to be clear on that."

"Why?"

He was smiling again. Jova became flustered. She wasn't explaining herself clearly. She'd tried to spare his feelings, but it wasn't working. "Listen, Davan. I just ended a bad relationship, unfortunately, several in a row. I don't want to date anyone right now. It's nothing personal."

"Nothing personal? It was obvious at the hair show we have chemistry."

Jova remembered the tuxedo clinging to his muscles and the scene on the catwalk. "There may have been an attraction—"

"There *is* a *mutual* attraction."

"I don't date everyone I'm attracted to. I'm just not interested in dating right now."

"You may not want to date anyone right now, but we're out on a date. Go figure." He turned back to the boats.

"You're not listening to me."

"You listen to me for a minute, Jova." He turned and watched her a long minute before going on. "I see the way you look at me. You want me." He let his hand glide down the length of her hair. "Now tell me this isn't a date."

Not able to think of a snappy comeback, Jova turned toward the water and drank several gulps of her lemon icee.

"That one's a beauty," Davan said, pointing out a boat. "I'd like to own a boat one day."

"You're sorta arrogant, you know?"

"I know. Hunt, kill, provide. Remember and we'll get along fine."

They left Hart Plaza by early afternoon. Jova drove slowly down Jefferson Avenue, pointing out landmarks. Since it was a sunny day, she decided to show Davan Belle Isle Park. By eight o'clock the strip along the riverfront would be jammed packed with cars. People would be out cruising, or picnicking with their family. Lovers would stargaze while teenagers hung out with their friends. Detroit's finest would make laps, keeping the crowd orderly.

It was still early, only a few families dotting the island, when Jova and Davan arrived.

"Do you have a blanket?" Davan asked.

"Maybe."

"How about we grab dinner and eat by the water?"

Jova drove a short distance to the Greek Town

entertainment complex. After circling the block three times, she found a metered parking spot. They placed an order at Pizza Papalis and walked around Trapper's Alley to wait for their pizza to be ready.

"Forty-five minutes is a long time to cook a pizza," Davan remarked. They stepped on the escalator in Trapper's Alley and ascended to the top shopping level.

"It's the best pizza you can get this side of Chicago."

"At twenty-five dollars, it better be."

Jova stepped off the escalator. "Cheap?"

"Frugal."

"Hunt, kill, provide. Remember?"

"I remember." He smiled begrudgingly.

"High-maintenance women can be hard to please," Jova teased.

"It's my weakness." He took her hand in his, and her knees buckled at the shocking current of excitement. "I specialize in pleasing high-maintenance women." He pulled her close and wrapped his arm around her waist. "Especially if they look as good as you."

Jova's stomach did a flip-flop while her sensible side warned her to pull away from Davan. A head taller than she, he was the perfect height for cuddling with her five-six frame. His body was solid and welcoming. She mustered up all her might, but she couldn't take that sideways step out of the comfort of his embrace. He tightened his arm around her as he stared at the contents of a gadget store's window display. His touch was meant to be casual, but Jova's insides were ricocheting with heated panic.

"Let's go inside," Davan said.

Having lost control of this tour/date a long time ago, Jova let him lead her by the hand into the tiny shop. He wandered from aisle to aisle, dismissing the salesman who offered to help him shop. He stopped intermittently and studied an interesting device. He held it up to her, anxious for her response. It was a man's store; she had no idea how the tools and devices were supposed to be used. She smiled and faked interest while he moved to another item.

"Will that be all?" the salesman asked when they reached the checkout counter.

Davan dug for his wallet. "See anything you like?" Realizing his words, he stopped digging in the wallet and smiled down at her. "Besides me."

The salesman laughed, but caught himself and stopped abruptly.

Davan shared a secret man-type nod with the salesman. "I think that'll be all."

With bag in hand, they sprinted across the street to pick up their pizza before returning to the car. They hummed along to Motown oldies as they drove down Jefferson Avenue. Once back at Belle Isle, Jova turned down the stereo and they found a spot to park and eat.

"Nice blanket." Davan sat on the blanket Jova had spread on the grass.

"You like it? I made it myself."

"Really?" He put the pizza box down and cracked open the soda.

Jova placed a slice of pizza on a paper plate and handed it to him. "I do a little crocheting in my spare time."

"I'm impressed." He bit into the pizza. "It is good."

"Told you. You should listen to me more often."

His voice dropped to a low rumble. "I will."

They watched the sunset in silence, their eyes glued to the horizon, while eating their pizza.

"Tell me about these men who have turned you off from dating."

Swallowing, Jova shook her head. "Nothing to tell. I made bad choices. And then I made a vow not to make any choices at all for a while."

"You should learn from your bad choices and move on. Not come to a standstill."

Easy for you to say. Your ex didn't sue you because you let him use your car.

"These guys still around?" Davan asked casually.

Her mind flickered to Herman. He didn't count. She'd been clear in telling him to leave her alone. "All my demons have been excised."

"Good." Davan's eyes darkened, turning into obsidian marble.

"You were married?"

Davan nodded. "We married too young. I wasn't mature enough. She didn't really want Davan David Underwood. She liked the packaging, but had plans to mold the inside to what she really wanted. I'm a simple man. I don't put on a show to impress. What you see is what you get. Hunt, kill, provide. I didn't do well with the remodeling, and I was too young to know how to handle it. Everything fell apart, we went our separate ways, our parents said 'I told you so,' and the rest is history."

"I didn't expect you to be so open about it."

Davan shrugged. "Wouldn't help me to get closer to you by hiding anything. Besides, I come from a family of talkers. We're close and share everything. I never learned artful deceit."

She watched him start in on his next slice of pizza.

"There's another problem we couldn't get past."

Jova waited for him to continue. She knew Davan couldn't be as perfect as he seemed. The fringe of his lashes shielded his eyes in a playfully sexy way. "What?" she prompted.

"I have a big appetite."

Jova watched him chew his pizza, his eyes glued to her cleavage. He wasn't referring to food. "Oh!"

"Mussing up my ex-wife's hair three or four times a day didn't fit her agenda."

Three or four times . . . a day! Oh!

"And then there was the issue of size—"

"Enough! That's enough information."

Davan smiled, pleased to have shaken her.

"You're joking."

He watched her with eyes that said he couldn't be more serious.

Eating through the charged moment, Jova wondered what Davan Underwood was all about. What were his flaws? Handsome, strong, principled— where was the catch? In her experience there was always a catch. She suspected Davan was no different.

His weakness had to be women. His answering machine had probably malfunctioned from all the telephone calls he was receiving while they were out together.

"Why haven't the women you're dating showed you downtown?"

Davan's gaze shifted to her. They darkened the way men's eyes tend to do when sex or a good meal is offered. He studied her. She squirmed, a little.

"Very creative of you, Ms. Parker." He rumbled

with laughter. "I've been too busy to date. The last three months have been spent moving, and helping my uncle at home and at the garage. Besides, I didn't meet anyone I was interested in dating until I met you."

Jova's face warmed. She'd brought up his marriage and his dating status. What was she doing? If she didn't want to date anyone, why was she prying into his personal life? And why did sitting on a blanket eating pizza feel this intimate?

"You should hurry, Jova."

"Hurry with what?"

"Hurry up and get over this 'you're not dating right now' thing before another woman comes along and snatches me up." He gave her a wink, then threw his head back and laughed at her startled expression.

Silence found them again while they sat at the river's edge and watched the boats glide by. Traffic on the strip began to thicken. Jova suspected their peaceful outing was about to take a dramatic turn and place them smack dab in the middle of Make-out Central Avenue.

"Uncle David wants me to bring you by to say hello." Davan found her hand and entangled their fingers. "No pressure. He knows this is our first date, but he asked anyway. If you don't want to go, I'll understand."

"No, it's okay. We should probably be heading out of the park anyway. Another hour and the traffic will be bumper-to-bumper."

Motown oldies ushered them across town to Uncle David's house. Not far from the salon and garage, the black and white house sat off the corner of a well-kept neighborhood. A lawn sprinkler rotated back and forth, watering the lush grass.

Davan took her hand, waited for the spray to pass, and ran up onto the small cement porch. He rang the bell and soon enough his uncle opened the door.

"Uncle David, this is Jova."

"My nephew doesn't have good manners." David swung the screen door open and invited her inside, leaving Davan looking puzzled on the porch.

David stood evenly with Jova. He wore dress slacks and a short sleeve dress shirt that had been starched to a crisp. The multicolored bow tie looked like it would strangle him.

"Why are you all dressed up?" Davan asked after closing the door.

"This is the way you dress when you're expecting lady company."

"Jova's *my* company, Uncle David."

"Then why are you dressed like *that*? Come have a seat."

Jova accepted his arm. "I don't know, I kinda like what he's wearing, Mr. Underwood."

"Uncle David. Call me Uncle David."

David wanted every detail of their date. He listened with unbridled enthusiasm, and admitted it had been so long since he'd dated, he wanted to relive their experience as his own. "I should've married," he said. "Now I'm too sick. No woman wants a man she has to take care of."

"How come you never married?" Jova asked.

He shrugged his spindly shoulders. "I fell in love once. I let her get away. At the time, getting the garage running was the only thing I cared about." He dropped his head. "I wish I had it all to do over."

Jova leaned over and patted his hand comfortingly. Davan had suddenly become very quiet. She didn't know what to say. Uncle David was still handsome, but frail and tired. Her heart broke for the sickly, aging man who always seemed to be in a bad mood. She'd always thought of him as an introvert, never making friendly conversation with anyone at the neighborhood watch meetings. She'd never considered he might be lonely.

"Have you had dinner?" Jova asked. "We have a couple of slices of pizza in the car."

"I've had my dinner." David withdrew his hand, brushing away his momentary emotional weakness.

"What about dessert?"

"Dessert?" David looked at Davan, who shrugged.

"Yeah, you have to eat dessert. Davan and I didn't have any either. I could make something."

David looked sheepish, his eyes roaming between Davan and Jova. "I don't know what I have in the kitchen. Davan does my shopping."

They both looked over at Davan. He watched the scene suspiciously. Jova wondered if she was overstepping her bounds, but David's confession of loneliness made her want to lift his spirits. She suspected his stoic attitude was a self-preserving mechanism. He was facing a debilitating illness alone. Even though Davan had come from Utah to help him get through it, a woman's touch was needed.

"Do we have time?" Jova asked Davan.

"Yeah, sure."

She turned to David. "Do you mind?"

David looked as suspicious as Davan. Did these men never have a woman cook for them? Both acted as if she'd arrived on the doorstep with her suitcases. All she wanted to do was whip up a quick dessert, and spend more time getting to know David. "How about it?" Jova asked, already getting out of her seat.

"No, I don't mind," David finally answered. "Make yourself at home."

Jova sent Davan away when he tried to show her around the kitchen. A few minutes later the television came on. She went through the cabinets and browsed in the refrigerator, searching for ingredients to make a quick dessert. Amazingly, the kitchen was well stocked. Thirty minutes later, she had whipped up strawberry shortcake with a side of ice cream. She apologized for having to serve chocolate ice cream, but it was all David had in the freezer—three quarts of it. The men waved off the apology. She doubted they would have known the difference if she had served lime Jell-O.

Sitting at the kitchen table, receiving compliments from Davan and David for her cooking skills, made Jova emotionally warm. She'd been very close with her mother, and missed her dearly. Months after her mother's death, she had exchanged her sorrow for ambition. Her goal was to make her mother proud posthumously by becoming a successful businesswoman. Having dessert with Davan and David let her experience the closeness of having a family, if only for one evening.

Jova was still humming when she pulled her Mustang up in front of Davan's apartment building.

Davan turned to face Jova. His face was partially hidden in the shadow cast by the streetlight, giving him a mysteriously sexy appearance. "I have never seen my uncle David so open and friendly. Never. He's stoic, and won't even discuss his illness with me. You come over and within minutes he's telling you his life story."

Now she understood his incredulous looks, puzzled stares, and confused glances during dessert. "A skill acquired with my profession."

"Again tonight, I'm impressed." His eyes danced from her mouth to her sundress. "Would you like to come up?"

"I better not."

He held her with eyes that promised many things—if only she would go up to his apartment. Her fingers crept to the door handle. She made a fist and placed it in her lap. This had to stop. She couldn't fall for a handsome face, perfect body, hypnotizing eyes, dazzling smile . . .

"I have coffee. You won't have to make dessert."

"It's getting late. I should go."

Davan reached across the console and stroked her chin. "I can't persuade you?"

Jova shook her head no. If she opened her mouth she'd scream yes. Her body reacted to the tender stroke of his fingers. Briefly, she debated the best and worst of what would happen if she went up for coffee. Coffee would probably turn into something a lot hotter, very fast.

Davan exhaled hard. "Call me the minute you get home." He stepped out of the car and walked around to her door. "I'll take a look at your car tomorrow, if that's okay."

Jova nodded yes.

Davan's laughter shattered the quiet evening. "You've gone all quiet again. It must mean you're struggling over coming upstairs."

Heat crept up Jova's neck. He could read her too well.

"Don't worry. I'll let you off the hook." He bent in the window, bringing his face inches from hers. "Tonight you get a free pass, but I only give one."

He stood abruptly, leaving her mesmerized. "Get home safely."

Chapter 7

Jova rolled over, almost falling out of bed. Her sweet dream about Davan shattered. Once she'd been able to stop thinking about him, the dreams had taken over, lulling her into a deep sleep. Their tour of the city had turned into a first date lasting the entire day, and some of the night. She forced one eye open. "Six o'clock. Who's at the door at this time of morning?" She trudged across the apartment, grumbling all the way.

"Good morning." Davan had transformed back into mild-mannered auto repairman.

"Mornin'," she mumbled.

"I came for your . . . car." He reached out to muss her hair.

Jova remembered the bandana and ratty dorm shirt, and ducked behind the door.

"Too late." Davan laughed.

"I thought the garage opened at seven."

"It does, but I get there at six-thirty to open up for Uncle David. I came in early to get a jump on your car. The knocking sounded worse when you drove off yesterday."

"C'mon in." Still not fully awake, Jova searched the living room for her keys. She moved across the room, retracing her steps from the night before.

"Did you make all these pieces?" Davan asked, examining her crocheted sofa cover. His voice crossed the small space of the studio apartment and she suddenly realized inviting him into her home meant inviting him into the intimacy of her bedroom.

"Yeah. I've been at it a long time."

"Looks great."

Jova froze as she passed the mirror on the dresser. She looked awful! She wouldn't have to worry about dating Davan after he'd seen what she looked like first thing in the morning. If this vision didn't scar him for life, nothing could. She glanced across the room at him. He didn't seem bothered by her appearance. He was looking around at her crocheting and photos of her mother.

"Here we go." She handed him the keys. "Would you like a cup of coffee?"

Davan sat on the edge of the sofa, his hands planted on his knees. "I already ate breakfast. More than two cups of coffee and I bounce off the walls."

She nodded.

"File that information away for future use." He flashed his smile.

"How can you be so *up* this early in the morning?"

"I don't need much sleep." He stood and headed for the door. "I'll try to finish today. I have to work between customers and running the office. If you need to go somewhere let me know."

"I plan to do the books for the salon today. Inventory and ordering supplies. I shouldn't need the car."

Davan stepped out onto the landing. "Go back to bed."

Jova watched him trot down the stairs. He turned

back. "My uncle is crazy about you, too." He walked into the early morning darkness.

She felt like a schoolgirl experiencing her first crush. A tingle of delight raced through her. Uncle David liked her, *too.* She felt giddy enough to jump up and down. How could she go back to sleep after Davan's visit? She tried, but ended up tossing and turning, thinking about him bent under the hood of her car with his muscles flexing. Finally, she gave in to curiosity and kneeled on the floor of her bedroom window, peeking out through the curtains.

The street was quiet. A few cars drove by, most likely her neighbors going to work. Davan had hoisted her Mustang up in the air. Every now and again she caught a glimpse of him passing by the garage door. He concentrated on his task, carefully selecting each tool he used to tinker beneath the car. A few times he stepped back and shook his head.

She prepared herself to be scolded when he returned. *When's the last time you changed the oil? Have the tires been rotated?* Hey, when she pumped gas she felt like a certified mechanic. Cars were for driving. When she'd had her Lincoln, the servicemen always called and reminded her to bring it in for maintenance. The only calls she received from Ben were reminders of his mother's standing hair appointment.

Davan came around to stand in front of Jova's car. He bent underneath the hood, giving her a full view of his posterior. She needed a man like Davan to take care of the mechanics on her car. And she'd bet he was a regular Mr. Fix-it around the house. Blue-collar working men knew how to use their hands—in all things. She shuddered, remembering the way his casual touch turned her to jelly.

"Stop it," she scolded herself. Hadn't she vowed not to date until the salon was financially stable? What happened to convincing Davan they were only friends? She gave up her position at the window, and headed to the shower. "As long as I'm up, I might as well be productive."

Jova spent the morning at Tresses & Locks. In between stealing peeks at Davan, she swept and mopped the salon floor. She rearranged the lingerie racks, and put together a new counter display. She hurried through the inventory, and called in her monthly order to her supplier. After balancing her books, she selected lingerie to place on special for the month. Just after noon she locked up the salon, and prepared to enjoy the rest of her day off.

"Jova."

She swung around, hand pressed to her chest. "Don't jump out at me! You scared me to death!"

"Sorry." Herman approached from the other side of the alley. "I know you told me not to come here again, but I didn't know who I could go to."

He looked beaten down and afraid. His clothes were dirty, the pants worn at the knees. He hadn't shaved or combed his hair. She took a step back. Bathing had not been a priority either.

"What about your family?" Jova asked.

Herman hung his head, shaking it no in response.

"Let's go upstairs." She remembered when things were really good with Herman. She had even believed they might have a future. She was still mad at him for dragging her into court, but she couldn't turn her back on someone she once cared for when he was this down and out.

She invited Herman to sit at the table she used to delineate her dining room area.

Herman picked at the tablecloth with dirty hands. The jewelry he'd often bragged about was gone.

"Have you eaten lunch?" Jova asked.

Herman shook his head no.

She moved to the kitchen to make him a sandwich. "Tell me why you're here."

"I can't come up with the money to pay the bookie. Hell, interest has made what I owe so high, I don't even know what my tab is today."

She placed the turkey sandwich and a glass of milk in front of him. "What are you going to do?"

Herman gulped his milk before answering. "If I don't have the money by six, he'll have my arm broken. Tomorrow, another arm."

She watched him tear into the sandwich. Did this actually happen in real life? Or was Herman running a scam on her? He'd proven he couldn't be trusted when he sued her. This could be an elaborate scheme to get the money from her.

"After both my arms are broken, he'll give the order to move on to my legs." He finished the milk. "God help me if I don't have the money when they finish with my legs."

"This is horrible. How did you get into this mess?"

Herman shrugged pitifully. Jova watched him devour the sandwich, eating like he hadn't had food for days. Obviously, he hadn't been home to change clothes, shave, or clean up. Her heart ached for him, but she couldn't get tangled up in his problems. Herman had proved to be the type of man who couldn't control his impulses, which landed him in deep trouble. Now he wanted her to bail him out. Him coming to her apartment put her in danger, too.

"Why did you come here, Herman?"

"I know you can't pay my debt, but I thought you might be able to loan me enough money for a bus ticket. I have family in Alabama. I can go there. I promise I'll send you the money as soon as I get work."

"I don't know . . ."

He grabbed her hand, squeezing it frantically. "Please, Jova. I'll go from here straight to the Greyhound station. I'll get lost down in Alabama forever."

She studied the desperation in his eyes. "How much?"

"A hundred dollars."

She pulled her hand away. "I'd have to go to the ATM."

"Thank you. Thank you. You're a lifesaver."

"Do you have a change of clothes?"

"No."

Jova made him another sandwich. While he ate, she searched her closet and found a jogging suit he'd left at her apartment when they were hot and heavy. "I have to go get the money. Why don't you take a shower while I'm gone?"

"Okay." He took the clothes from her, his hand lingering on hers. "Thank you for this."

She pulled away and headed for the door.

"Jova, one more thing. Can you give me a ride to the bus station?"

The racket in the garage stopped when Jova stepped in. Three men rushed up, asking if they could help.

"Is Davan around?"

"Should've known," one of the guys mumbled. The others walked off. "He's in the office."

She'd been to the garage a few times before, usually to see if the cashier had change for one of her customers' large bills. There were four bays where cars were suspended in air, waiting to be repaired. Several people sat in the modest waiting area watching television. Invoices and key rings hung on a Peg-Board behind the front desk. Handwritten signs were posted above the time clock with warnings about clocking in for a coworker. The office Davan now shared with David was behind the front desk.

"Hi." Davan came out of his seat, around the desk to greet her. The office was small, clean, and neat. The back door opened up to the bays where the men were working. The window over his desk looked out on the alley behind the garage.

"What's up?" Davan asked, smiling under his baseball cap. His overalls were clean, which probably meant he'd spent most of his day in the office.

"How much longer on my car?"

"I found the source of the knocking and took care of that this morning." He waved for her to follow him to the back of the garage. "When's the last time you had the oil changed?"

Jova cringed. The car care lecture would come next. She'd modified her speed while driving with him. What more did he want? She followed him through the bays to the back of the garage near the parts storage. Various pieces of her Mustang were scattered on the ground.

"This is a beauty of a car, Jova. You should take better care of it. Do you know to how to check the tire pressure? Have the tires been rotated?"

The theme from *The Twilight Zone* played in Jova's

head. If it were up to men, there would be laws regulating the care and maintenance of your vehicle. Skip an oil change, and go directly to jail.

Davan walked around the car pointing out things he planned to do to the car. She interrupted his lecture. "How much longer?"

"I'll have it done by closing. Tomorrow morning at the latest."

"An unexpected errand has come up."

"No problem." He fished his keys out of his back pocket. "You can use my Dodge. It's the black truck around back."

"I don't know if I can drive a truck."

"It's one of the compact trucks. If you can drive an SUV, you can drive my truck."

Jova fingered the keys. "Are you sure?"

Davan smiled. "I know where you live."

She thought of Herman waiting at her house. "It won't take long."

"Take your time," he called after her. "And don't speed."

Jova spread a blanket on the seat of Davan's truck before she let Herman get inside. Davan obviously spent a great deal of time maintaining his truck. The interior was immaculate, the finish pristine. The motor hummed, and the chrome shined. The last thing she wanted to do was leave the stench of another man behind.

Jova had never felt more relieved than when Herman stepped on the Greyhound heading for Alabama. She'd sat with him in the downtown terminal, waiting for his departure. She took no chances that he would miss his bus.

No hulking men dressed in black came after them. They weren't followed. In a day, Herman would be safely tucked away with relatives down South. No longer her problem.

After returning Davan's truck, Jova came home, a little miffed that her off day had been squandered on working in the shop and helping her ex escape his troubles. The Indian summer heat left her sticky, and Herman's odor made her feel funky. Maybe she could enjoy the rest of the evening. She took a long shower and pampered her body. After towel-drying, she caressed her body with flowery oil and sat in front of the window air conditioner while she gave herself a manicure and pedicure. She brushed out her hair and placed it in a long braid that hung past her shoulders. She slipped into a comfortable pair of denim shorts and a pink tank top. After starting dinner, she sat in front of the television with crocheting in hand.

Around eight, Davan rang her bell. "She's ready," he announced, holding up her keys. He gave her a rundown of what he'd done. "You don't have the foggiest, do you?"

Jova shrugged. "The only thing I know about cars is that they need gas and once a year I have to go to the DMV for my registration."

Davan laughed. "Good thing I came along."

Chapter 8

Jova's week started off strangely and ended badly.
The credit card company called and informed her of a suspicious spending pattern on her Visa. She found a local branch office, which turned out to be downriver, and went to straighten out the mess. She was issued a new card and the charges were removed, but she lost an entire day of customers.

She had no doubt that Herman was somehow involved in the credit card purchases. She had obtained the card to use in case of salon emergencies only. She kept it in the dresser, rarely using it. He must have stolen her number when she left him to borrow Davan's truck and make the ATM run.

Thank goodness Herman was out of her life. She would never see him again, and if she did, she'd turn him over to his bookie personally.

Dawn still wouldn't say more than two words to her. All week, Dawn ignored her, pouting when Lisa teased Jova about her date with Davan. Jova had tried over and over to make small talk. She'd even apologized, trying to salvage their friendship. Nothing worked.

Saturday evening, Jova counted the day's earnings while Dawn toiled at her station. Being alone in the shop and not speaking made Jova uncomfortable. She went in the back to toss in a wash of towels. When she returned, Dawn had packed up her station.

"Today's my last day. I'm going to rent a booth at a salon in Redford."

"What? Dawn, don't leave. You can't be this mad about Davan. It was one date."

Dawn's face was set with unforgiving anger. "You stabbed me in the back. I refuse to work for someone like you. I won't make you any more money."

"You're more than an employee. We're friends."

"No, we're not." Dawn hiked her bags on her shoulder and headed for the door.

"Dawn?" Something more was going on. Jova just didn't know what. "We were friends. You could at least explain the real reason why you're leaving."

Dawn swung around, dropping her bags to the floor. "I tried to be your friend, but you're two-faced. I saw Herman first, but you had to have him. And then you threw him away, always complaining about him not being good enough for you. Like to say, 'Hey, I'm done. You can have him now.' And when Davan walked into the shop, I made it clear I liked him, but you had to have him too. Well, I'm outta here. You can have every man that walks through this door."

Jova stood shocked at her friend's revelation. She didn't know Dawn had had a thing for Herman. And she couldn't seriously be upset about Davan. He was never anything more than kind to her.

Dawn snatched up her bags. "I'd better warn Lisa about you." She stomped out the door.

Jova was still standing frozen in disbelief when Davan came through the door. "I just helped Dawn load up her car. She said she quit, because you pushed her out. What's going on?"

"I don't think I know."

"Why don't you sit down?" He tried to help her into the salon chair.

She stepped back, avoiding his touch. "I need to be alone for a while."

"You need someone to talk to. I'm here, but I won't let you beat yourself up about Dawn."

"One thing you should know about me, Davan," she snapped. "If I say I need to be alone, I really need to be alone."

"I'm not leaving until I'm sure you're going to be okay."

"Don't push me." She blurted out the details of conversation with Dawn, subtly accusing him of having played them against each other and causing the fallout with Dawn.

"I understand you're upset about Dawn quitting, but I didn't have anything to do with it. I was never anything more than friendly to her. I can try to talk to her and clear everything up if you want."

"No." Jova forced herself to calm down. "No, I shouldn't have implied . . . I'm sorry. You're right. I'm upset. I've lost a friend, and my best employee."

A moment of silence cooled the air between them. Davan leaned his head to the side questioningly and asked, "Who's Herman?"

Had she blurted out Herman's name?

"You said Dawn accused you of taking Herman, and now me, away from her."

"Herman is my ex."

"How ex?" His dark eyes narrowed, questioning.

"Ex." Jova didn't know why she felt compelled to explain, but she did. She didn't want him to think she was interested in another man. Curious, how he made her feel this way when she'd firmly decided not to date. Ever since making that declaration, Davan had proceeded to tear down every wall she built. Here she was telling him about Herman.

"Very ex. He left town. I drove him to the bus station Monday."

"Monday?" Davan's expression hardened. His dark eyes filled with storm clouds. "I had your car all day Monday."

She'd said too much.

"Jova, did you borrow my truck to drive your *ex*-boyfriend around?"

Yep, she'd said too much.

"Hmm." He nodded knowingly. His obsidian eyes were cold and angry. He spoke through clenched teeth. "I don't know how I feel about that."

He turned and left the salon without saying good-bye.

Chapter 9

Davan used his key to open the door of David's house. He followed the volume of the television into his uncle's bedroom. "How are you doing?" he asked, pulling a chair to the bedside.

"Tired today," Uncle David answered, pausing between his words. The house felt stuffy, and David lay underneath a blanket, perspiring.

"Are you warm?"

He shook his head. "Cold. Always cold. Because of the anemia."

"Have you eaten?"

"Fixed some soup a little bit ago. Not hungry now. Tired. Where's that pretty girl?"

"At the salon."

David smiled. "Jova's nice."

Davan didn't want to talk about Jova. He had no right to be, but he was jealous about her having seen her ex-boyfriend. She'd loaded him into his truck and driven him around town. It didn't seem right. He was working to get closer to her and she was still seeing her ex. He let his jealously go for the moment, and concentrated on his uncle's health. "When do you see the doctor again?"

"Next week."

"I'll drive you." He expected his uncle to protest,

but when he didn't Davan settled in to spend the evening. "I think I'll stay and watch television."

Uncle David nodded, too tired to speak.

Davan stayed with his uncle until he fell sound asleep. He felt so helpless when it came to Uncle David. The man had a will of iron and a stubborn streak to match. Davan was tempted to move his things into the house despite his uncle's objections, but he couldn't go against his uncle's wishes. He owed David his dignity, among other things. He could continue to check on Uncle David every day. He would also drive Uncle David to the doctor's office and get a report firsthand. If it didn't sound good he'd call his mother to come to town and take over.

Davan sulked on the drive home. Uncle David refused to let him move in to take care of him, and Jova pushing him away earlier didn't help him to feel any better. What was it about her that drove him nuts?

"Man, you've got it bad." He ran a hand over two-day stubble. He jumped through hoops like a schoolboy for her. At the garage he couldn't concentrate for watching the comings and goings of the salon, hoping to catch a glimpse of Jova passing by the window.

The simplest gestures meant much to him. He possessively claimed that every one of her smiles was meant for him. Meticulous with her hair, Jova never had one strand out of place. Finicky about her clothes, she dressed in the latest fashions. Her studio apartment was small, but it fit her perfectly: well kept and fashionably decorated with her own creations.

Davan had just arrived home when the buzzer rang. "Yeah?" he asked into the intercom.

"Davan, it's Jova. Can I come up?"

Jova? He pushed the button, buzzing her inside the building. He tossed his baseball cap on the hook beside the door and ruffled his hair to life. No time to change out of the overalls. He opened the door and stood in the hallway, waiting for Jova to come off the elevator.

Jova walked to him like a vision in a dream. She wore burgundy shorts with a matching blouse, the V cut giving a modest hint of her cleavage. Snappy sandals completed the outfit. Her silky black hair was parted down the middle and two long braids hung to her shoulders. She carried a large straw bag on her shoulder, another in her hand. She waltzed up to him and dropped the bags on the floor. "This is my second visit today. You weren't home earlier."

Sassy, he thought.

"Davan, I did the wrong thing."

He crossed his arms over his chest and leaned against the doorjamb.

"I don't want you to be mad at me."

He liked where this was going. "Why?"

"Why?" Jova shifted her weight from one foot to the other. "Why? Because we have a good friendship and I need all the friends I can get right now."

"Friendship?"

"Well, yeah." She couldn't hold his gaze.

"I want to be more than your friend." He stepped forward, wrapped his arm around her waist, and pulled her against his body. He pressed her close, erasing her resistance. He lifted her chin in his palm, lowered his head, and kissed the corner of her mouth.

"Oh, my!"

Davan severed their connection. "Good evening,

Mr. and Mrs. Steinkeller." The elderly couple living across the hall shuffled away to the elevator. Embarrassed Jova, hurried into his apartment.

"What's in the bags?" Davan asked, hauling everything inside.

"Peace offerings." Jova dropped to her knees and rummaged through the first bag, pulling out a Tupperware dish. "Fried chicken." She produced two more containers. "Corn and salad." She stood, dusting her knees. "Friends again?"

"Friends?" He took a menacing step forward. "Do I have to kiss you again?"

"N-no," she stammered.

"We agree this is a date?"

Jova looked hesitant, but agreed. "Okay."

"I guess that means I still get to kiss you again."

She looked as if she had fallen into a bear trap. "But—"

"What's in the other bag, Jova?" He kneeled and searched through the bag, finding Monopoly, Twister, and two videotapes. He grinned up at her. "I'm not into the chick flicks, but Twister has possibilities." He rubbed the hem of her shorts between his fingers.

Jova staggered back. "Maybe we should eat."

"Yeah." He looked her up and down, appraisingly. "I'm famished. Wasting away." He wasn't referring to food.

"I haven't finished unpacking," Davan said as they moved to the kitchen. He ripped the tape from a box sitting on the kitchen counter. Not finding what he wanted, he set the box on the floor, and moved to the next.

"You've been here three months."

"I know. I just haven't gotten around to finishing.

I hate decorating, but I like the comfort of a homey house. Like your place."

"Why do you do that?"

"What?" He pulled two plates from a box and handed them over to her.

"Say things to fluster me."

"You mean flirt with you?" He retrieved glasses and silverware.

"Yeah."

"Why do people flirt, Jova?" He turned to her. "Should I be more direct?"

She began rinsing the dishes, avoiding his gaze.

He moved next to her, drying the dishes. "I'll tell you a secret." He emptied his hands and refilled them with Jova's waist. "I'm very attracted to you," he whispered next to her ear. "I want to date you. I want to get to know you better." He reluctantly pulled away. One more second and he would be kissing her. "There are other things, too, but I probably shouldn't go into them right now."

Jova's big brown eyes stared up at him. "Can you be more direct?"

He grinned. "Now you're playing with me."

She watched him, not giving a hint of her emotions.

"I can be more direct. Are you attracted to me?" He watched the sway of her backside as she sauntered over to the kitchen table and started dishing out food onto their plates.

"See, I came with a peace offering, and look how you treat me."

"The pouting is kinda sexy." He moved behind her, his body close enough to touch hers. She stiffened at the contact. "Are you attracted to me, Jova?"

"I came here as a friend."

"Twice?"

"Are you bent on ignoring me, or just stubborn? I told you at Hart Plaza I'm not interested in getting involved with anyone right now. No offense."

"Oh, none taken." He moved closer, inhaling the scent of her hair. "If you aren't interested—you know I am because I've made that clear—why didn't you just drop off the food and leave? You could have apologized tomorrow at the garage. You not only came by *twice,* you brought movies and games. It kinda tips your hand that you plan to stay awhile."

"I-I—"

"Are you attracted to me, Jova?"

"No," she answered, her voice soft and low.

He pressed into her. "If you're not attracted to me, why do you watch me from your shop window?"

He had touched a nerve. If possible, her body became tighter.

"It's okay. You don't have to answer." He stepped away and she visibly relaxed. "Let's have dinner."

Davan helped himself to seconds, praising Jova for her cooking skills. Could she be any more perfect? Beautiful, easy to talk to, sweet with a touch of D-town toughness, and a good cook too! As icing on the cake, she carried herself with the dignity of a princess and dressed as regally as a queen.

"Tell me about your mother," Davan said.

"My mother was beautiful. We were best friends. I miss her."

"What was she like?"

"She was very determined. My father left us when I was a baby, so I don't really know him."

"You never talk to him?"

She shook her head no. "He left when I was two. I don't even remember him. He left and never looked back. I don't know where he is, or if he's even alive."

Davan's story wasn't much different. His father divorced his mother soon after he was born to start another family with another woman. His mother never remarried, and rarely dated. She never spoke negatively of his father, but it was clear by the lengths she went to not to mention him, he'd hurt her badly. Davan had vague memories of his father at Christmas. His father sent a card on his birthdays, until he turned eighteen. After that, his father faded away. Unlike Jova, he knew exactly where his father lived. They just didn't have a close relationship.

Jova continued. "My mother worked hard to keep a roof over our heads. She worked jobs she hated. She insisted on dropping me off and picking me up from school every day. We didn't have a car until I went to high school, so she walked everywhere. Once I got old enough to stay at home alone after school, she went to junior college. Became a paralegal."

"Sounds a lot like my mom. When my father left, she got a total makeover. She finished college, and found a good job working with the local government. There are even family rumors she had some cosmetic surgery—my father left her for a much younger woman."

Jova ate a few bites before she spoke again. "I think my mother was a little disappointed when I didn't go to college. Four years of fighting to come up with tuition wasn't for me." Jova lit up with memories. "You should have seen her when I graduated from cosmetology school. You would have thought I had graduated from medical school at Harvard. My mother didn't want me struggling to pay the bills. She wanted me to do the things she couldn't, like travel. She would have been proud of me opening the salon."

"You miss her?"

Jova nodded, her eyes shining with tears. She dipped her head and started eating.

"I'm going to miss my uncle."

Her head snapped up in surprise. "Your uncle?"

"I told you he was sick. It doesn't look good."

She reached across the table. He met her halfway. He stroked his thumb against the softness of her hand.

"I'm going to his next doctor's visit to find out more. You wouldn't know it by the way Uncle David showed off for you, but he's very private, and very proud. He doesn't want anyone fussing over him. He doesn't want his lifestyle disrupted until absolutely necessary. He won't let me move in to help, and he doesn't want my mom here until he's completely incapacitated. It's frustrating."

"It's hard being helpless, but if it's what he wants."

"I know. That's why I try to back off. He raised me like a son. I owe him."

"Maybe that's why he doesn't want you and your mother moving in. Pride. He still sees himself as the leader of the family. He doesn't want to look weak. The fact he says it's okay for your mom to come when he's unable to take care of himself shows he knows he needs you."

"You might have something," Davan said.

"He took to me easily. And I fell for his charm right away. I could look in on him. If you wouldn't mind."

He tightened his hold on her hand. Jova's compassionate smile and knowing eyes made him feel he could handle anything. They made a connection in the silence. His initial attraction to Jova had been based on her sexy curves and beautiful face. The more time he spent with her, pulling away the layers of her hesitation, the more he appreciated her wonderful personality.

Jova pulled her hand away, leaving him bereft. "Why don't I clear the table while you put on a movie?"

In the living room, they debated over which movie to watch. Davan wouldn't budge. "You have to put the rules down about these things early in a relationship," he told Jova.

She countered with, "This is not a relationship, so watching the movies is okay."

"Yes, it is, and no, it's not. If you want to watch a movie I have Sylvester Stallone packed away in one of these boxes. Sylvester, Bruce, and Arnold, those are real movies."

"Forget the movie." She placed her hands on her hips. "We should unpack these boxes."

"Too domestic. Wouldn't want you to get any ideas, little Ms. I'm-not-ready-for-a-relationship-right-now."

Jova rolled her eyes, fighting a smile. "And I thought you were nice when I first met you."

"I was making a good first impression. I have you now. I can guzzle beer on the sofa and ignore you while I watch the big game."

"You'll never have me."

"Really?" He gave her the heated glare he'd noticed earlier made her step falter. "Don't even joke about that."

Jova's body language softened, Davan's eyes darkened. The quiet of the apartment became palpable, dangerous. Silence stretched between them. Davan wanted to pick her up, carry her to the bedroom. Chick flicks were crammed with moments like this. She would like being tossed over his shoulder and carried into his bedroom where he would ravish her. He would have to fight past her insecurities and inhibitions before she would reveal her true passion, but he was up to the challenge. He exercised self-restraint. There were better ways to seduce Jova Parker. Subtle, and not so subtle, ways of letting her know she turned him on . . . and warmed his heart.

"How about a game of Twister?" Davan asked.

Caught in the heated moment, Jova nodded.

"You set up the game. I'll move these boxes out of the way. I'll have to finish unpacking this weekend. I can't entertain you here with boxes all over the place."

During Twister, Jova dropped her guard, laughing and smiling as they wound their bodies into pretzels. Third game in, Davan's coordination faded and he made them topple to the floor. They laughed a long time, Jova's chest heaving.

Davan looked down at her, highly aware of their bodies being pressed together. "Do you know why I like women who fuss over their clothes and die if a hair is out of place?"

Jova's laughter faded. Her hands moved to his waist. "No. Why?"

"It's fun messing them up." He kissed the corner of her mouth. "How about it, Jova?" he whispered over her lips. "Can I get you a little dirty?"

He kissed her lips, his mouth barely touching hers. He pulled back, studying her reaction. Her lashes curtained her big brown eyes. Her lips parted slightly. She held a strange power over him.

One look made his insides quiver. As badly as he wanted her in his bed, he knew he needed her for much more. He reached up, loosening one braid and then the other, his eyes never leaving hers. He combed his fingers through her hair. When the silky tresses were arranged around her face, he thought he would melt. He had dated pretty girls, but none were as adorable as Jova. None ignited his protective nature, or made him think of curtains and commitments.

"I know how I feel about you driving your ex in my truck now," he said.

Jova cleared her throat. "How?"

"Don't *ever* do it again." He cupped the back of her head, and brought their lips together. He'd expected her to resist, but her hands tightened on his waist. Soft and full. He wanted more of her kiss. He teased her mouth tenderly until her arms wound around him. The first taste of her inflamed him. The kiss deepened and Jova responded with a long moan. He used his knees to pushed her legs apart and settled into her softness.

Jova's hands came up, pushing against his chest.

Davan pulled away, questioning her response.

"It's getting late," she said.

He tucked a soft tendril behind her ear. "You don't have to leave." His eyes darkened, clarifying his meaning.

"I do have to leave."

"I don't want you to go. Not yet."

"That's why I have to leave."

"One more kiss, and I'll walk you to your car." His thumb caressed her bottom lip. "Just one more kiss."

Chapter 10

Davan leafed through a fishing magazine while waiting for his uncle. David had shooed him out of the examination room when the technician came in to perform an abdominal ultrasound. The waiting room looked more like a page out of *House Beautiful* than a doctor's office with its leather sofas and oak tables. Soft lighting from table lamps cushioned the blow of the doctor's bill.

"I did one smart thing," Uncle David commented when they first arrived. "I bought good medical insurance."

A woman seated nearby had added, "Dr. Greenville is the best. I know. I've checked. I wouldn't trust my husband's heart to anyone but the best."

Davan wondered if she still felt the same way when she ran from the office an hour later in tears. He tossed the fishing magazine aside, and paced the length of the room. No sense bothering the receptionist again. The nurse would call when he could go back into the exam room with his uncle. He found a pay phone and dialed the garage. Everything was running smoothly. Things were quiet. He would get to the garage by closing to lock up.

"Davan Underwood," the nurse called. "The doctor will see you now."

He followed her down a long corridor to the doctor's private office. Plush carpeting and dark wallpaper gave the office a warm, homey feeling. A large, built-in wall aquarium bubbled as exotic fish swam by. The nurse closed the door as she left, making the room a soundproof cocoon.

"Dr. Greenville." The doctor rose from his chair behind a large oak desk, his hand extended. Not what Davan expected, Dr. Greenville was young, probably mid to late twenties. He wore dress slacks that hung with expensive ease down legs that propelled him to over six feet tall. He had the classic "I've got it all because I'm a handsome, rich cardiologist" smile. "Sorry we had to meet under these circumstances. Have a seat, please."

Davan sat in one of the twin leather chairs facing Dr. Greenville's desk.

"The nurse is finishing up with your uncle. He gave me permission to talk to you without him." The doctor opened a chart. "He's a man of his convictions."

"Stubborn," Davan added affectionately.

The doctor nodded his understanding. "Let's get right to it. Your uncle has an abdominal aortic aneurysm."

Davan looked askance.

The doctor pulled out a color chart mapping out the arteries, veins, and chambers of the heart. He illustrated his words as he explained. "An aneurysm is the out-pouching of a blood vessel. Many things can cause it, but with Mr. Underwood I suspect it's caused by a hardening of the arteries. An abdominal aortic aneurysm, or AAA, is an aneurysm located in the abdominal-aorta region. Your uncle's aneurysm is located here."

Davan studied the chart. "Can't you repair it? It looks like you could tie it off or something."

"I'm afraid it isn't so simple. True, it can be surgically repaired, but the location, size of the vessels involved, and rate of growth have to be taken into account."

"What are you doing for my uncle?"

"We're trying medical management."

Davan braced himself. "My uncle is under the impression he's going to die from this."

An uncomfortable expression colored Dr. Greenville's face. "I advised Mr. Underwood to have surgery immediately upon diagnosing the aneurysm. He refused." The doctor leaned forward, planting his elbows on the desk. "The aneurysm is growing at a steady rate. I won't be certain until the tests we did today are read, but it has grown to five centimeters in diameter."

"Five centimeters is bad?"

"Five centimeters is large and poses a dangerous threat to rupture. Mr. Underwood also has chronic lung disease and kidney problems that complicate the situation further."

"What are you saying, Dr. Greenville?"

"The aneurysm and complicating factors make surgery too risky, at this point. I would have to recommend a CABG, or coronary artery bypass graft, followed by surgical repair of the AAA."

"Why don't we do the . . ."

"CABG."

"Why don't we do the CABG and then repair the AAA?" Davan didn't understand what they were waiting for. He wasn't a medical expert, but time seemed to be of an essence.

Dr. Greenville frowned. "To speak frankly, Mr. Underwood, your uncle probably wouldn't survive the surgery."

"But it's worth a chance."

"To who?" the doctor asked quietly. "Your uncle doesn't want to take the chance. He has expressed his wishes to live out the remainder of his life without heroic intervention."

"Can't you force him to have the procedures?"

"No, I can't. It's his decision. I have to honor the way he wishes to live out his life."

Desperation moved through Davan. "I've heard about situations like this. Can't his family go to court and get permission for the procedures?"

"There are situations where the family can petition the court for guardianship. However, I don't think that is appropriate here. Your uncle is of sound mind. You're certainly free to investigate further, but I don't think you'll be successful."

"Dr. Greenville—"

The doctor held up a hand, stopping him. "At this point, Mr. Underwood, I wouldn't perform the surgery. I don't know if any surgeon would. Odds are your uncle wouldn't make it off the operating table."

Davan collapsed back in his chair.

"Excuse my bluntness, but I wanted you to understand fully."

The desperation seeped into his lungs, making it difficult to breathe. "There has to be something we can do."

"I'm sorry."

"I love my uncle, Dr. Greenville. I don't want him to die. It's that simple. I don't understand why it wasn't a simple decision for my uncle when there

was a chance the operation would help him."
Davan sat forward, burying his face in his hands.

"I know this is very difficult for you and your family, Mr. Underwood. Believe me, I hate to have to deliver such terrible news." Dr. Greenville came around the desk and clasped Davan's shoulder. "Consider everything I've told you today. Talk with your uncle and try to understand why he made the decision he did. Do these things before you do anything rash. I've seen families torn apart in these situations. Isn't it more important to spend this time loving your uncle instead of fighting with him?"

Davan nodded, his face still buried in his hands.

"Why don't you take a moment?" Dr. Greenville left him alone to grieve.

Chapter 11

"What are you doing?"

Jova's face broke into a smile when she heard Davan's voice. She clutched the phone close to her ear, willing him near. "I'm drinking hot cocoa and eating animal crackers."

The soft rumble of laughter tickled her ear. "Hard day at the salon?"

"I interviewed a couple of stylists to fill Dawn's position. No luck." Whoever took over for Dawn needed to fit in with the salon's image.

"I'm across the street. Can I come by?"

Jova did a mental assessment of her appearance. Her hair could be more imaginatively styled than a ponytail, but it would do. The pink and white sundress fell two inches above her knees. She wiggled her painted toes. She was standing in front of the mirror, checking her makeup, when she told Davan he could stop over.

Davan is dangerous, she thought, remembering their last encounter. *"One more kiss,"* he'd said. He stayed true to his word and gave her one last kiss, but he hadn't warned her it would leave her mind stunned and her body tingly. No man had ever kissed her with such authority and passion.

While she was styling hair, Jova's mind often wandered to thoughts of him. What might have happened if she hadn't left his apartment? Her days and nights were spent dreaming up romantic endings to that question.

Afraid she might miss his call, Jova often ran for the phone. She examined every word between them, hoping she'd said the right thing. She waited anxiously for him to ask her for another date, but he hadn't so far. She had mixed feelings about that. She wanted to see where a relationship with Davan might go, but she had made a vow to put Tresses & Locks first in her life.

Jova realized her musings were only to satisfy her ego. Davan had weaved a spell on her mind and body that couldn't be undone. If she didn't stop watching him from the salon window, she'd be reported as a Peeping Tom. She wanted Davan—badly. She was formulating the ways when Davan tapped on the door.

One look at his downturned mouth and sad eyes and Jova knew there was a problem. "What's the matter?" She pulled him inside.

"Is it obvious?"

Yes, to her. "What's wrong?"

They sat on the sofa together while Davan gave her the details of his visit with Dr. Greenville. Sadly fascinated, she listened to the morbid details of the doctor's report. Learning the specifics of David's failing health left Davan shaken.

"I'm so mad at him," Davan said. "I took him home and got out of there as fast as I could."

"Mad? At your uncle?"

"Yes!"

"Why?" Jova thought his anger misplaced.

"He had the power to stop this." Davan jumped up, pacing from wall to wall. "He could have agreed to the operation when he was first diagnosed. Instead he did nothing. He's still not doing anything." He shook his head, running a hand across his chin. "This is not my uncle. I don't know who this man is, or what he's trying to do, but this is not my uncle David. My uncle is a fighter. He wouldn't lie down and die without trying every trick in the book to beat it."

"The doctor might be right. David has his reasons. You should talk to him."

"What reasons? Tell me what reason he could have for walking out on me."

"He's not walking out on you, Davan." Jova added gently, "He's dying."

"He's dying because he doesn't love me enough to fight." Davan loosened his tie. "You don't understand. Uncle David is the only father I've ever known. He finds out he's sick and he doesn't consider how much I need him. He doesn't consider his family's feelings when he decides not to get treatment. He doesn't think about the pain this is causing my mom. He just says, 'I give up.' I never thought I would say this about my uncle, but he's selfish and cruel."

"Davan," Jova said tenderly. "Come sit down."

He stopped midstep, looked at her, and calmed instantly. She reached out to him, and he dropped down next to her.

"Davan." She placed a comforting hand on his cheek. "I understand you're angry about your uncle's decision, but it was *his decision*. For whatever reason, this is what he has decided to do. You can't let him see you this angry. He needs your support."

"How can I support this?" Davan's spoke softly, the anger shifting to pain. His dark eyes locked with hers, searching for answers. "I'm going to lose my uncle."

Jova pulled him to her. She fought back tears, thinking her heart would break for Davan and the painful road ahead.

He buried his head against her chest and admitted, "It hurts."

Jova held Davan for a long while in silence. She didn't know what to say, and doubted he felt like talking. Hearing about David brought back sad memories of her mother's death. Diagnosed with breast cancer at thirty-five, she lost her battle with the disease ten years later. It was an emotionally hard time for Jova, but once her mother went into remission after the first bout of chemotherapy, they learned the value of life. They had always been the best of friends, but the illness brought them closer, urging them to appreciate every moment they had together. When her mom did pass away, Jova was sad, but she had no regrets. As she held Davan she understood his feelings of anger and betrayal, but she wanted him to cherish the time he had left with his uncle. He would never forgive himself if David died while they were fighting.

"Are you okay?"

Davan lifted his head, but did not move away. "I'm better."

Jova's stomach flip-flopped when he stroked her cheek with the rough pad of his thumb.

"You're a good person to talk to," he said. His warm breath shimmered over her cheek. "Thank you for listening."

Jova swallowed, finding her voice. "That's what friends are for."

"Again with the friends?" He grinned. His hand slid from her cheek, over her neck, to the back of her head. He brought her to him and kissed her, timidly at first, then with a hunger that made Jova back away. His arms held her, bringing her back into the kiss. He teased the corners of her mouth, and she fastened her arms around his neck. His tongue licked her lips, encouraging her to accept his offer of passion.

Earlier, Jova had been thinking of all the reasons she should leave Davan alone. His kisses made her think of all the reasons she couldn't. He was skillful, the art of his tongue taking her to another world. When she opened her eyes, the room spun and she was on her back. Davan straddled her, massaging her breasts, watching her with intensity hot enough to set her on fire.

"Davan—"

He dropped down, kissing her neck. "Yes?" He nibbled her ear, making her forget her objections. "Would you like to go to your bed?" His eyes moved slowly from her to the bed in the far corner.

"No."

"Here?" He opened the top button on her sundress.

"No!"

His hand gripped her knee, moving upward. She clasped his wrist. "No, Davan."

He watched her, searching for the truth. "It's too soon?"

"Too soon, and you're upset. It's not *right.*"

"And things should be right." He sat up, helping her up too. "When we decide to make love, I want it to be perfect. You're special, Jova."

She smiled, dropping her head to hide the warm flush in her cheeks.

"Let's go out."

"Do you want to visit your uncle? Make sure he's all right after the doctor's visit today?"

"No. I want to take you out on a date. I want to get my mind off Uncle David for a little while. How about a movie?"

"I thought we agreed we couldn't go to the movies together."

"Since you've been so wonderful I'll let you pick the movie. Even if it's a chick flick."

"Well, this is a surprise. C'mon in."

Jova stepped inside David's house.

"My nephew isn't here."

"Actually, I came to see you."

"Well, if I had known you were coming I would have dressed." A Detroit Tigers T-shirt hung from David's frail body. Worn jeans were secured at his waist with a brown belt. "Let me help you with those bags."

"I'm fine. If I could put them down in the kitchen."

"Sure, go right ahead." He followed, watching as she dropped the organizer from her shoulder and placed the grocery bag on the counter.

"I need your help."

"Me?" David took a seat at the table and invited her to sit with him.

"My stylist quit. I need help finding a new one. I have several resumes here, and I thought, since you hire for the garage, you could help me choose the best candidate." She placed her organizer on the table, flipped it open, and turned it to face David. "I know it's a lot to ask, so I brought dinner." She placed her hand over his. "Thought I might be able to bribe you."

"Well, a pretty girl like you doesn't have to bribe me to do anything. Sure, I'll help you."

"Great! Let me get you something to eat while you take a look at the resumes."

Jova served dinner thinking she was pretty sly to have come up with this plan. Uncle David had made it clear he didn't want anyone fussing over him. He wanted to be independent and remain in control of his life. But he needed to eat. And someone needed to check on him every day, and since Davan was still wrestling with feelings of betrayal, why not her? They liked each other. She had the perfect excuse to drop by with dinner. Hey, as far as she was concerned, it was a win-win situation.

They became fast friends over dinner. David shared stories of his life out West in Utah, describing his family as an eccentric mixture of fun-loving characters. He told stories of Davan's wild childhood. Jova quickly realized why Davan's mother called for help in raising the rambunctious child. David wanted to know everything about Jova. She talked extensively about her mother, and shared her loneliness growing up as an only child. David never mentioned his health and Jova didn't pry.

"How's my nephew treating you?" David asked between reading resumes and slurping his second bowl of homemade chicken noodle soup.

"Davan is nice."

"Nice?" He peered across the table, reading her. "Well, I know it's not good when a woman describes you as 'nice.'"

"When it comes to Davan and me, nice is a good thing. We've only been out twice."

"You like him though?"

Jova avoided answering by swallowing a spoonful of soup.

"Well?"

"It's complicated."

"Complicated? Are you trying to insult me? Do you think I'm not smart enough to understand?"

"No." She hesitated to discuss her relationship with David. They were family. The impatient look David leveled at her told her to give him something. "Davan and I have only gone out twice. Right now we're just friends." She thought of Davan's heated responses when she classified their relationship in those terms.

"Friends?" David laughed. "I bet you don't say that in front of Davan."

Chapter 12

"This has to be the largest mall I've ever been to," Davan said.

"I know. Great Lakes Crossing is the best. They even have a hotel package."

Davan squeezed Jova's hand. "Is that an invitation?"

"You have a dirty mind. Do you know that?"

"Hmm." He steered her into the Rainforest Cafe. "I'm hungry."

"You have a dirty mind, and you're always hungry."

They stepped into the replicated Costa Rican rain forest. A fine mist blew across the aisles. After browsing in the gift shop, they ducked trees, vines, and automated wild animals to reach the hostess. With the soft lighting and sound effects, they easily fell into the rhythm of the restaurant. Davan placed his name on the seating list and Jova suggested they wait for their table at Steven Spielberg's Game-Works. He purchased game credits and they ventured into the adult playground. Jova found an interesting pinball machine and settled in to play. Davan observed her from behind, moving in when she added hip action to guide the silver ball.

"I should have taken you to Jeepers," Davan teased.

"Believe me, if I could have fit into the kiddie roller coaster, we'd be there right now."

"You're blowing the prudish image I have of you."

Jova turned to him. He placed his hands on the corners of the pinball machine, trapping her. Tonight she wore dark jeans, sassy sandals to show off her pedicure, and a sexy white shirt with tiny buttons. Her silky black hair was combed back and flipped upward at the ends. Her big brown eyes watched him, expectantly, almost a challenge.

"You're beautiful," Davan whispered. "I look at you and I want to pamper you, take care of you."

"Whoa."

"Did you say 'whoa'?" He smiled. "I have you all figured out. You didn't make a conscious decision not to get involved in a relationship. You're commitment phobic."

"I am *not* commitment phobic. If I was to show up at your apartment with a pair of drapes, you'd drag me back to the truck and I'd never hear from you again."

"You wanna bet?"

"You'd lose."

"I'd win—in several ways."

Jova's heavy lashes dipped, but Davan brought her back to him by cupping her chin in his palm. "You told my uncle we were only friends?"

"He cornered me."

"And you called me *nice?*"

"Nice is good. You make it sound like a bad thing."

"Hearing the woman you're crazy about calling

you *nice* is definitely a bad thing. There are other adjectives. Sexy, hot, spectacular . . ."

"I get the point."

Davan pressed their bodies together, keeping her trapped between the muscular wall of his chest and the pinball machine. "You need to learn the difference between a friendship and a relationship. Kiss me."

Jova looked around. GameWorks was filled to capacity. Couples were drinking, friends laughing.

"Kiss me, Jova." Davan embraced her. As he transferred his heat to her wrapped in a kiss, she didn't care how many people were watching. She forgot about propriety as she closed her eyes and snaked her fingers through his hair. He pulled her closer, his hold unbreakable. The buzz of the Rainforest Cafe beeper made them separate.

"You really have to learn the rules of this relationship, Jova."

Davan took her hand—she was standing dazed in the middle of GameWorks—and led her out.

They were finishing dessert in the Rainforest Cafe when Davan brought up their relationship again. "We joke about what's happening between us, but I really want this relationship to work out." He pulled her chair across the floor, bringing her next to him. "I want to be your best friend, but I want to be more than that, too."

"Relationships get messy. A friendship may not survive the drama."

"True, but we can try. You've told me you've had bad experiences, but you're not a quitter. If we're right, do you want to throw it away without finding out? All I know is that from the first moment I saw you in the parking lot, I knew I wanted to make a serious attempt to build something between us."

Jova dropped her head.

"Tell me what you're thinking."

She found his eyes. "I'm thinking I should have learned my lesson. I shouldn't get involved with anyone until the salon is profitable and my life is stable."

The light died in Davan's eyes. As quickly as it faded, Jova wanted to jump out of her chair and hold him until it returned. She placed her hand against his cheek. "And I'm also thinking I would miss you if you stopped coming around."

"Are you saying you're willing to give us a chance?"

"I am."

He took her hand, leading her to the exit. "Let's get out of here and go somewhere where I can kiss you."

Davan did not want to leave Jova, but the evening was coming to an end. Instead of their time together satisfying him, every minute they shared made him want more. Taking Jova home after she'd agreed to give their relationship a chance seemed cruel. He wanted to take her to his apartment and celebrate by lavishing her body with kisses and caresses.

Davan thought of himself as tough and rugged, too big and bad to be *whipped* by a woman. Jova changed all that in a matter of three dates. If she wanted, she could make him drop to his knees and promise her anything. He wanted to give her the entire world. More. She was the Beauty to his Beast; he was ensnared in a fairy tale.

Davan stood on the landing outside Jova's door fingering her collar, his fingers grazing the soft skin of her neck. "Would you like to go out for dinner tomorrow?"

"I'd like to, but I've already made plans."

His stomach clenched into a painful knot. "What kind of plans?"

"I'm cooking for your uncle. On the pretense of him helping me straighten out my books. He could stand a haircut too, if I can talk him into it." She smiled with angelic innocence. "Jealous?"

"Damn right." He tried not to smile, but with Jova it was impossible.

"David said he hasn't seen you in two weeks. Since his appointment with Dr. Greenville."

Davan cast his eyes low.

"He talks about you a lot. He misses you. You should come by tomorrow—"

"The garage is going to be really busy tomorrow."

"Davan." She placed a comforting hand on his arm. "You can't ignore your uncle forever. Talk to him and tell him how you feel—before it's too late. You'll regret it if you don't work it out."

"I don't want to talk about this." He wrapped his arms around her waist, pulling her in for his kiss. "Tonight has been perfect. I don't want to ruin it."

Davan watched Jova's lips part as he dropped his head. He met her with restrained anticipation. Holding Jova's warm, soft body caused a sexual awakening in him stronger than he'd ever experienced. He delved deep into her waiting mouth, searching for the key to her heart. After the first kiss, she relaxed, falling under his spell. She sought refuge in him, initiating another kiss. Davan nibbled her ear. His body tightened with unspoken possibilities. He held her tight as his lips traveled to her neck. Her arms were around his waist, holding him tightly. He moved to her mouth, kissing her with a measured amount of urgency, sensing the night was coming to an end. They held each other on Jova's porch, kissing until her mouth appeared pink and swollen with unspoken passion.

"I better go in," Jova said, breathlessly.

"I could come in with you."

She smiled at his attempt. "Do something for me?"

"Anything." How could he ever tell her no?

"Come to dinner tomorrow night at your uncle's house."

Davan stepped back, breaking their connection. "Jova," he groaned, turning away.

"For me." Her hand pressed into his back.

He turned, fighting the urge to take her in his arms. He didn't want to give in, but if he held her, he would.

"I'm trying to help." She stepped closer, taking his arms and wrapping them around her waist. "Do this for Uncle David. Do this for *you*."

"You don't understand."

"I don't understand? I'd give anything for one more dinner with my mother."

Her words didn't settle well. She was right. He'd regret leaving things on bad terms with his uncle. But he was still angry.

"Davan?"

He sighed heavily. "What time?"

The intricately designed tablecloth was one of Jova's best creations. After going through David's cupboards she found beautiful place mats and brass napkin holders. She finished the table setting with a cluster of vanilla candles.

"Uncle David," she called from the kitchen, "ten minutes until dinner."

He grumbled, but pulled himself out of the recliner and shuffled off to the bathroom to wash up. Jova warmed all over. David could be feisty, but no matter how much he mumbled and complained, he enjoyed having her around. Over the past weeks, she'd grown found of him, too. Having David didn't replace her mother, but he provided a parental bond she had lacked until meeting him.

Meeting Davan had drastically changed Jova's life. She had David to look after. Davan made her days—and nights—brighter. The clientele list at the salon was growing steadily since the hair show. David's astute business sense helped select the perfect stylist, and Jova would be making her an employment offer soon.

Jova checked her watch. Davan had less than ten minutes before they sat down to dinner. Nervous that he may have changed his mind, she went to the window and searched for his truck. His stubborn streak might be as wide as David's. She quickly discarded any negative thoughts. Davan would do the honorable thing. He said he would come, and he would keep his word. Certain Davan would show soon, Jova moved to the kitchen and began spooning dinner into serving dishes.

David emerged from the bathroom as the doorbell rang, dressed for dinner in khakis, a white shirt, and a tan tie. Jova stood in the kitchen doorway and watched for his reaction. He tried to maintain the stoic set of his mouth as he let Davan in, but his eyes told the truth. They both hated arguing, but were too stubborn to relinquish their viewpoint. She moved into the small foyer with David and Davan.

"Jova invited me to dinner," Davan explained.

"Jova's taking over my house, isn't she?" David huffed. He made his way to the kitchen, his gait slowed by his struggle to catch his breath.

Jova blew out a puff of air and rolled her eyes. "I must be a saint to deal with you two."

"Hey, I'm here like I promised." Davan kissed her and produced a bouquet of wildflowers from behind his back. "For the cook."

She inhaled the sweet fragrance of the flowers while assessing him. He had gone home to change before coming to dinner. The white linen suit deepened the dark tone of his skin. She watched him walk into the living room, wondering if the pants were sheer enough to see . . . black. And they weren't boxers.

"Davan." If she could get him to turn around, she could get a full frontal view of his—

"Yeah?" He turned.

She gulped.

"Yes?"

Caught!

His crooked smile thrilled her, and teased her at the same time.

"Dinner's ready."

He held out his hand for her.

Once the silence was broken, dinner conversation remained generic. The men complimented Jova on her cooking. They discussed the salon and the garage. When the silence threatened to make the situation uncomfortable, Jova brought up the weather. She wanted Davan and David to work out their problems, but understood they'd have to do it in their own time. At least they were sitting down together. The next time they might discuss more pertinent issues.

Davan started on his second helping while David struggled to finish his first. Jova watched him with worried eyes. She'd deliberately made dinner light, befitting the hot weather. David's doctor had recommended he eat six light meals a day. Eating frequently kept him from being hungry. Eating light meals decreased the amount of energy needed to digest his food, energy he needed to get around.

David pushed back his chair.

"Are you finished?" Jova asked. "You hardly ate a thing."

"Not much appetite these days."

"I know, but you have to keep your strength up. I'll shop for you tomorrow. I'll buy fruit and healthy snacks. Then you can grab a little something whenever you want it."

Davan gave her a look she couldn't read.

"Don't bother yourself." David patted her hand.

"Yeah," Davan added, "don't bother." He mumbled, "He probably plans on starving himself to death."

Shocked, Jova dropped her fork. David froze, staring at Davan in disbelief.

Jova broke the mounting tension. "He didn't mean it, Uncle David."

"Don't take up for him. He said it, he meant it." David's glare swiveled to Davan. "Do you mean what you said?"

Davan pushed his plate away angrily. He slid back from the table, his chair making a screeching noise. "There was a chance. You opted not to take it."

"It's my life!"

Davan colored the room with a string of curse words.

"I know you're upset about my decision—"

"Yes, I'm upset," Davan shouted. "Why aren't you? How can you throw your life away so easily?"

David pushed away from the table.

Davan pleaded with his uncle. "I love you. Mom loves you. Why would you hurt us like this?"

"You see me as lowdown enough to hurt my family?"

Davan didn't answer.

"Maybe I'm handling it this way so I won't hurt my family." David pushed himself up.

Jova motioned for Davan to stop him. He didn't move, but the anger was gone. Replaced by hurt and devastation. Dinner had deteriorated too quickly for Jova to save it. "Uncle David, don't go away. You and Davan should talk it out."

He stopped after several steps. He turned, directing his words to Jova. "Thank you for dinner. I'm sorry it couldn't have been more pleasant." He glanced at Davan, and then refocused on Jova. "I'm not feeling very well. I'm going to lie down. Can you see yourself out?"

"Yes, but—"

"Good night."

Jova tried to remain neutral, understanding both men's feelings in the emotionally charged situation. Before she could comfort Davan, he rushed from the kitchen, slamming the front door behind him.

"How did I get myself wedged between these two stubborn men?" Jova mumbled as she cleared the table. Good thing she was there to buffer the situation. Neither would even have made an attempt to clear the air if it weren't for her gentle prodding. Watching the heated words exchanged between them left no doubt they loved each other. She knew from experience, people handled death in different ways. She wouldn't give up on either of them, because if David died while they were angry at each other, Davan would be riddled with guilt.

After cleaning the kitchen Jova checked on David and headed home. Emotionally beat, she showered and jumped into bed. She was dozing when the phone rang.

"Hello?"

"You're mad."

Jova took a deep breath. "Davan, I'm not mad at you."

"I called to apologize for the way I acted at dinner."

She dropped back on the bed. "Have you talked to your uncle?"

"I called, but he didn't answer. I'll call him tomorrow."

"I could—"

"I appreciate what you're trying to do, but I have to do this alone. We'll work it out in our own way, in our own time. I love my uncle. Trust me to take care of it. Understand?"

"I understand." He was asking very nicely that she butt out. Jova wasn't offended. The goal was to repair their relationship. She didn't care how they achieved understanding.

"You cooked a wonderful dinner, and I ruined it. I was at my worst tonight, and I hate that you had to witness it. I'm not dealing with my uncle's situation very well. I'm sorry."

"No apology necessary. I just want to see you two speaking again."

"I want to make it up to you." His voice deepened, giving her goose bumps. "This weekend, you and me?"

"Sounds good." Jova's call waiting interrupted their conversation.

"Is your phone ringing?"

"Yeah."

"This late?" Davan questioned.

"It might be important. Talk to you tomorrow?"

He hesitated, but said good-bye.

Jova clicked to the other line.

"I need your help."

Herman! Jova slammed the phone into the cradle. It rang back immediately.

"Don't hang up!" Herman yelled.

"I've done all I'm going to do to help you."

"This Alabama thing isn't working out. They expect me to get up at four-thirty every morning and help with the farm. I'm a city boy. I don't know anything about cattle and crops."

"Not my problem."

"I want to come back to Detroit."

"Again, not my problem."

Silence filled the line for a brief moment. "I can get bus fare from my aunt. If you can put me up for a couple of days—"

"No. Absolutely not. And I'm telling you, if you show up on my doorstep I'm not letting you in. Enough playing on my sympathy."

"I don't want a handout. I'm talking about you and me giving it another shot."

"Are you crazy? You totaled my new car and then sued me to pay off your gambling debt. And would you happen to know anything about charges on my Visa?"

"I apologized about taking you to court, and I don't know anything about a Visa card."

Actually, he had never apologized about dragging her into court. She hadn't expected him to confess about the Visa. "What about the money you owe the bookie? Aren't you afraid he'll come after you if you come back?"

He hesitated. "I've come up with a solution to that problem, too. If you'll help me."

"We dated for less than a year! Why do you keep asking me to help you?"

"This is the last time—"

She'd heard that before. She didn't need to hear the details of his scheme. "Sorry, I've gotta go." She hung up with him calling her name.

The phone rang back immediately. She ignored it. Enough time passed for her irritation with Herman to grow before the phone rang again. She snatched it from the cradle. "What?"

"Hey, are you okay?"

"Davan. I'm fine. Sorry."

"I wanted to make sure you didn't have an emergency . . . the late night phone call."

"Everything's fine."

Davan held the line in silence, obviously waiting for an explanation. The phone call would bug him until he had all the details. *Not tonight,* she thought. She had been through enough for one day. *Tonight I'm too tired to deal with jealous men or exes looking for a handout.* "It's getting late, Davan, and I have a full day tomorrow."

Chapter 13

"Davan, it's six o'clock in the morning." Jova leaned against the doorjamb, her eyes barely open.

"We have a date."

"Now?"

"Now." He spun her around and sent her away with a swat on the behind. "Get dressed."

She mussed her wild mane. "I haven't even done my hair."

"A ponytail is fine." He stepped inside and searched for the television remote.

"Where are we going?"

"You'll see."

"If you won't tell me where we're going, I don't know how to dress."

He dropped onto the sofa. "Casual."

She rolled her eyes, trudging off to the bathroom. After she dressed, Davan ushered her out and they'd started on their road trip. Two hours into the drive, he stopped for breakfast, which he had to coerce Jova into eating. Too early in the morning, she lamely protested, but he made her eat a light meal anyway.

Jova slept in the cab of the truck most of the way, her head resting on Davan's shoulder. He fingered the tiny strap on the white corset top she wore.

Flowers were randomly embroidered on front,
around the tiny hooks binding it to her breasts.
The dainty top teased his imagination, hardened
his body, and made him wonder if he could remove
it with one well-placed tug. It stopped above her
navel, leaving a good four inches of her perfect
belly exposed before the top of her stretch jeans
came into view. She had brushed her hair back into
a ponytail, but insisted on lugging a bag of hair ac-
cessories. Her cheeks were rosy red, her lips pink.
He bet she tasted like expensive champagne: bub-
bly against the lips, but smooth going down.

Jova stirred beneath his arm. She definitely
wasn't a morning person. "Are we there yet?" She
stretched with the practiced seduction of a feline.

"Almost."

"Can I know where you're taking me? Or am I
still being kidnapped?" She moved across the cab
into the passenger's seat. He wanted to pull her
back, but let her have this small distance.

Davan pointed toward the passenger's window.
"Look."

Jova pressed her nose to the glass. A few moments passed before she could make out roller
coaster tracks. "Cedar Point? We're in Ohio?"

"I've never been. I thought it would be fun."

"I love Cedar Point, but the salon's been so busy
I didn't think I'd make it this summer."

Situated on the Lake Erie Peninsula, halfway between Cleveland and Toledo, Ohio, Cedar Point is
known for its fifteen daredevil roller coasters. Taking Cedar Point Amusement Park by storm, Davan
planned to ride them all. They ran from ride to
ride, more excited than the children visiting the
park. Davan insisted they ride every coaster and ex-
treme thrill ride. Jova was more a Ferris wheel type,

and after she rode on the three-hundred-foot-high Millennium Force, her shaky legs reduced her to keeping Davan company in the long, twisty lines.

They stepped off the coaster, Davan trying not to laugh, as he held her around the waist, bearing her weight. "Are you okay?"

"No more," Jova grumbled. "No more roller coasters."

"We'll take a break." He helped her to Coasters Restaurant. Remembering her light breakfast, he seated her and ordered two big burgers with fries, two extra-thick chocolate milkshakes, and a double order of fudge brownies. She picked over the fries until her stomach settled, then devoured lunch.

"Let's go watch a show," Jova said, steering Davan away from the monster rides. Her legs were still shaky from a combination of the humidity and aftereffects of the Millennium Force. If she could keep Davan occupied, she might divert his attention away from the coasters. He agreed to watch the three shows the park offered. Afterward, they walked along the beach, but Jova's nerves were still too fragile to ride any more roller coasters.

Davan embraced her around the waist from behind. "Ride one more coaster with me."

"Isn't there a merry-go-round we can hop on?"

He planted feathery kisses on her neck. "C'mon."

With each caress of his lips, she felt herself succumbing. "Which one?"

Davan stopped suddenly. Palming her chin, he turned her head toward the coaster in question. He read the description from the park map. "The Wicked Twister is the world's tallest and fastest 'double-twisting' impulse coaster. Riders zip out of the station at a maximum speed of seventy-two miles an hour in 2.5 seconds!"

"You're a maniac!" Jova took off in the opposite direction.

He caught her by the shoulders and trapped her within his arms. "Come on. It'll be fun."

"Davan, no. Look at that thing!"

"I'll hold on to you really tight and you can scream in my ear."

She planted her hands on her hips.

"For me?" When he flashed his crooked smile, Jova found herself standing in the line for the Wicked Twister. Twenty minutes into their wait, rain started to fall, saving her.

Davan checked out the darkening sky, hopeful. "It'll pass."

"I don't know. Maybe we should head back to the truck. If we get our hands stamped, we can come back once the rain stops."

"I think you conjured up this rain just to get out of riding the Wicked Twister." He took her hand and led her out of the park.

Lord knows, she'd been praying for divine intervention. By the time they'd reached the truck, the rain was falling at a steady pace, and storm clouds darkened the area. She climbed into the truck while Davan stopped to speak to a man loading his family in the car next to them.

"He says there's a tornado warning for this area. News radio says one has been spotted." He turned to her. "It's already getting dark. The highway must be jammed. We shouldn't try to drive home in this mess."

"It's not safe to sit here."

"You're wet. We need to get you warm and dry." He started the truck and pulled out of the parking space, following the stream of traffic.

She searched the skies. "Tornados scare me. I

don't want to be on the highway, out in the open, if one touches down."

"We could stay . . . overnight. We passed some hotels on the drive in."

A clap of thunder, accompanied by a vicious streak of lightning, helped Jova decide. "Maybe we should."

Judging by the traffic, most people visiting the park decided not to brave the storm. The string of hotels neighboring Cedar Point buzzed with cars. After being turned away from two overbooked hotels, Davan parked in the Comfort Inn lot. "Stay here. I'll get the room."

Watching the gloomy skies, Jova said, "I'll come with you."

The implication of staying overnight in a hotel with Davan didn't hit her until the desk clerk asked what type of room they wanted.

Davan turned to her. "Is two double beds okay?"

Requesting two rooms seemed immature, and expensive. They were adults. Davan had always been the perfect gentleman on their dates. It wasn't like she hadn't learned to control her raging hormones every time he touched her.

"Jova?" Davan asked again, his obsidian eyes simmering.

"Two doubles," she agreed, wondering if driving home in the storm would have been safer than spending the night in a hotel with Davan. Her stomach jumped as she followed him into the gift shop where they purchased what they would need for the impromptu overnight. Long dates that ended with heated kisses were safe compared to spending a night together without barriers to curve their desires.

Jova supposed Davan felt the subtle tension

building between them, too. He was unusually quiet as he led her down the corridor to their room. He opened the door, allowing her to enter first. Classic, reliable Comfort Inn. Always clean and comfortable, the room had two double beds with a bedside table separating them. The standard coffeemaker, television, and sitting area completed the room.

Jova stepped into the darkness of the room. Darkness that brought Davan too close for comfort. He clicked on the lights. She jumped.

Davan wandered to the window, pulling back the curtain and checking on the weather. Embarrassed by her jumpiness, Jova retreated to the bathroom. She finger-combed her hair in the mirror. "Calm down," she told herself. "It's not like you haven't been alone with him before. Keep your head on straight and nothing will happen."

What's so wrong with something happening? Dangerous thought.

Davan appeared in the doorway. "Did you say something?"

She shook her head. "No."

"I'm going to call Uncle David and let him know we're staying overnight. He'll worry about you." He winked and her knees wobbled.

She joined him as he ended the call.

"He gave me a lecture about your virtue."

Watching the sexy brush of Davan's lashes on his cheek, she could use a dose of lecturing herself.

"I promised him you were safe with me, so what do we do to pass the time?"

They decided to gather in the hotel bar, along with many other Cedar Point visitors stranded in the small town. The audience cheered patrons on as they took the stage to sing karaoke. With much prodding, Davan jumped up and totally obliterated "My Girl," by The Temptations. Every woman in the bar envied her when he serenaded her. But the intimate kiss he gave her for his finale brought the house down. Thoroughly embarrassed by her brazen response, they called it a night and returned to the room.

The jumpy stomach returned when Jova changed for bed. The extra-large T-shirt hid more than the corset top she'd worn all day, but it didn't help ease her nerves. She'd been alone with Davan many times, and she knew he would never force her into doing anything she didn't want. Why then was she so nervous? Maybe because she did want to experience Davan covering her body with intimate kisses. Maybe she did want to feel the weight of his naked body against hers. Maybe it was Davan who should have the nervous stomach. She brushed her teeth, feeling silly for worrying over nothing. When she came out of the bathroom, Davan was leaning against the headboard, long lean legs stretched across the bed.

"Come watch television with me." He reached for her, pulling her to sit between his thighs. His arms tightened around her waist. She tried to focus on television, but once she leaned back against his solid chest, her thoughts scattered. No man had ever made her body weak and her heart flutter. She felt comfortable with him, safe and warm. She could stay with him in their private world forever.

"Did you have fun today?" Davan's lips grazed her ear, leaving behind the heat of his words.

"Great. It was great."

Davan slipped the clasp from her hair, using his fingers to comb it out in even waves. "We should come back." His fingers grazed her scalp, sending shock waves down her spine, and she couldn't answer. His lips touched the back of her neck. He caught the silky strands in his fist, and pulled her head back to his waiting lips. He kissed her tenderly, being careful not to break her.

Suddenly, Jova's worries vanished. As he kissed her, her mind raced, picturing what was to come. With precision, he laid her on his pillow, his body stretched out beside her. He kissed her slowly, cautiously.

Davan propped himself up on his elbow, trailing a finger down the length of her arm. "I've been meaning to ask you something. Who was the late night phone call from?"

"What?" Jova asked, dizzy from his kisses. "You're asking about a phone call? Now?" Of course he would ask now when he had her at a disadvantage. Davan had the memory of an elephant. He might not have pressed her for details at the time, but just when she thought the matter had been forgotten, he searched for answers.

"The other night, we were talking and your line rang. You said it wasn't an emergency."

Jova sobered, remembering Herman's latest crisis. She debated on opening the subject with Davan, but saw no harm in being truthful. "My ex."

An eyebrow quirked with interest "Do you have a lot of exes?"

"Not at all."

"This isn't the first time you've mentioned an ex coming around."

"He didn't come around. He called."

"Very late at night." Jealousy caused the corners of his mouth to harden.

"Are you going to start a fight about my ex calling me?"

"No." The anger melted. "No. I was curious."

She stroked his cheek and he came to her, pressing his full lips to hers. He lavished her in kisses that made her head spin. He had to be the best kisser she'd ever dated. He read her mood perfectly, and delivered the attention she needed without hesitation. Playful or erotic, sensual or caring, his kisses fit her wonderfully. He pulled away first, and Jova could see by the lines at the corners of his mouth that he was absorbed in thought. "I'm a little rusty. What's supposed to happen now?"

"I don't know what you mean."

"We've been dating for several weeks. I don't want to see anyone else. I sure as hell don't want you to see anyone else. How can we accomplish that without jumping into an engagement?"

"I think I know where you're going, and if I'm right, you are rusty."

"How about this?" His lips were close enough to touch hers when he spoke. "I'm sick of the exes. You're my woman, and I want it to stop."

"That's one way of getting your point across. You sound like you're haggling with an unreliable worker."

"This might be more to your liking." He placed his hand on her thigh, inching it up under her T-shirt as he spoke. "I'm crazy about you. I'm not dating anyone else. I don't want you to see anyone else."

"Better."

"Better," he mumbled, kissing her. "Is that all I get, 'better'?" He kissed her again, but this kiss sent a different message. He hungered for her. If the way he watched her during the kiss with those dark, sexy eyes didn't get his meaning across, his palm massaging the swell of her behind did. He watched her with the concentration of a predator. His lips caressed her lips—her mouth—with a tenderness that proved he treasured her.

Jova's sensuality awoke as the kisses deepened. He kissed the corners of her mouth as he worked the T-shirt up, exposing the round curves of her breasts. She purred and he cupped his palm over the beckoning swell. Her fingers stroked his silky dreads, holding his mouth to her breast, encouraging him to taste her. He worked magic with his tongue, lapping at her straining peaks. Her body liquefied at his touch. Fascinated by his control over her sexuality, she closed her eyes and relished the mastery of his tongue.

Davan pulled away, leaving her cold. He watched her reaction as his palm pressed against her mound, his fingers applying a light caress. "You don't have to sleep in the other bed." He applied his wanton stroke to the blossoming nub between her thighs.

In answer, Jova sucked in a sharp breath, arching her back. She fought the riotous sensation. "Yes, I do."

"I don't have to sleep in this bed."

"Yes, you do."

"Why?" He rolled her rigid nipple between his fingers.

There was a very good reason. Jova just couldn't think of it with his tongue licking her breast, his lips pulling at her nipple.

"Why?" Davan asked again as he covered her body with his. The steel part of him pressed against her mound. He kissed her, working to remove his shirt and leave them skin to skin.

Jova ran her fingers over the taut muscles of his back. She sought out the heat of his mouth and kissed him feverishly. She moved to his neck. He moaned, giving her encouragement to explore further. Her tongue found his Adam's apple and the hollow below it.

The sound of his zipper buzzed through the room, zinging off the walls. She would have protested if she could have broken the kiss. He kicked off his jeans, trying desperately not to put too much distance between their hungry bodies. He crushed her, bare chest to bare chest. The steel hardness of him pressed against the supple place between her thighs. He pushed her legs apart and sank into her, the thin fabric of her panties the only thing separating them. His fingers were inside the waistband when Jova found her voice.

"Do you really want me to stop, Jova? Because what we're doing feels very good."

"Very good, yes." Her mind was turning to mush.

Davan worked his hips into a rhythm that made her gasp. "There's no one here to stop us. There's no *reason* to stop."

Jova fought her way through the quicksand hindering her judgment. "It feels good, but it doesn't feel *right*. Not yet."

Davan reversed the rotation of his hips and hit a spot that made Jova arch her back with a moan. He lingered there, adding pressure and taking it away. He pressed down hard between her thighs, giving her a preview of what he offered. Possessed by his sexuality, Jova wrapped her legs around his waist. He cupped her bottom, whispering in her ear promises of what making love would feel like. She moaned, but he drowned the noise with his sultry words. Emotions mixed with arousal, driving them to gyrate faster and more uncontrolled. Breathing heavily, they called out together.

"Davan." Jova wanted to apologize for her lustful behavior; explain why she wasn't ready to go any further.

Davan kissed her words away. He lifted her, still panting, in his arms and carried her to her bed. He tucked her in, kissed her forehead, and shut off the light.

Chapter 14

Davan stepped into David's foyer. Spending the weekend with Jova opened doors he'd long closed. When his marriage failed, he gave up on wanting a wife and children. Jova made it all seem possible again, but he had to start with his uncle. No matter how angry Uncle David's decision made him, he had to get past it and enjoy what time they had together. "How are you feeling, Uncle David?"

"The new medicine Dr. Greenville gave me is working wonders. I have enough energy to come in this weekend." David walked upright, no shuffle in his step, to his recliner.

Davan sat on the corner of the sofa. "Are you sure? If you don't feel up to it—"

"Just a few hours. Sitting in this house is driving me nuts."

Davan nodded. The conversation was civil, but tension filled the room. He pulled a bag from his jacket. "I picked up your prescriptions."

"Thank you." David took the bag and turned on the television. "How's Jova?"

"Good."

"She's a pretty girl. Beautiful inside and out." He ran his hand over his graying hair. "She gives a good cut, too."

"Yeah, Jova is a good person." He relaxed back on the sofa. "Didn't she stop by today?"

"It's been two days. She's working hard at the salon since Dawn up and quit on her. It's a shame."

Davan smiled at his uncle's concern for Jova. It made her seem like part of the family already.

"I like having her around. She brightens up this place. Good cook, too." He gave Davan a pointed look. "We made a mess of things at dinner."

"It was my fault," Davan admitted. "I apologized to her. She's not upset. She cares about you and wants us to get along. I explained we'd work it out on our own."

Both turned their attention to the television. Better not to speak at all than to rehash their argument.

"She'd make a man a good wife," David said without ceremony.

Davan concentrated on the television commercial. He didn't want to discuss his relationship with Jova. He wanted to know why his uncle didn't have the operation when he could. He wanted to understand his uncle's reasoning. Asking those questions would start another fight, and he didn't want to fight. He loved his uncle.

"Well?" David asked.

"Well, we're a long way away from marriage."

"When are you going to see her again?" David pushed.

"This weekend. If you're coming in to the garage, I can spend the whole day with her."

"That would be a nice thing to do."

Silence stretched between them, giving them an excuse not to discuss the important issues they needed to face.

David broke the silence. "Your mother called."

"She's worried."

David didn't answer.

"We're both worried about you." Before David could protest his sentiment, Davan went on. Emotions he had tried to bury surfaced with a vengeance. He tapered his words, not wanting to push his uncle into a corner. "If I wasn't worried about you, I could handle your decision a lot better."

"It's my life. I have the right to decide what I want to do with it."

"But why, Uncle David?" He wanted desperately to understand.

"I've lived a good life. I don't want to end it with pain and suffering. I don't want my family to go through that. I don't want my friends to see me that way. I want to die with dignity."

"Death wasn't the only option."

David waved the words away. "I know what Dr. Greenville told you. He said the same things to me. The truth is, my health has been bad for some time. Risking the surgery to remove the aneurysm didn't guarantee me any more time." He tilted his head back against the chair, closing his eyes.

After a long moment where Davan carefully measured his words, he asked, "Didn't you want a little more time to spend with your family?"

David rolled his head toward Davan. "How much time do we need? We have time now and we're spending it fighting about my decision. That's why I like having Jova around. She doesn't look at me like she's waiting for me to keel over. She smiles and tells me about her day. She makes me feel alive." He turned to the television. "Been a long time since I felt alive. I have enough time. Let me enjoy it without having to justify my decisions."

With new insight, Davan sank into the sofa. Could he accept his uncle's decision, and just be happy that they were together now? He thought of Jova's sentiments about her mother. How she was happy to have had time to say good-bye before she died. If David had made his choice, what could he do to change it? Whether he liked it or not, the foundation had been laid. It was his job to love his uncle, not judge him.

David snapped his recliner back and clasped his fingers together on his stomach. "Have you eaten? I made dinner, and the Pistons' first preseason game is starting. Can you hang around?"

"Yeah, I can hang around. I should check out my new home team."

Lisa waved the phone in the air. "Jova, it's Davan—again."

"Tell him I'm with a customer." She ignored Lisa's sigh and pulled the curling iron through Mrs. Nash's cherry-red hair.

"Who's Davan?" Candi, the salon's new braider, asked without inhibition.

A week ago Candi had answered the sign in the window advertising the need for a stylist. Jova hadn't considered having a braider at the salon. It seemed a conflict with the "personal spa" type of atmosphere she wanted. But Candi's dynamic personality wouldn't allow her to say no.

Candi brought a solid clientele, but with braiding styles lasting up to three months, she needed to pick up new customers to keep a steady stream of income flowing. Jova volunteered to be her model, letting Candi French-braid her hair in thin, neat rows. The style radically changed her looks. When her clients saw the new style they made appointments with Candi for their teenage girls. This brought an entirely new generation of customers to the salon, a segment Jova hadn't thought about marketing to.

The same week Candi joined the staff, Josh stopped in asking to speak with the owner. Fresh out of barber school, Josh needed a place to work. His funds were limited and he couldn't afford to lease a chair at the area's going rate; Jova's fifty-fifty policy worked. Josh eased into the salon's festive atmosphere, holding his own during sparring matches with Candi.

Lisa placed her hand over the phone receiver. "Davan says he can hold."

"Tell him I'll call him later."

"Who's Davan?" Candi asked again. "And why don't you want to talk to him?"

Lisa placed her customer's freshly painted nails in the hand dryer. "Davan is the hunk who helped her win the lottery."

"Sexist women," Josh interjected. Being a male in the cosmetology industry came with stereotypes the five-foot-three Josh fought every day. He overcompensated for his short stature with tall tales about his love life. He spoke to his customer, waving the clippers to punctuate his point. "If we started a lottery about what we want in a woman, they'd run us out of here."

Candi jumped in. "That's because men all want the same stinkin' thing. Big breasts and an even bigger behind."

The women in the shop all agreed.

"Tell me I'm wrong?" Candi challenged.

"That's not true," Josh's customer cut in. "We want a woman who can cook and clean, too."

A collective grumble came from the women, while the men shared a high five.

"I saw the slips of paper in the lottery jar," Josh said. "So none of you should talk."

Guilty, the women quieted down.

Candi's fingers worked at lightning speed, twisting strands of hair into braids. "We're off the subject. Jova, why won't you take Davan's calls?"

"It's personal." Jova clacked the curling iron, accentuating her point.

The shop hummed, all eyes turned on her.

Jova selected a strand of hair and applied the hot iron. "Now you guys are playing into the 'beauty shop gossip' stereotype."

"Best place to get therapy," a customer called out from the waiting area.

Candi agreed. "Help us help you, Jova."

"I don't need any help."

"You don't?" Lisa asked, grinning. "Good, because Davan's coming across the street right now. And he doesn't look very happy."

Two women cruising the lingerie racks hurried to the window. "Damn," one of them said. "He's a lottery winner all right."

The shop fell silent when the door to the salon jerked open. Customers sat down, wanting a front seat for the action. The stylists pretended to concentrate on their customers, but their eyes followed Davan through the shop.

"Hi, Davan." Lisa greeted him with extra dynamism.

He nodded his hello and marched up to Jova. "I need to speak with you."

She couldn't meet his dark glare. "I have a customer."

Mrs. Nash turned to face her. "It's okay. I could

stand a potty break." Davan stood aside and she rushed off.

"I've got the phones covered," Lisa offered.

"Where can we talk?"

Jova wouldn't beat Davan's determination today. Under the watch of everyone in the salon, Jova led him to the supply room.

Davan closed the door, turned to her, and used long strides to close the distance between them. He used the wall of his chest to back her into a corner. He locked her there by placing his palms on the wall on each side of her. His height made their bodies fit together with the precision of a jigsaw puzzle. "You haven't spoken to me since Cedar Point—two weeks ago."

"I've been busy."

"Don't give me that. Why are you avoiding me?"

Because whenever you're around my heart beats double time. Because when you kiss me, my stomach drops to my toes.

"Is it because of what happened in the hotel? We wanted each other, Jova. It's no crime to make out."

She had wanted much more. She awoke the next morning with Davan sleeping in the bed beside hers, snoring lightly. Even asleep he was hard with desire for her. And she had wanted it so badly. She had watched him, more afraid of what she would do than about any advances Davan had made before they fell asleep.

"I miss you," Davan whispered. His lips grazed hers and made her feel silly. His tongue licked the corner of her mouth. "Do you miss me?" His fingers gripped her waist and he kissed her, leaving her dazed and confused about the volatility of her desire for him. "Don't you miss me even a little bit?"

Jova fell into his arms. "A little bit."

He placed his palm on her cheek. "We made out. No tragedy. It's okay for modern women to be hot."

She swatted at him.

"I told you about my hunt, kill, provide nature, but I forgot one important thing."

"What?"

"Protect. I protect what's mine."

"I'm not a *thing* for you to possess," Jova protested.

Davan caressed her bottom lip with the pad of his thumb. "You can put whatever spin on our relationship you want, no one has to know. But between us, in private, know this. You are *mine*. I will hunt, kill, and provide for you to be sure you have everything you need." He kissed her gently. "Mine to protect." He backed away, walking backward out of the supply room. "Stop running from me."

It took Jova a moment to recuperate from Davan's bold command. She gathered her composure and returned to her client. All eyes were on her, waiting for an accounting of what had just happened between her and Davan. Jova ignored the collective curiosity of the salon and started working on Mrs. Nash's hair.

"He laid one on you," Candi boldly commented. The salon erupted in laughter. Jova swiveled her chair so no one would see the red flush creeping up her neck.

Lisa rescued her. "Leave Jova alone. You're making her blush."

"Thank you, Lisa." Jova held her head high, as if offended, but thinking of Davan's kisses made her smile. The salon lapsed into its routine discussion of current events, forgetting about Davan's visit, but

Jova couldn't erase the taste of his lips. Her mind wandered to hot sandy beaches while she finished Mrs. Nash's hair. She started her next client while wishing she were alone with Davan on a desert island. He had told her to stop running. She might be able to retreat physically, but her mind never left him.

"Have you heard anything from Dawn?" Lisa asked, frantically filing her customer's acrylic nails.

"Not a word."

"I know someone who works in the Redford shop. She says Dawn pretty much keeps to herself, but she doesn't have a kind word for you."

Jova placed her patron under the dryer. She flopped down in her chair to rest before the next customer arrived. Without Dawn in the shop to take some of the walk-ins, and Mimi shampooing less than part-time because of a political emergency in Lansing, she was exhausted.

"Maybe you should try to talk to her again," Lisa advised. "She has to see how dumb the whole fight is. But you know Dawn has too much pride to make the first move. You should call and try to work things out with her. You need her back. You're working from opening to closing, and you still have to turn some of the walk-ins away."

Lisa's customer craned her neck around to see Jova. "Too bad the new stylist didn't work out."

Jova was glad to find Candi, but regretted that the stylist she and David had selected hadn't worked out. "Her boss wouldn't let her out of her lease. She had to sublet her booth rental or pay the fees until the owner finds a replacement. She said it's too much hassle to leave until the lease is up."

"Another reason to work it out with Dawn," Lisa added.

Remembering their argument, Jova swiveled her chair to face Lisa. "Did you know she had a thing for Herman?"

Lisa shook her head. "No idea. She knows what happened between you two. Why would she be mad about him?"

"Davan is the turning point."

"Yeah, she really wanted him." Lisa glanced up from her work. "But don't let it worry you. Davan asked *you* out."

Jova wanted to run to the window and see if she could catch a glimpse of him underneath the hood, repairing a car. Restraining herself, she crossed the room to check the timer on the dryer. But Davan's kisses had stirred a nervous energy only he could satisfy. She lifted the hood and spoke to her customer. "You have thirty minutes left. Do you mind if I run out for lunch?"

"No," the woman shouted over the whirling dryer.

"I'll check to see if she's dry," Candi volunteered.

"I'll hurry." Jova smiled and lowered the hood of the dryer.

"Don't rush, I'm not in a hurry. This is the only time I get away from the kids."

Jova left through the back door. She drove four blocks to a string of fast food restaurants. Cars were wrapped around the restaurants' drive-through windows. She kept driving until she found a restaurant that wasn't so busy.

"Hey." Davan lit up. "This is a nice surprise. Come in."

Jova stepped into his office, closing the door behind her. She held up a Subway bag. "I brought you lunch."

He held his arms open, snuggling her into his

lap. "I guess our talk earlier did you some good."
He thanked her with a heated kiss.

She locked her arms around his neck. "Maybe
you do deserve a little more of my attention."

He pulled his head back to see her clearly. "Really?"

She pressed her face into his neck, nuzzling the
collar of his overalls. The smells of the garage clung
to him, oil and grease—all man. He could wear
these scents with the same finesse as designer
cologne.

"You're going to get dirty." His voice sparkled
with delight.

"I don't care."

"Wow."

Jova slipped from his lap, checking out his office
while he ate.

"I've been talking to Uncle David."

She swung around, anxious to learn if they were
getting along any better.

"We're getting there. He's commented about not
seeing you much lately."

"I know. Tresses & Locks has been very busy. I
plan to stop by this evening."

"He'll like that a lot, but I don't want you wearing
yourself out. If you're too busy to stop by because
of the salon, Uncle David will understand."

"I won't stay long, but I want to check on him."
Jova hugged him tightly. "I have to get back to the
salon. I have a customer under the dryer."

Davan laughed, the sound rough and tumble.
"You left a customer under the dryer to bring me
lunch?" The light in his eyes said he was highly impressed. "Don't even try to leave without giving me
a kiss." He caught her around the waist.

She was more than happy to comply. After a long, heated kiss she headed out.

"Don't forget what I told you earlier," Davan called after her.

"Not a chance."

For the rest of the day, Jova thought about the possibilities of what a relationship with Davan held. Several times, she was caught daydreaming, and had to take the teasing of a lifetime. She had it bad for Davan, and no matter that she wasn't ready to admit it, everyone else could plainly see it.

She'd pushed Davan away after their make-out session at the hotel, and now she regretted it whole-heartedly. She missed David, too. The minute the last customer left, she grabbed the dinner she had prepared the night before and headed to his house.

"Just soup today, please, Jova," David said.

She placed the TV tray over his middle. When she turned to leave his bedroom, he stopped her.

"Pull up a chair." His words came between deep inhalations. "Can you sit with me for a minute?"

"No problem." Jova dragged a chair from the corner of the room and placed it next to his bed. She laughed at a sitcom while David watched her with a weak smile. After he finished his soup, she removed the tray and handed him his evening medicines.

"Well, I need to ask a favor of you," David said. He turned off the television and angled his body in her direction. "That stubborn nephew of mine would keel over if he heard about this."

She smiled, agreeing with the stubborn part.

David went into his bedside table and pulled out a large white envelope with commercial advertising on the front. He fingered the edge while he explained, "I've made my arrangements."

"Arrangements?"

"Funeral arrangements."

The morbidity of the conversation made her stomach sink. But this seemed important to David, and right now his feelings were more important than her rolling stomach.

"I don't want my family to have to handle any business—after I'm gone. I've made a will. It didn't make sense not to take care of my funeral arrangements, too." He held the envelope out to her. "Well, it's all done, and paid for."

"Uncle David, I don't know if I'm the one you should be giving this to."

"I want you to keep a copy. When the time comes, I want you to share this with my sister and Davan." He swallowed, his Adam's apple bobbling. "It'll be painful enough for them. They shouldn't have to bother themselves with these kinds of details."

Jova pressed the envelope to her chest and clasped his hand.

"Will you do this for me?"

"Are you sure there's no one in your family you'd rather put in charge?"

David shook his head. "I know this is unusual, especially since we haven't been acquainted very long, but I want you to take care of this for me. Of everyone, you'll be the most sensible—when the time comes."

"This is a big responsibility. You can count on me."

"Between us?"

"Between us."

Chapter 15

"Good morning, ladies."

Jova turned, beaming at the sound of his voice. Davan had come to have that effect on her. He only needed to be near to make her day bright. She hadn't seen him much this week because one of his mechanics had been called for jury duty, and the garage was keeping him busy. He talked briefly with Josh, a typical male conversation about cars and sports, before greeting her with a kiss. The simple brush of his lips across her cheek made her want to swoon. "Quiet today?"

Jova nodded, looking up at him from her salon chair. "I came for your car. I'd like to winterize it before the weather gets much colder."

Candi whispered, too loudly, something about Davan winterizing her.

Jova shot her an angry look. "Let me get my keys."

Davan followed her to the back. As soon as the supply room door closed, he pinned her against the counter. "I might as well steal me a kiss. Since I walked all the way across the street, and all."

How convenient, Jova thought as she explored his mouth. If she could combine the salon and the garage in the same building, in order to have access to Davan's kisses every minute of the day, she would.

But still she held back.

And Davan knew it.

Jova ran her fingers through his miniature dreads. "Why don't you come by later and let me do your hair again?" She took his hand from her hip and examined his fingers. "I'll throw in a manicure."

"I don't want a sissy manicure."

"Come into the twenty-first century. You have to take care of your hands." *Because you need them to touch and caress me,* she would never say aloud. She'd seen the way he'd been watching her lately. Waiting for the tiniest sign it was okay to pounce. "What's 'sissy' about a manicure?"

"Man-i-cure. The cure to being a man."

"Silly!" She swatted at him.

He ducked, and darted out of the supply room. "I'll bring dinner."

Wednesdays at Tresses & Locks were notoriously slow, and the threat of bad weather made the day even lighter. Jova got the jump on her monthly inventory. She sat at her computer in the supply room and worked on the books. At lunchtime, she gathered orders and made a noon run. Thinking of Davan and the guys, she had three large pizzas delivered to the garage. This earned her a sizzling phone call from Davan. After organizing her workstation, she called David. He sounded good, energetic. His next appointment with Dr. Greenville was in two days.

By the time Davan arrived at her studio, Jova thought she would go out of her mind with anticipation. This had been happening lately, her being hyped to see him, to have him near. She prattled on about the salon over dinner. He didn't seem to mind, watching her with sincere interest. Later, she ignored his protests as she soaked the motor oil from beneath his nails. They wrestled over the bottle of clear polish when she produced it, ready to paint his nails.

"No, Jova. No polish," he said emphatically.

"For me?" she cooed.

He begrudgingly released the bottle. "I don't know the point of all this anyway. My hands are just going to get dirty again tomorrow."

"Wear gloves."

"Gloves! I'm a *mechanic*. I work with my hands. I have to be able to *feel* my way around."

Jova glanced up at him. It took a second to register, but Davan realized the inadvertent seductive meaning of his words—and her response. She pressed a hand to her stomach, attempting to quiet the butterflies swirling there. He followed the movement, seeming to contemplate his response. She refocused on his fingers, and the moment was lost.

Davan claimed to be hungry again after Jova finished the manicure. The way he went on, you'd think he was starving. Of course his fingernails were wet, so she would have to feed him. "Of course," she muttered. She fought a losing battle to give him a chastising glare, and fed him fresh fruit.

After his crafty manipulation with the fruit was finished, Davan settled between Jova's legs. She sat on the sofa above him, her fingers balancing the comb while she wrapped small sections of his hair around it. He flung his arms over her thighs, increasing the level of intimacy. Working on his hair, his head resting on her thigh to give her better access, held an unexplainable intimacy Jova had never felt with her customers. They enjoyed being close, always maintaining contact with the subtlest of touches. The better part of an hour passed with them in comfortable silence.

"David needs a few things from the store," Jova told him.

"I'll stop by tomorrow."

"He gave me a list." She steadied his head, positioning him the way she wanted. "He should need refills on his prescriptions, too."

Davan turned to her. "You keep up with that?"

She turned his head back into position, pressing his cheek against her left thigh. "I coordinated my monthly inventory with how long his prescriptions should last, so I wouldn't forget."

"Hmm."

She and David had adopted each other. She saw him as a father figure. Davan's cool response made her wonder if she was becoming too domesticated with the Underwoods. "I didn't mean to overstep—"

"No, you didn't." He wrapped his fingers around her ankles. "It's sweet of you."

Darkness had engulfed the neighborhood by the time Jova began twisting the hair at the nape of Davan's neck. He used the remote to turn off the stereo and switch on the ten o'clock news. He rushed to the window when the weatherman spoke of accumulating snowfall.

"Jova! Come quick!"

She hurried to join him at the tiny window near her bed. She peered out in the darkness. The street seemed quiet enough. Her car was parked beneath the window intact. His truck was still there, too. No need for the alarm shaking his voice. "What's wrong?"

"Look!"

She scanned the darkness again. "What is it, Davan? I don't see anything."

"It's snowing."

"*So?* You scared me. I thought something was wrong."

"*So?*" he mocked her. "The only time I've seen snow is on television." He stepped behind her, wrapping his arms around her waist, and pressing his arousal into the cushion of her bottom. "See the snow through my eyes."

Jova glanced back.

"Close your eyes," he instructed.

She closed her eyes, and he freed one hand to block her vision. "Open them."

She did.

"Imagine seeing snow for the first time. Look through my eyes."

Perfect white flakes dotted the sky. A fine layer coated their cars. The streetlights made the flakes dazzle and shimmer in the artificial light.

"It's beautiful," Davan whispered near her ear.

She fell into the beauty and innocence of his world. A place where snowfall signified a miracle. Watching the snowfall, she tried to size Davan up. A man whose values were derived from a hunt-kill-provide philosophy. A man who made his living working with his hands, and showed how much he cared by doing little things. Little things that added up to huge displays of affection. Caring for her car, bringing her lunch or dinner when he noticed the salon buzzing with customers. Giving up his life in Utah to move across the country and care for his ailing uncle.

She turned in the circle of his arms. He smiled down at her; the crooked, sexy smile. How could she forget it when she listed his endearing attributes?

"Let's go outside," he whispered.

She nodded, emotions brimming too close to the surface to speak.

He captured her cheeks in his palms. "Are you okay?"

She answered by throwing her arms around his neck and pulling him down for her kiss.

Davan joined David in the living room after putting away the last of the groceries.

"You picked up everything I needed."

Davan handed him Jova's list. "She told me to refill your prescriptions, too. I'll bring them by tomorrow. And she reminded me about your appointment with Dr. Greenville. The shop is booked solid so Jova's going to drive you."

"Well, Jova is something else, isn't she?"

"Jova's the best," Davan answered. He'd come to that conclusion long ago. He ripped open a bag of chips and settled back to watch the basketball game.

"You better do something about Jova soon," David announced during the commercial break.

"What do you mean?"

"If you don't make your move, some young buck is going to come along and steal her from you."

"You don't have to tell me." No ex-boyfriends were hanging around lately, but Davan sensed someone was looming, waiting for him to make a mistake, ready to step in and magnify his imperfections.

"Well, she cares about you. You only have to see

the way she lights up when I mention you to know it."

Davan's head snapped in his uncle's direction. "I hadn't noticed."

"Look!" David grumbled unintelligible words. "You have to pay close attention to your woman. You're not in Utah anymore. These cats around here will swoop in and take Jova away before you even know what's happening."

Davan had never thought of himself as a jealous person, but his uncle's chastisement hit a nerve. He wanted to race to Jova and do bodily harm to any man hanging around. He had to admit a mild twinge of anger pricked his nerves whenever she mentioned the *ex*. He'd told Jova he considered her *his,* but maybe it wasn't enough. It didn't feel like enough. Visions of commitment and curtains danced in his head—again.

"Have you seen someone hanging around Jova?" Davan asked.

"Can't say I have."

"Has she mentioned something to you about someone else?"

"It's more what she's not saying." David was being deliberately cryptic. Davan didn't know his purpose, but it fanned the flames of jealousy.

Jova liked spending time with him. Davan knew that for certain, but it wasn't enough. His feelings had quickly grown out of control. He'd skipped *like,* cruised past *caring,* and was now in a zone he didn't want to label. Not until he could identify Jova's feelings. The information he needed lay directly below the surface. There were times when they were together he knew she would confess her feelings, but she always backed off. Always, just out of reach.

"Uncle David?"

He turned his attention from the game to his nephew.

Davan hesitated to share the intimate details of his relationship. His uncle's bold comments opened the door. He'd told him about the birds and the bees, why not talk to him about his concerns? Hell, Uncle David had taken him to the drugstore to buy his first box of condoms. Davan would get good advice and a straight answer, without judgment.

"What?" David asked.

"I can't seem to close the deal with Jova."

David took a second to decipher the words. "You've tried?"

Davan nodded. The make-out session on the Cedar Point trip looked like a G-rated movie compared to their encounters since.

"Do you think she wants . . . to seal the deal with you?"

"I do," Davan answered without hesitation. He didn't know why she wouldn't drop her guard and let him pierce her layer of protection, but her reaction to his touches confirmed she wanted him as badly as he wanted her.

"You really care about her?"

"More than she knows."

David took minute to formulate his advice. "You should let her know."

Davan nodded. Maybe he hadn't made it clear. Maybe she hadn't opened up to him because he hadn't opened up enough to her.

"And, Davan?"

"Yes?"

"Sometimes you can't take no for an answer."

Chapter 16

Jova held the phone to her ear with her shoulder, pulling a brush through her customer's hair. "Davan, I'm sorry. I'm running late. I don't think I'll make it in time for the movie."

"It's okay. You're off tomorrow, right? Come by when you're finished."

She admired his easygoing nature. "No matter how late?"

"No matter how late. *Ten days*. It's been ten days since we've spent any time alone together. I want to see you."

Ten days since she'd last kissed him. Her nerves were frayed because of it.

"Where are we going?"

"Why?" he teased.

"I have to know what to wear and how to do my hair."

"Dress." Davan wouldn't get any more specific. She loved dressing up for him. He took his appreciation to an entirely different level, but after being whisked off to Cedar Point, she knew to get the details. He wouldn't spill. He teased her, hanging up with the parting words "We're going where I should have taken you a long time ago."

Jova couldn't get out of the shop fast enough.

Jova radiated with pride as she serviced the last customer of the day. Tresses & Locks had begun to turn a good profit every month. The creditors were paid. Her employees were happy. The only downside, long hours keeping her away from Davan.

The salon picked up over the winter holidays, while the garage slowed to a nice pace, allowing Davan to spend more time with his uncle. They were getting along much better. Davan's anger would still flare when David had a bad day, and they would argue. David continued to defend his decision, becoming more stubborn about the little things. To Davan's credit, he was learning to contain his anger and redirect it into the garage. And Jova had learned how to get around David's obstinate moods.

These were the two men in her life, Jova thought fondly. They might not be perfect, but they were hers.

Right now, Jova wanted to be perfect for Davan. Tonight felt special. It wasn't their anniversary or a holiday, but somehow she felt it would be more special than those days.

After a luxurious bath, she spent a long time styling her hair. She used the flat iron to curve her hair in even layers from a symmetrical part. Davan hadn't seen her since she'd removed the French braids, streaked her hair with modest brown highlights, and cut it to frame her face in a serious bob.

Feeling sexy would give her a boost of confidence when Davan's sensuous gaze made her melt. For this she selected a hot-red, racy, silk, and lace bra and panty set from her lingerie rack. When they arrived in the store many women ogled them, but none wanted to pay the hefty price to own them.

"Okay," she said aloud, searching her closet. "Davan said to *dress*. I'll knock his socks off."

She selected a black silk georgette ruffled skirt with floral embroidery and beading. The intricate layers were romantic and ultrafeminine. A black silk peasant blouse with jet beading completed the allusion. She debated on panty hose, but decided against diminishing the effects of the hot-red panties. The tea-length skirt would be warm enough to fight the chilly weather along with the black kid boots she would wear. She added a spritz of designer perfume in all the places Davan might kiss. No elaborate jewelry tonight, gold pearl earrings only. She wrapped a winter-white crocheted scarf around her neck, buttoned up her vanilla canvas hooded coat with the fur lining, and stepped out the door.

Jova expected her anticipation to diminish once she was in her Mustang on the way to Davan's apartment. It didn't. It bloomed and radiated into a pulsating desire she'd never felt before. She watched the numbers pass in the elevator, too slowly taking her to Davan's floor.

He was standing there when the elevator doors parted. Dreads shiny and neatly twisted. Freshly shaven, wearing a russet suede shirt opened down to the defining curve of his abdominal muscles. The large cuffs brought attention to his fingers: long, lean, and neatly manicured. Black dress slacks and black shoes completed his outfit. Wherever they were going, they would be the most attractive couple there.

"Jova." He greeted her with a smile that lit his eyes. Her own was as bright. They embraced in the hallway, Davan breaking contact to lead her into his apartment. "Hungry?"

Her day had been so busy, she'd forgotten about dinner. Being safely with Davan, she could remember to perform the necessities of life. "I am. Did you cook?" Heady aromas tickled her nose.

"I did, but it'll be a few minutes. Sit down. I'll bring you a drink." His fingers lingered on her shoulders, helping her off with her coat from behind. "Wow."

She turned, catching his keen stare.

"You look great," he ground out. "I better check on dinner." His tone said he'd much rather do other things. He strutted out to the kitchen.

Jova fashioned herself on the sofa; when he came from the kitchen, she would be the first thing he saw. He had been working on the apartment. All the boxes were unpacked. The furniture had been neatly arranged. Drapes hung over the blinds at the massive windows. He hadn't added any personal touches like photos or artwork, but his place was comfortable. A sign he was settling in and making a home.

Davan emerged from the kitchen, martini glasses in hand. "About ten minutes." He handed her a glass rimmed with a cocoa and sugar mixture.

Jova took a tentative sip. "Umm, what is this?"

"Chocolate martini."

"It's good. You've unpacked and decorated."

"Not as homey as your studio, but it'll do." He watched her over the rim of his glass.

"I feel very comfortable here."

"Good," he said emphatically, as if putting an end to a long argument. Jova watched him with piqued curiosity. He was different tonight. He watched her with heated intensity, making her wonder if it was safe to be alone in his apartment. Mood music was provided by Motown oldies. "Sexual Healing" by Marvin Gaye was playing now, and it reminded her of the time he'd walked into the salon catching her and Dawn's routine.

Davan checked the food, announcing dinner when he returned. He seated her at the dining room table and disappeared again in the kitchen. "Do you need help in there?" Jova called, thrilled with all the attention he was lavishing on her. The table had been set for two with a white tablecloth and burgundy runner. Matching votives flickered.

"No, you stay seated." He brought out the first serving dish. "Sherry-basted roast chicken," he announced before going back into the kitchen.

"I didn't know you could cook."

"I have a few dishes I can whip up, mostly pasta. I knew you would be late, and hungry. I wanted to feed you. I took these recipes directly out of *Essence.* Cross your fingers."

"So far, so good," Jova said, inhaling the aroma of the chicken.

Davan made several more trips to the kitchen. When he sat across from her, the table was covered with candied yams and apples, string beans, rice pilaf, and golden rolls.

"I didn't have time for dessert, but I picked up some fresh fruit." He watched her, waiting for approval of his efforts.

"Everything looks wonderful, and smells great. The fruit will be fine."

He surprised her by reaching for her hands and saying grace before they began. Once Jova dug into the food, she couldn't stop complimenting him. She helped herself to two pieces of chicken, and seconds on the candied yams and apples. Thinking she wouldn't look sexy *or* romantic in her clothes if she kept eating, she declined Davan's offer for more rice and rolls.

"No one's ever cooked for me," Jova said, pushing her plate out of reach—or else.

"I like spoiling you."

It wasn't the *words,* but his *expression,* that made Jova tilt her head in question. He took a long drink from his water glass, watching her predatorily. She glanced away, but he continued to brazenly watch her. His eyes slid downward and she could feel his caress. She didn't understand when or why, but a line had been drawn in the sand.

"Did I tell you how beautiful you are?" Davan asked, running a finger around the rim of his glass. "I like your hair this way."

Sexual energy charged the air. Jova tucked her hair behind her right ear. "Thank you."

He nodded, still watching her with obsidian eyes, peering right through her. "You dressed for me. You're so damn sexy."

She cleared her throat, sexual tension making it hard to swallow. "I'm sorry we missed the movie."

He didn't answer, didn't stop watching her. His finger strummed his glass. The innocent gesture seemed obscene in the thick darkness of the candlelit apartment.

"It's late. I should be—"

"Don't go," Davan commanded. He pushed the glass away and firmly planted his elbows on the table. The movement made his shirt gap open, revealing the smooth planes of his chest. "I want you to stay."

"I—"

"I want to make love to you."

Heat rushed to her cheeks. Her body threatened to melt under Davan's demanding gaze. She dropped her head, making her hair fall around her face in a curtain.

"It's time, Jova," Davan said as if it were simple reasoning.

"I'm not ready."

"Will you ever be *ready*? What does *ready* mean?"

She couldn't explain it. And she couldn't explain why she hesitated when her body felt beyond wet and ready. When he occupied every crevice of her mind. When her heart begged him to take her to the point of ultimate fulfillment.

"We've been dating four months," Davan said as if being ready were related to the calendar.

No matter how tempting he looked in the suede shirt, she couldn't cross the line he'd drawn. Not yet. She had to be sure. She had to be ready. Ready to take the leap of faith, and sure he wouldn't abuse her heart afterward.

"Stay. Make love with me."

She threw her head back and met hungry eyes that would not take no for an answer. Anxious eyes that had previously understood, and had been willing to wait.

"Davan—"

"Don't say no." The crack of his voice made her jump.

"I should leave before we fight."

"We're about to have one hell of a fight if you think you're leaving here." His voice sounded tighter than a drum. "Do you want me, Jova?"

She knew better than to fall into this trap. She didn't answer, because there was no right answer. Yes, she wanted him. But it wasn't so simple. Emotions and old hurts were involved; they'd have to consider the future and define the meaning behind the sex. It wasn't as simple as *I want you. Let's make love.* Davan, her heart, her body—she was the only one thinking rationally.

"Make love to me, Jova."

"Davan, no—"

He bolted from the chair, rounding the table in

a flash. Jova jumped, but didn't move quickly enough. Davan gripped the back of her chair and pulled it back from the table, scraping the floor. "I told you not to say no. Not tonight, Jova. I've waited so long—do you know how long?"

Her fingernails bit into the sides of the chair. She sat paralyzed, trapped in a cage and afraid to move. The menace in Davan's voice showed he meant business, and for the life of her she couldn't figure out how things had gotten out of control.

"I need to leave," she said quietly. No use rattling the lion's cage.

"You're not leaving."

"I want to leave. Are you going to try and make me stay?"

"Try? You're not leaving," he repeated forcefully.

Becoming angry, she tossed her head back and glared at him. "Are you going to force me to sleep with you, too?"

"I'm not going to have to force you to sleep with me." He rotated the chair around to face him. He kept his hand on the back of the chair, blocking her escape with his body. "The only thing I'm going to have to force you to do is deal with your feelings."

"I don't get you," Jova said, feeling desperate now. "You've never been like this before."

"It's simple. I want you. You want me. Why are you complicating it?"

"Because it *is* complicated."

"No, it's not, Jova." His tone softened, but his hand continued to grip the chair. "Why are you fighting me?"

She used her hair as a concealing curtain.

"If you don't answer me, we'll be here all night."

As she didn't plan to answer him, or be there all

night, she plotted her escape. She could be as stubborn as Davan. If she wanted to leave, she would leave. He couldn't force her to lay her private fears at his feet for his dissection.

"Tell me why you're afraid to make love to me."

Jova kicked him in the shin with the toe of her kid boot. He released his grip on the back of the chair to grab his shin. She raced to the door, but he caught her around the waist just as she reached for her jacket. He carried her to the sofa and dumped her there, ensnaring her body with his.

"Damn it, Jova! That hurt! Stop struggling before you hurt yourself."

Realizing she could never outwrestle him, she stopped struggling. "Let me up."

"Are you afraid of me?"

She choked out a sarcastic laugh.

"Do you not feel as strongly about me as I feel about you?"

The twinge of hurt in his voice stopped her cold. She stared into his obsidian eyes and realized making love wasn't about fulfilling carnal desire for Davan. Making love was about validating their feelings.

"No," Jova said, "it's not that I don't care about you."

"What is it? Tell me why you won't make love to me."

"I'm scared," she admitted.

"Scared of what?" He brushed the hair away from her eyes.

"Scared I might lose you."

"Me?" Puzzlement crooked his brow. "You're not going to lose me. What's going on in your head?"

"I'm keeping the barrier between us." He would have knocked it down long ago. "If I let my guard

down, and you hurt me, I don't think I could recover, Davan."

"This is because of the exes."

"Maybe some, but you mean more to me than
anyone ever has. If I give my all to you, and it
doesn't work out . . . I can't take that chance. My
heart can't withstand one more crack."

"Jova, have I ever given you a reason to doubt
how I feel about you? Have I ever complained
about you spending time with my uncle, becoming
part of my family? Have I ever looked at another
woman?"

"No." No, to all those things.

"Is there ever a time when you don't know where
I am, and what I'm doing?"

"No." She was beginning to feel foolish.

"Do I yell at you? Hit you?"

"Never."

He held her face in his palms. "You're special to
me. I try to prove how important you are every
day."

"I know."

"If it isn't enough for you, tell me what you need.
If I can do it, I will. You know that, don't you?"

"I do." She did.

"Jova, you have to let go of the woman who
doesn't trust men. Forget about everything you've
gone through in the past. Stop running. Look in
your heart, and trust me."

"I do, Davan."

"Then let me make love to you. Because right
now, right here, it's what I need to do to prove how
much I care for you."

Chapter 17

Jova lay in a sea of reds and browns, propped up on her elbows, watching Davan undress. Next to the chocolate martini glasses on the beside table were two candles that shed light on the rippled muscles of his abdomen. He opened the buttons on his sleeves last, letting the shirt fall to the floor. His eyes were serious as he opened his belt, then the snap on his pants. The zipper. He eased the zipper down—so slow, too slow—and pushed the slacks past his narrow hips. Unlike his chest, his legs were peppered with dark hair. He wore black silk boxers, jutting out in the front, ready.

"Jova." He held out his hand.

She came to him, expecting him to undress her. He took her hands in his and guided her thumbs into the waistband of his boxers. She molded her hands to the indentation of his waist. He kissed the top of her head, encouraging her. If this was her time to enjoy, she wanted to take her time exploring him. Her hands slid over the lush silk and cupped his hard behind. He took in a sharp breath. She enjoyed the feel of his muscled bottom gliding against the sheer silk, a sexy contrast. She teased him, finally letting him guide her fingers into the waistband and pulling them down to his ankles.

She kneeled before him as he stepped out of the boxers.

He crushed her to him, hard and ready. This would be different from the make-out sessions. His manhood stood at full attention, wanting *her*. Begging for her attention.

Davan stroked her neck with his tongue as his hands cascaded over her shoulders, back, behind, and thighs. "I want you so badly," he said. He slid his hands inside the waist of her skirt, pulling it over the round curve of her bottom. She worked to kick off the kid boots. He pulled her shirt over her head, releasing another sharp breath when he saw her lingerie.

"I wish I could make love to you with these still on." He whipped her around, cupping her breasts from behind. He massaged ruthlessly until the peaks of her nipples strained against the satin and lace. A snap later, the bra fell to the floor.

The ridge of his sex pushed demandingly against the small of her back. She wanted to turn and grasp him firmly in her palm. He dropped to his knees behind her, planting kisses along her panty line and each hip. His tongue swirled in the small of her back. He grasped her hips, tugged, and the panties disappeared.

How had she managed to wait this long?

He stood, taking her into his arms from behind. Her head fell back and he lavished kisses along the column of her throat. He lifted her and they fell to the bed together.

She reached for him and was surprised by the heaviness of his sex. He elongated with each stroke, grew thicker with the pressure of her fingers. She lay beneath him, pulling him to straddle her.

"I only have so much control, Jova." He stilled

her hand, turning to rummage through the bed-side drawer. In her hurried haste to have him inside her, she had forgotten to protect them. But Davan would never forget.

She watched him with curiously eager eyes as he ripped the package open and rolled the latex from the tip downward. He stopped midway, distracted by her intense observation. He fell back on the bed, leaving the task incomplete. She rolled onto her side, facing him. She formed a ring around his manhood with her fingers, moving the latex sheath down the shaft. He twitched beneath her fingers. His fists were clenched, grinding into the mattress. "Hurry," he whispered.

Brazenly, she straddled him. He encouraged her new boldness by grasping her hips. She guided the tip of him between her wet folds. She braced her palms on his chest and lowered herself an inch. "Good, very good." She rocked back, taking another inch and another. He filled her so completely, yet she held more in her hand than she engulfed. Another impaling inch and she questioned her sanity. She stopped, his girth stretching her to the limit.

Davan grasped her hips and tossed her to the bed, immediately straddling her thighs. He entered her again quickly, but stopping where they'd left off. He lowered his chest to hers, ravishing her mouth. Suspended above her on his elbows, he chanted, "Make love to me, Jova."

She fell into the hypnotic rhythm of his words, pushing up to take more of him. He nibbled the hollow of her neck, whispering a promise of what was to come. She accepted more—but, then no more.

Being partially inside Jova was torturous. "I need

you, Jova." He flexed his hips, pushing deep, giving all he had. He took her hands and guided her to cup his behind. With every one of her strokes, he flexed. He kissed her with soul-stirring thoroughness and there was no more pain. Only a pleasure beginning at her core, and radiating through her body to push through the protective barrier surrounding her heart.

Instinctively, Jova moved beneath him, contracting her hips, encouraging Davan's rhythm. She bucked wildly. He flexed slowly, with a steady, sure beat.

"You're torturing me," Jova panted.

"Trust me," he answered, grabbing her hips and slowing her cadence. "Make love to me."

Their eyes met, mesmerizing her. She matched the thorough rocking of his hips. He adjusted his hips and began a delicious glide against her hardened nub, the meeting of hard and wet. *There.* If he would apply friction *there* the world would open, and all would be hers.

Davan's eyelids flickered. He'd found the place he needed to be. She rocked against him, kneading the muscles of his behind. The pressure swelled. Davan moaned, gliding against her wanton nub, sending a white-hot chill down her spine. The pressure building, building, until she couldn't concentrate, and lost the rhythm of her stroke. Davan pressed her hips into the mattress, and buried himself deep. One last gliding motion pushed her over the edge, and she screamed. Seconds later, her body shook, vibrating with newly released energy. Davan stiffened, groaned—pumping hard until he collapsed. She kissed his eyelids and stroked his chest as his body trembled.

He rolled onto his back, taking her with him.

"Jova," he moaned a hundred times. "Jova," he whispered until she fell asleep.

Jova stared at the stucco ceiling, recalling why her body felt achy and thoroughly loved. She turned to the dying candles. She inhaled the scent of love, remembering . . .

Davan.

The culprit was nowhere in sight.

She climbed from underneath the comforter, and hurried to the bathroom. Davan's things were neatly lined on the counter, aftershave and shaving items, lotion, soap—the usual *man* stuff. The shower curtain and accent rugs matched the burgundy and tan color scheme of the bedroom. The shower tiles were wet, his towel neatly folded across the rack. A clean set hung next to his.

"Oh, no!" Jova said, noticing herself in the mirror. Her hair went every which way. Her mascara had melted, leaving dark circles underneath her eyes. She rummaged through his medicine cabinet, finding a comb and brush. She grabbed the gel she had given him to use on his dreads and applied a light coat to her bob. She couldn't help smiling, as she thought of the tussling involved to get her hair this disheveled. She cleaned away the circles underneath her eyes. She washed and powdered before slipping into the robe hanging on the back of the bathroom door. She rolled the sleeves and tied the belt to hide her nakedness.

"Not bad in a pinch," she said, checking herself out in the mirror.

She found Davan in the kitchen placing dishes in the dishwasher.

"What did you do?" He looked horrified.

"What?" She thought she had done a good job of making herself presentable.

He palmed the back of her head. "You did your hair . . . and stuff."

"So?"

"I was proud of my work. Do you know how much back I had to put into it? And you go and get—fixed up."

Jova rolled her eyes.

"I accepted the challenge of getting a prim and proper woman good and dirty, but you went and ruined it."

She swatted at him, ducking under his hand.

"Now I have to do it all over again."

"Stay away from me." Jova sprinted across the living room, making it just inside the bedroom door before Davan scooped her up and threw her over his shoulder. He landed on top of her on the bed. She hadn't laughed this hard in years.

"Do you need anything?" Davan asked, laughter rumbling softly in his throat. He peered down at her, enveloping her in the warmth of his obsidian gaze.

"I'd like you to hold me."

He took her in his arms, snuggling his face in the crook of her neck from behind. "Any regrets?"

"I regret waiting so long."

"You understand I care about you?"

She answered by snuggling closer.

"We're good together."

She wiggled within the circle of his arms to face him. "You know what? We *are* good together."

"Absolutely." He kissed her nose, her cheeks, and her chin. "Don't sound so surprised. If you'd listen to what I've been trying to tell you for months . . ." His fingers opened the belt of the robe, pushing the ends apart. "We could have been here a long time ago." He caressed her breast. "We have a lot of time to make up for." Her nipple became rigid beneath his palm, validating his ability to excite and entice her. He dropped kisses on the taut peak, using his other hand to bring her other breast to life.

Jova rose up on her palms. "I take full responsibility."

Davan helped her remove the robe, his lips holding firmly to her nipple. "Hmm," he hummed, sending electric vibrations through her.

Looking down at him feeding off her sexual energy set Jova afire. Her fingers drummed through the pattern of his dreads, short and silky. His tongue lashed out, beating against her nipple with the precision of a whip. The sensation ricocheted through her body and she called out his name. Shamelessly, she writhed beneath his skillful hands and expert tongue. Never had this much attention been paid to satisfying her breasts.

Davan grasped her shoulders and firmly pushed her against the mattress. His hand drifted down her perspiration-slicked body, outlining her hourglass shape. "You have a perfect body." He explored the swell of her belly, the curve of her hip, and her voluptuous bottom. "And it's all mine." His fingers plunged into the luxurious fluff between her thighs.

She arched her back, sucking his fingers into the rapture.

Jova felt Davan harden along her thigh. Her uninhibited response to his touch made him impatient to possess her. He watched the dark, torturous expressions that must have been crossing her face as he strummed the nub that made her his marionette.

"Come to me," he said, watching her hips shimmer against his hand, begging him to push her out of control. His manhood throbbed against her leg, driving her to the crux. She screamed, boldly announcing her completion.

Anxious to share the all-embracing joy, he pulled the bedside drawer out too forcefully and it landed on the floor. Jova giggled as he hung off the side of the bed, scrambling for a condom. He growled, hurriedly applying the latex.

"Shhh," Jova soothed, reaching for him, and at the same time slanting her body to accept him.

He sank into the wet heat, flexing his hips and filling her cavern with every inch of him. He moved with restrained vigor, priming her. He tried to describe the warmth building at the base of his manhood. "You're torturing me."

"And tantalizing." Jova relished in her power.

Satisfaction appeared on the horizon and he took her with brisk, robust thrusts that left him soaked with perspiration. He closed his eyes, guarding against the soft moans escaping her lips. He fought to prolong the explosion when he wanted it so badly. She grabbed the hard muscles of his behind, bringing him into her. He growled, his self-control teetering as he pinned her wrists to the bed. It was too late. She'd succeeded in throwing him overboard. He stiffened. He ruptured, his conclusion coming hot and hard.

Davan collapsed in a heap, struggling to catch his breath. He pulled Jova onto his chest, his grip possessive and rough, because in the aftermath he realized he could never lose her.

Chapter 18

Davan greeted everyone in the shop before taking a seat in Jova's chair. She stood in front of him, hands on hips. "What can I do for you, Mr. Underwood?"

"Do you want me to say it aloud?" He wiggled his eyebrows.

"Ugh," Candi said.

Jova threw her a look and Candi swiveled her chair in the opposite direction.

"The garage is slow. Uncle David is feeling better so he came in today. That makes me free to take off. Do you want to catch a movie tonight?"

"It's pretty slow here, too. I'm sure we'll close by six, and then I'd love to go to the movies with you. As long as I get to choose the movie."

"Deal, but no chick flicks."

Overhearing their conversation, Lisa said, "Why don't you take off? I'll close."

Jova wanted every minute she could steal with Davan. He stayed on her mind. "I'll clean my station and we can go."

"I'll wait." Davan looked on while she straightened up.

Suddenly, a tense hush fell over the salon. Jova turned slowly, not wanting to know the cause. Seeing Lisa's shocked expression in the mirror, she continued to turn, her heart beginning to drum. Davan was talking to her about what movie to see, oblivious of the silent commotion in the salon.

Jova stopped, immobilized.

He stood on the other side of her chair, behind Davan—the best, and worst, of her world colliding.

Davan saw the reflection in the mirror behind Jova. He looked up at her, his eyes narrowing to black slits, questioning pits.

"Jova, I need to talk to you," Herman said, angrily. As if he had the right to be angry with her. He wore clean jeans and a flannel shirt. No coat, although it was very cold outside. He didn't wait for her to answer his request. He turned, heading for the supply room.

To Jova's horror, Davan did not miss a beat of the interaction. His gaze flickered between her and Herman. Already he composed his questions.

Jova closed the door of the supply room and spun around, furious. "What the hell are you doing here?"

"I found my way back to Detroit—since you wouldn't help me."

"I told you I never wanted to see you again. What are you doing at my salon?"

He forced the anger to fade, his expression giving away the difficulty to let it go. "I learned my lesson the hard way. I'm going to rebuild myself. I'm going to get a job, car, and apartment. I've given up gambling."

"I'm happy for you, but this doesn't have anything to do with me." And she never wanted it to have anything to do with her again. He was pitiful. Half dressed with nowhere to go. Comparing him to Davan would have been an insult.

He advanced on her. She took a step back, and he dropped his arms. Anger passed over his face, but his voice remained humble. "I need help getting back on my feet."

"No!"

"Just a little, and then I won't bother you again."

"No. Why do you keep coming to me? Don't you have friends or family who can help you?"

His voice dropped. "I remember how kind you were when we were together. I thought you could help me this one last time, and then—once I've gotten myself together—we could get back together."

Is he trying to seduce me? "Absolutely not. Listen, Herman. I've tried to be firm but honest with you. There is no chance we'll ever get back together. I don't want to be with you. There's even less chance I'll give you any money. I'm not getting tangled up in your problems."

"You'd leave me out on the streets?"

"I've done enough. Go to your family. Go to Gamblers Anonymous."

"Once my bookie finds out I'm back in town, he'll come after me," Herman pleaded.

"You shouldn't have come back." She guessed the work had gotten hard and he'd run away. "There's nothing I can do for you, Herman. You need professional help." She hated being cold, but nothing else seemed to work.

"I'm asking you nicely . . . one last time."

"What does that mean?"

"Don't find out." The raging anger had returned, evidenced by the fine tremors shaking his body.

"Are you threatening me?"

He clenched his fists.

"Don't threaten me, Herman. You don't scare

me. You need to leave my salon—and never come back."

"I remember a time when you would have begged me to come to this funky little shop!"

"A moment of stupidity on my part."

Herman glared, but she didn't back down. "You'll be sorry you treated me this way." He stormed past her. "Bitch!"

Chapter 19

David suggested they have catfish, grilled outside even though it couldn't be more than twenty degrees. While he tended the fish, Jova made salads and lemonade. Davan wouldn't be joining them for dinner today—and she felt relieved.

Davan had been letting her stew. He was too angry to make love to her, and too prideful to ask what had transpired between her and Herman. A week had gone by since Herman's tumultuous visit to the salon, and Davan hadn't said a word about it. He visited her every day. He brought her lunch or dinner when he noticed the salon was busy. After work, he might drop by with a video. They kissed and talked as usual. He offered no intimacy. He remained a good, polite boyfriend—minus the intimacy. They had only made love twice, but Jova felt like an addict going through withdrawal.

It unnerved her—Davan not inquiring about Herman—because she could plainly see he wanted every detail. As the days passed, the mistrust grew. He would always be good and polite, but distant. He was building a wall, and she feared once it was solidly constructed, Davan would leave her. This worried her. She expected a phone call ending them every day, which explained her relief with him not joining her and David for dinner. If she could avoid him, he couldn't end their relationship.

The mature thing to do would be to tell Davan everything. She should have told him everything the day Herman appeared. She shouldn't have let it fester, feeding Davan's doubts and cultivating mistrust between them. But she didn't want to share any part of her past relationships with Davan. She had confessed making bad choices in the past. Couldn't that be enough? Did he have to know every detail of every mistake? How come they couldn't start fresh and leave the past behind them?

She reversed the tables and placed herself in Davan's shoes. The only reason she hadn't pried into his past was that his past was hundreds of miles away in Utah. She didn't need to know, because there was no chance his past would come waltzing into the garage demanding favors.

"Jova," David asked gently, "is there something bothering you?"

She looked up from her dinner.

"You've been really quiet today. Well, it seems like something's been bothering you all week."

"It's hard, you know?" Her voice sounded strained and there was a huge lump in her throat. "Not having my mother here to talk to."

"Well, we're not blood, but I consider you family. You're as good as a daughter to me. And I'm not saying that because you're seeing Davan. You're my family always, separate from your relationship with Davan."

She swallowed back the growing lump. "I feel the same way, Uncle David." An overwhelming urge came over her to share her feelings. She never thought about David being near the end of life, and she never treated him with fragility, but the uncertainty of her relationship with Davan made her share her emotional revelation. "I've pretty much felt like an orphan since my mother died. My father's out there somewhere, but I don't know him. I'm not sure if I want to know him, seeing he ran out on my mother and me."

An unreadable expression crossed David's sunken facial features.

Jova continued. "The time I've spent with you the last few months has been great, Uncle David. You've made me a part of a family again. I can't tell you how much I need this."

David cast his eyes away, and Jova suspected he was fighting back tears. "I had a chance at having a family and I threw it away. I ruined a good relationship with a woman who meant everything to me. Only I didn't realize it until she was long gone. I concentrated on building my business, making a future—like you're doing. But what good is building a business and making a future if you don't have anyone to come home to every night?"

Jova read his message clearly.

"Don't get me wrong. I love my nephew, and I'm glad he brought you to me. There are just some things you can only share with a wife."

Jova wanted to comfort him, but knowing David, he would perceive it as pity.

"You're young, Jova. You have time to figure out what's important in life. Pay attention to what I'm telling you. Take a look at your life. Decide what you need to be happy—truly happy—and go after it."

"I met Herman over a year ago." Jova wrung her hands, watching for any negative reaction from

Davan. "Herman helped me through a very hard time in my life. No matter what I tell you, I want you to know I couldn't have made it through my mother's passing without his help. I think that's why I put up with him when things started falling apart. When he saw I couldn't handle planning my mother's funeral, he jumped in and took over. I'll always be grateful to him for that."

"I understand. Go on." Davan sat on her sofa, his hands gripping his knees.

"Bad luck found Herman. One thing after another started going wrong for him. He was injured trying to break up an altercation between two prisoners."

Davan raised a questioning brow.

"Herman worked as a prison guard at Jackson," she explained. "When he was injured, the doctors took him off work for weeks. He wasn't sure he'd ever be well enough to go back to work. He became depressed, and looking back, it's when he started gambling. At first, he went to the casinos to pass the time. Next thing I know, he was spending all his time there."

Davan remained silent, no disapproving expression.

"Disability didn't pay enough to cover his monthly bills, so I loaned him money to get by. Even with that, I noticed a few things around here missing. He needed more and more money. Just when it seemed to be spiraling out of control, the doctors let him return to work. He was happy again, and our relationship went back to normal."

She paused, filtering out the details of her personal time with Herman. "It didn't take long for the gambling to start again. I questioned him about it, and he stopped. Or so I thought, but he actually just hid it from me. It became a problem. Our relationship suffered. We started drifting apart, but neither of us ended it.

"Then came the day he borrowed my new car. He stayed out all night drinking and gambling. The next morning I get a call saying he's in the hospital. He recovered quickly enough. At this point, I'm ready to end it, so I did."

Still, she couldn't tell what Davan was thinking. She continued. "Time goes by and I find out he's suing me for his injuries from the accident. The day I met you I had just left court."

Davan nodded. Jova could see him mentally piecing his own time line together. She finished the story, ending with the scene he'd witnessed at the salon. She waited for him to comment, to pass judgment on how she had handled Herman.

His black gaze scrutinized her. She'd told too much. Did she dwell too long on her relationship with Herman? Did she glaze over it too fast, and now he suspected there were secrets she wasn't telling him?

"Why are you telling me all of this, Jova?" His voice was deep, a black hole that provided no clue of his emotions.

"I—I thought you should know. You were there when Herman came to the salon."

"So? So what I was there? *Why* are you giving me all this information about Herman? Why is it important for me to know about your relationship?"

"I didn't want you to mistakenly think I was still seeing him."

"Do you care what I think?" Davan asked stonily.

"Yes! Yes, I care."

Anger raised his voice an octave. "Why now? You

let me wonder what the hell was going on for a
week."

"I know. I should have come to you right away,
but I didn't."

"So why now? Why not let it go on? Why not let
me go on thinking you're seeing someone else?
Why end my suffering now?"

"Suffering?" She hadn't thought—

"Are you still in love with him?"

"No! I never loved Herman." What did she say
that led Davan to believe she ever loved Herman?
He'd misunderstood somewhere along the way.
And the only reason she hadn't spoken to him
about this whole mess was that she feared his reaction.

"Why are you telling me all of this?" Davan asked
again. "Is this your way of letting me down easy? Am
I supposed to walk away now?"

"No! You have the wrong idea."

"Then explain."

"I don't want you to leave me, Davan."

He watched her for an agonizingly long time.
She was taking their relationship to an emotionally
new high.

Jova answered his unspoken question. "There's
no one else in my life."

Davan believed her; she could see his anger melting.

"I don't want anyone but you."

He caressed her with a gaze of molten liquid.

Jova stood, looking down on him. He held her
eyes, but didn't speak. She climbed into his lap,
straddling him on the sofa. "Forgive me?"

He answered with his touch. His hands slipped
beneath her sweater.

"I could earn my penance."

He growled, his fingers working at the hooks on her bra.

"Since you're not speaking to me, I would need a sign—"

Jova received her sign, hard and demanding, pushing against the cushion of her bottom. She kissed him hungrily, working at the buttons of his shirt.

Davan pulled her sweater over her head, and tossed her bra over the sofa. He fondled her breasts roughly, impatiently grunting for her to get his shirt off.

She responded to his aggressive touch by going up on her knees, giving access to his hands as they searched underneath her argyle skirt. With one jerk, her panties and tights were at her knees. He had worked them down her calves by the time she unzipped his jeans.

There was a chorus of grunts and moans while they rummaged through his wallet for a condom. And then nerve-shattering silence as Jova braced herself, placing her palms on his shoulders. His manhood bobbled between them, encouraging them to proceed quickly.

Jova licked her lips, watching Davan as she removed one hand from his shoulder and grasped his shaft. He was hard and thick and long—and desperate for her. She lowered herself onto the steel rod. He blinked, grabbing the sofa cushion to still himself. She took more of him inside, and the muscle in his jaw jumped. Hot and pulsating, she forced more inside; hard steel gliding into her slickness.

"All of it," Davan growled.

They'd done this dance before—balancing the insertion with the snug fit. It took time. Their de-

sire raged too hot for time and patience to matter.
Jova inhaled, bolstering her courage, and then she
took it all.

Having survived the torment, Davan toppled
over the edge. He grabbed her bottom possessively,
meeting each of her wanton thrusts with a matching stroke.

"Davan," Jova moaned. Her head hung down,
pressed against his chest. Her fingers dug into his
shoulders. She moved with pistonlike precision,
this position allowing her to dictate the force of
Davan's hammering movements. He filled her to
capacity, sliding delicious friction across her en-
gorged nub. She could go on like this forever.

The sex was hard and angry. Davan's eyes were
soft and adoring. During a moment of lucidity, Jova
wondered how he could make her feel all these
emotions at once.

"Come with me, Jova," Davan demanded softly.

He lifted his hips, burying himself deep. He
slipped a finger between his lips, and then slid it between them, touching her overly sensitive core. She
would do anything, *anything* to keep the sensation
alive.

"Come, Jova." His fingers bit into her bottom,
bracing her and driving hot steel deeper.

Emotion clustered near Jova's heart. Sensation
swarmed and settled where her throbbing en-
gorgement fought Davan's steady deluge.

"Come, Jova," Davan taunted.

"No," she panted, working her hips franticly. "I
don't want this to end."

"Jova—"

"No! I don't want this to end." She worked feverishly.

"Shhh." Davan cupped her face in his palms. "Look at me."

She couldn't, because he would make her stop.

"Jova, look at me."

She tossed her hair back testily, giving in.

"Come . . . *with me.*"

The intensity in his obsidian eyes was enough to push her to the limit. Her orgasm came loudly and without mercy. From this day forward, it would only take a glance from Davan to shatter her. He wrapped his arms around her tightly, pushing her body into his as he grasped the apex of his climax.

He held her, stroking her hair with calming fingers. His breathing was still ragged when he carried her to the bed, and disappeared into the bathroom.

He hurried, but she knew. She knew her aggressive lovemaking had caused the condom to come off.

She turned on her belly, burying her face in the pillows. She rationalized her scandalous behavior: her desire for Davan had been out of control. If that was true, then why now, completely sated, did she feel a repressive joy over the possibility of carrying his baby?

Chapter 20

"Hi, can I help you?"

"I'm Patricia Hornsby." The woman answered as if Jova should know her.

Jova took in the dark trench coat and winter suit. The woman carried a briefcase overflowing with papers. She looked all business. This wasn't a casual sales call. Correctly reading Jova's confusion, the woman handed her a business card. *Right Way Realty.*

"What can I do for you, Ms. Hornsby?"

"Patricia, please. I'm stopping by to make sure your move is still on schedule. When your phone became disconnected, I thought you might have already vacated the premises."

"What?" Jova shook her head. "I'm confused. Vacated the premises?"

"I know we settled on thirty days, but like I said, when your phone became disconnected—"

"My phone isn't disconnected, and I don't have any idea what you're talking about."

"Do you mind if I come in?" Her perfect pale complexion had reddened from standing in the cold.

Jova invited her in. "You should start from the beginning," she said once they were seated on the sofa. "You said something about me vacating the premises. Why would I do that?"

Patricia batted her baby blues. Now she was confused. "Ms. Parker, you act as if this is unexpected. Did anyone lead you to believe you would be able to continue living here?"

"I still don't understand."

"When the building was sold—"

"Sold! What do you mean my building has been sold?"

Patricia placed her briefcase on her lap, and flipped it open. "You're right. I better start from the beginning."

Jova spent a horrifying hour with Patricia Hornsby of Right Way Realty. Frantic phone calls were made to the home office. Patricia produced a signed contract of sale to Jova. An attorney representing Right Way Reality arrived at her studio with more papers. Jova countered by showing them the deed to the building. They were apologetic, but the bottom line was the building had been sold and in fourteen days, Jova needed to be out of it.

She was alone now, her hands trembling as she tried to make sense of the legal documents. She knew she hadn't signed the papers, and she didn't recognize the attorney's name on the forms giving him license to act on her behalf. The documents looked so authentic, she began to wonder if she had developed an alter ego.

Panic set in.

"I'll get a lawyer." She crumpled the papers. According to these documents she already had a lawyer.

Fourteen days. Two weeks to pack her things, dissolve the shop, and find a place to live.

Could a lawyer stop the sale of the salon with only fourteen days to work with?

Funds. Once the shop was closed, how much money would she have to live off of?

How could this have happened? Patricia had plainly explained *how* it happened.

Who would do this to her? Who would snatch the salon out from under her?

It hit her like a ton of bricks.

"You'll be sorry you treated me this way."

Herman's words.

Could he be desperate enough to rob her of everything? He knew all she had was tied up in the salon. He knew she lived in the building. For a time, he had spent his nights here, too. Could he— would he be desperate enough to rob her of everything?

With a bookie threatening to kill him?

Yes, yes, he would do this to her.

Davan ran to his truck, and raced at top speed to his uncle's house.

"Davan, come quick. Jova's here. She's really upset. I can't stop her from crying."

He parked four feet from the curb, and ran across the lawn. "Uncle David, open up." He banged on the door, rushing inside when David answered.

"I can't make out what she's saying." David shuffled behind him to the living room. "Something happened at the salon."

"Jova?"

She bolted up from the sofa and ran into his arms. He held her, watching David over her head. It didn't take long for him to quiet her. He knew how to comfort her. She liked her hair stroked. She needed to be held tightly.

He helped her back to the sofa. "Jova, what's wrong?"

David stood nearby, worried.

She pulled beaten papers from her purse. Davan handed them over to his uncle. "Tell me what's going on."

"You sold the salon?" David asked, incredulously.

Davan's head snapped around. She wouldn't sell the salon without mentioning it to him. He knew how much the business meant to her. It was the beginning of a legacy made available by the tragic death of her mother.

"*Someone* sold the salon. A real estate agent showed up today to remind me to be out in fourteen days."

"What do you mean someone sold the salon?" David asked. "I thought *you* owned the salon."

"She does," Davan answered. Already a picture was forming.

"It's not my signature on those papers, Uncle David," Jova explained. "I don't know who that lawyer is."

Davan and David listened as she told them about how the drama had unfolded over the afternoon. "I've never heard anything like this," Davan said, shocked by how her salon could have been sold without her knowing anything about it.

"It happens," David said. "Unfortunately, we hear about this sort of scam a lot around here. A poor family can't get credit approval for an apartment. They answer an ad in the paper for a house to rent. The landlord says he's had hard times before and he's willing to give them a chance—if they can come up with a deposit. The family comes to move in and two other families are there, too, ready to move in. Or, like in Jova's case, they find out the house is owned by someone else, and their deposit it gone."

"What do I do, Uncle David?" Jova's face clearly displayed her torment.

"Well, I'll call my attorney and see if he can do anything. If he can't, I'll see if he can refer someone."

"Thank you."

David took the papers and went into the bedroom he used as an office.

"We'll fix it," Davan said, his heart breaking. He took Jova into his arms, wiping the tears from her cheek.

"What if—"

He placed his finger over her lips. "No matter what, Uncle David and I will help you."

She wrapped her arms around his waist, and buried her face in his chest.

"Do you know who could have done this?" Davan asked.

"Herman said I would be sorry for not helping him."

He stroked her hair. "My thought exactly."

An hour later, David emerged from his office. He didn't look hopeful. "Well, I faxed the papers to my attorney. He took a quick look."

Jova sat up, waiting.

"It's going to be a long, involved fight."

Jova whimpered, and Davan held her closer. "Did he say what her chances were, Uncle David?"

David sat on the edge of his recliner. "He said these cases are hard to prove, but he's not an expert in real estate law. He's going to have one of his partners call Jova. After he looks over the papers and makes some phone calls."

Davan's anger bubbled to the surface. "How long is it going to take?"

David shrugged. "A few days to get back to Jova. Longer than two weeks if they have to go to court."

Jova turned to Davan. "What am I supposed to do in the meantime?"

"In the meantime," David answered, "my attorney says you have to abide by the contract."

"I have to leave my salon? My home?" Jova started crying again. "I don't have anywhere to go."

"Davan will rent a U-Haul and get the guys in the garage to help move your things here until this is settled."

"No! I can't do that, Uncle David."

"If you don't come here, where?" David raised a finger at Davan, cutting him off. "Forget it. You two aren't married. Jova won't be moving in with you."

Davan took her hand. "It's up to you, Jova. You know you're welcome to move in with me." He took her chin in his palm. "And it doesn't have to be temporary."

Her tearstained eyes moved between him and his uncle.

"It's not proper," David snapped.

"Uncle David." Hadn't he told him to go after Jova in the first place?

Jova interrupted, quieting the explosive situation. "I'll move in here. Thank you, Uncle David."

"I knew that dog was up to no good," Lisa said when she heard the news.

"I'm sorry." Jova looked at each of her employees in turn. "As soon as I get this settled, I'll

ask you all back to Tresses & Locks. I know you
have to make a living, so if you choose not to return, I'd understand."

Jova had called the meeting to assure Lisa,
Candi, and Josh of her efforts to save the salon.
By the end of the gathering, instead of her comforting them, they were comforting her. They
understood working as a stylist in the Hair Capital of the World was as easy as driving to the next
shop. Starting your own business an entirely different matter.

"What I don't understand," Candi said, "is how
the new owner got into the building without anyone knowing. I mean, they had to check out the
place before making an offer. Right?"

Jova and Lisa looked at each other, silently questioning.

"I'm hardly ever out of the salon during business hours. I can count on one hand the days I
missed."

"Go get your calendar," Candi said.

Together, they strummed through the last three
months—during the time Patricia Hornsby said
it took to close the deal. For tax purposes, Jova
charted her every move. She even accounted for
time spent having lunch with Davan and early clos-
ings. She easily retraced her steps.

Josh made the proclamation. "It had to be
here." He pointed to a date on the calendar.

"The day I went downriver to straighten out my
stolen credit card. I never thought . . . I left Dawn
in charge of the shop. Lisa, you worked a half day.
Remember, you left at lunch."

Lisa nodded.

Candi crossed her arms over her chest. "Dawn's
a real piece of work."

"Would Dawn help Herman steal the salon from you?" Josh asked.

"A few weeks ago, I wouldn't have believed she'd up and quit on me. She told me she liked Herman, but I interfered." Jova turned to Lisa. "Do you think she'd be this vengeful?"

"My gut tells me she had something to do with it. Herman couldn't have pulled this off alone."

Anxious to share her theory with Davan, Jova hugged everyone good-bye and hurried to dinner at David's place. He listened closely, commenting after she pieced it all together. "I don't know, Jova. It seems a little out there."

"How mad was she when she quit?" David asked.

"Pretty mad. Her anger seemed out of proportion. She'd been my friend since the day she walked into Tresses & Locks, but she turned on me because of one date with Davan."

"She doesn't sound rational." David took his dishes to the sink. "You should go talk to her, find out what she knows. Maybe she could give you something to take to the attorney."

"Good idea," Jova agreed.

"I disagree," Davan said. "If Dawn is irrational, you shouldn't approach her, and if she does have something to do with all this, will she tell you anything that might land her in jail?"

"I have to do something, Davan."

"It could be dangerous. I don't like it."

Jova sought allegiance with Uncle David. "What do you think?"

"Davan's right, it could be dangerous. Tell the attorney and let him handle it."

Knowing it would be useless to argue with the two most stubborn men on the planet, Jova con-

ceded. "I'll tell the attorney, but it still seems like
I should do something."

"Jova . . ." Davan's tone pleaded for her to leave
it alone, but his eyes sent a stronger warning.

"You two work it out. I'm going to bed." David
threw Davan a pointed look. "Jova, lock up when
Davan leaves. Good night."

Jova picked up the conversation once David left
the kitchen. "I can't believe Dawn would be this
treacherous." She wouldn't help Herman destroy
her, would she? But Dawn did reveal the fact she
had wanted Herman all along, and blamed Jova
for getting in the way. No. Dawn had witnessed
firsthand Herman's manipulation. She knew
about his battling a gambling addiction.

"Dawn wouldn't stoop this low," Jova tried to
convince herself. She watched Davan finish his
dinner. He had been the prize; the one that got
away. "She did get sizzling mad when she found
out about our date."

"Stop worrying yourself over this, Jova. If Dawn
is involved, we'll find out soon enough. We can't
do anything tonight." He reached for her hand.
"I'm worried about you. I want you to stay focused,
and do exactly what the lawyer tells you to do."

"I will."

"You call me any time you need me. I'll be here
in ten minutes."

"I don't know what I'd do without you."

After finishing dinner and cleaning the kitchen,
they moved to the living room. Jova laid her head
on Davan's chest, letting him remove all her worries. He stroked her hair, a soft rumble bubbling
in his chest as he laughed at a sitcom. Being with
him like this was all Jova needed to feel everything
would work out. She wrapped her arms around

his neck, angling her head for a kiss. Without hesitation, he turned his attention from the television to her need. He held her close, sharing his strength through the art of his kiss.

"In all the excitement, we haven't had a chance to talk about us," Davan said.

Jova reached for her glass of wine, avoiding his dark gaze.

He went on unhindered by her avoidance. "The last time we were together, the condom—"

"I know."

A hundred questions crossed his face. He added wine to his glass, taking a sip before continuing. "Are you on the pill?"

She shook her head, bringing down the curtain of her hair.

"I can't tell you what to do with your body, but would you consider the pill?"

Unexpected grief pierced her heart.

"Why do you look so crushed?"

"No reason." Jova understood bringing a child into her life right now would be stupid. She and Davan weren't serious enough to be considering marriage, and she didn't want to be a single mother. Her child would need every advantage to succeed in the world. She knew these things, but it didn't keep her from wanting Davan to care about her enough to want a family with her.

"I'd like to be a father some day," Davan clarified. "I want a wife, a family."

Her melancholy had nothing to do with having a baby. It was about becoming a family with Davan. About being his wife. When had her feelings become this strong?

Davan continued to explain. "It's not the right

time. With Uncle David being sick, and your salon being sold . . ."

"I'll make an appointment with my doctor."

"You understand?"

She nodded. Yes, she understood. She was falling in love with Davan.

Chapter 21

"*Davan*," Jova said, exasperated with his thirty-minute tirade.

"He treats you like you're a virgin princess." He stalked across his apartment barefoot, wearing a faded pair of jeans that molded perfectly to the hard haunches of his backside. "A few weeks ago, he wanted us to get together. Now he's doing his best to keep us apart. If I didn't know better, I'd think Uncle David wanted you for himself." He whirled around, crossing the distance separating them with three bounding steps. "He hasn't hit on you, has he?"

"Davan! Of course not. David still wants us to be together, and he has specific ideas about how it's supposed to occur. He's protecting my honor."

"*Hello*, Jova. We aren't in the sixteenth century. Besides, *I'll* protect you if you need protecting." He dropped down on the sofa beside her. "You living with my uncle isn't working out. You have to move in here."

"You need to relax. You're all wound up over nothing."

"I'm wound up because Uncle David won't let me within five feet of you to do any *unwinding*."

"Maybe he does need to protect my honor," she teased.

"Not funny. We get along well. You're my girlfriend. Why can't you move in here?"

"If we decide to take our relationship to a deeper level, I want it to be based on our feelings for each other, not because I'm going through a hard time."

Davan barked out his frustration. "The truth is you are going through a hard time. So we move a little faster than we'd anticipated. It doesn't mean it won't work out."

"Davan."

He persisted. "We'll move your stuff in this weekend."

"Now you're trying to bully me. Don't push me." Jova stroked his long fingers. "I can't repay David for everything he's done. I'm virtually a stranger, but he took me in and is helping with the lawyer and straightening out the mess with the salon. The least I can do is live by his house rules."

Davan grunted.

"You know I'm right."

"I know you could be living here, with me. We wouldn't have any problem finding time to be together then. I could roll over in the middle of the night and—"

"Davan!"

"Okay, okay. Uncle David is right, and I'm a sex fiend."

"Are you making all this noise over sex?" She expected him to start pouting any moment.

Davan pulled her into his arms. "I miss you. We don't have any time alone together anymore."

"We're together now."

A crooked smile bloomed. "We are, aren't we?"

"I told David I wouldn't be home, and to call here if he needed anything."

"You did?" Already his fingers were dancing over her belly.

"Uh-huh. I could make you breakfast in the morning."

"I could break away from the garage and come home for lunch." Davan's fingers slipped underneath her sweater.

Jova's hand climbed up his thigh. "As the boss, can't you take extra-long lunches?"

"As the boss, I don't have to go back after lunch at all."

Chapter 22

On Tuesday, February 14, Jova sat between Davan and David in the plush surroundings of Mr. Hammermill's office. Lawyers seemed to intimidate her, and she did her best to stay away from them. It was another reason Herman's lawsuit had upset her, even if it had been proven frivolous. She reached over and took Davan's hand. He sent her a concerned glance, but quickly turned back to the lawyer, not wanting to miss a single word.

A middle-aged man with thinning sandy-brown hair, Mr. Hammermill had a confidence that radiated U of M Law School. Pictures of his family were neatly placed on the credenza. A wife, two boys, and a German shepard posed smiling into the camera, standing on a lush lawn with a huge home in the background. Maintaining a very businesslike attitude, he described Jova's case with words like *real estate fraud* and *forgery.* "The first thing we have to concentrate on, Ms. Parker, is proving you didn't sign the power-of-attorney papers."

"How do we do prove it?" she asked.

"I'll have a handwriting expert take a look. He'll need a sample of your writing, of course."

"Sounds okay." She looked to Davan for confirmation. He nodded.

"Next, I'll meet with the attorney who 'acted on your behalf.' We'll need to find evidence he knew he wasn't dealing with the real *you*. I know this attorney. He has a reputation for being very crafty. He knows the law and how to maneuver loopholes. He works within the law, barely, but he knows how to cover his tracks."

"Doesn't sound very encouraging," David said.

Mr. Hammermill reared back in his chair. "I have to be honest, Ms. Parker, whoever pulled this off did his homework."

"Herman Norman," David interjected. "She knows who's responsible."

"It would be wonderful if we could prove Mr. Norman responsible. All we have is Ms. Parker's suspicions."

Jova tried to convince Mr. Hammermill. She told him about Herman's repeated visits, asking for her help to bail him out of debt. She gave him the details of the day at the salon when he had threatened revenge. "It couldn't have been anyone else."

"It sounds very likely that Mr. Norman is involved, but many people had to play a part to bring this deal to heel. The court deals in facts that can be indisputably proven. We have to give the judge paperwork, expert testimony, and witnesses if we expect to be successful."

Davan cleared his throat. "Mr. Hammermill, can you stop the sale of the building until Jova has her day in court?"

"The sale has gone through—three months ago. I can't stop it. I've filed an injunction to keep the new owners from altering the property until the case is settled. It might deter them; maybe they'll put pressure on Right Way Realty."

David rubbed wide circles across Jova's back, showing his support.

Mr. Hammermill continued. "I've scheduled meetings with Right Way Realty's attorney. I'll also meet with the attorney who claims to have your power of attorney. Give me a few weeks and I should have more to report."

"A few weeks?" Jova questioned warily.

"Unfortunately, these things take time. I know this is difficult, but hang in there. You obviously have a lot of support."

David spoke up. "Davan and I are in your corner."

The attorney tried to reassure her with a smile. "My assistant will talk with you about the handwriting analysis. I'll contact you as soon as I have something to report. Stay positive."

Jova huddled into the warmth of her coat. She walked across the parking lot still dazed by Mr. Hammermill's assessment of her situation. Davan helped her into the car. David took the backseat. They tried to stay upbeat, throwing out suggestions of what to do next.

Stay positive, Mr. Hammermill had said. She searched for a positive side to what was happening to her. She'd closed Tresses & Locks, and was losing money every day. She couldn't go back to her studio apartment. She'd had to let her employees—her friends—go. No job, no home. She couldn't find anything positive to hold on to.

Meanwhile, Herman undoubtedly sat at a casino gaming table spending the profit from the sale of her salon. He as good as spat on her mother's grave. It had turned out nothing was genuine about Herman.

There had to be something she could do. Waiting for the weeks to pass before Mr. Hammermill called would be torturous. She needed something to fill her days. She'd fallen into a comfortable routine with Uncle David, and Davan stopped by almost daily, but she needed to define her own self-worth. Her mother had taught her the value of being independent and making a life separate from what a man offered. Her mother's only regret was becoming mentally and financially bankrupt when her father left.

Jova realized closing the salon didn't negate her stylist skills. She would find work somewhere until she could reclaim Tresses & Locks. Salon owners might have a problem with her being a previous owner, afraid she might steal industry secrets. But if she tried hard enough, she could find a booth to rent.

She had formulated her plan by the time they reached David's house. Davan wanted to spend time with her, so they settled David in before leaving for the evening.

"How are you holding up?" Davan asked. They were still parked in front of David's house.

"I won't let Herman beat me."

Davan smiled. "I want to get your mind off of the salon, and Herman, and all your troubles. How about we get something to eat, and then I'll take you wherever you want to go?"

"Anywhere I want?"

"Dinner and whatever. You're the boss. As long as we end the evening at my place."

She sank back against the seat. "I would like the biggest, juiciest corned beef sandwich Mr. Fufu can make. Add a slice of lemon pound cake and I'm all yours. Then I'd like to go to your apartment and spend a nice quiet evening alone with you."

"I was hoping you would say something like that." Davan pulled away from the curb. "But who's Mr. Fufu?"

"You haven't had Mr. Fufu's yet?" Jova exclaimed, clearly determining it a tragedy. "Mr. Fufu's makes the best soul food in the city. Sandwiches this big." She measured the distance with her hands. "He also does a lot for the community, which is why I don't mind driving clear across town for a meal."

"Mr. Fufu's it is."

Davan hiked Jova's overnight bag up on his shoulder. "Can you get the door?" He juggled the bags from Mr. Fufu's restaurant, handing off the keys.

"I told you to let me carry my bag, Mr. Hunt, Kill, Provide." She searched for the key to open his apartment.

"And protect. Don't forget protect."

Jova opened the door and stepped aside.

"Get the lights. The switch is on the left."

She flipped the switch and gasped, clamping her hands over her mouth.

Balloons. Balloons everywhere. Red and pink helium balloons filled the living room, announcing Jova's birthday. She parted the red and pink ribbons hanging from the stems of the balloons, making her way into the center of the room. She stood enveloped by the balloons, giggling like a little girl.

Davan emptied his hands and joined Jova, taking her into his arms. "Happy birthday, baby."

"With everything going on I totally forgot my own birthday! You remembered!"

"Of course I remembered. No wonder you're so sweet. You're a Valentine's baby." He led her into the dining area. "Have a seat."

The fateful chair that had been her sexual undoing was draped in red and pink streamers. In the center of the table was a large box wrapped in pink paper with tiny red hearts. "Can I open my gift?" Jova clapped her hands together excitedly. She hadn't been this happy about a birthday since she was ten. Somewhere along the line, the magic had disappeared. Tonight Davan brought the magic back, accompanied with a flood of emotions Jova never thought she could experience.

"One second." Davan helped her sit before going into the kitchen. He appeared minutes later carrying a round cake, alight with twenty-eight red candles. The detail of the red roses was amazing. *Happy Birthday, Jova* was written in the center of the white icing. They wouldn't taste the cake until much later. Not until Davan licked icing from the tips of her nipples, and she slid a sliver between his ravenous lips.

"Davan!"

He placed the cake on the table and proceeded to sing "Happy Birthday"—off-key. Jova giggled, enjoying every note of the chorus. He ended with a flourish on bended knee, his long arms extended. "Make a wish and blow out the candles."

Jova closed her eyes and wished for many more nights like this with Davan. She draped her arms around his neck. "I can't believe you did all this . . . for me."

"Look here." Untangling her from his neck, he opened the jacket of his suit.

She reached inside and pulled out a pink envelope. She opened it, expecting a birthday card.
"Two tickets to the Motown Revue at the Fox The-
atre! How did you get these? It's been sold out for
months."

"A chauffer, who drives for several Motown stars,
brought his limo into the garage for repairs. I remembered how much you love the Motown oldies,
so I repaired the car in exchange for the tickets."

"There can't be a more considerate man on the
planet." Jova wound her arms around his neck,
pulling him down for a succulent thank-you kiss.

"Wow." He helped her back into the birthday
chair and placed the gift box in her lap. "Open it."

She tore at the paper.

"Remember, you called me the most considerate
man on the planet."

Jova inhaled a sharp breath. She pulled a sheer
black gown out of the box and let it dangle from
her fingers. The lace was delicate enough to melt
in her hands. Silk ties crisscrossed in a lattice design, framing a V-neckline that would plunge to her
navel. She believed the ties were meant to hold the
two swatches of material together enough to conceal her breasts. The back of the gown crisscrossed
down to the small of her back, and ended with a
dramatic fishtail hem.

"You are going to look *sooo* sexy in this gown."
Davan's voice was husky with need, and she hadn't
even tried it on yet. "There's more."

She handed the gown over to Davan and peered
into the box. She pulled out a pair of black garters
and nylons.

"This is when you're supposed to remember how
considerate I am."

"You've been plotting this moment since rummaging through the lingerie racks at my salon."

"Guilty as charged." His eyes blazed desire. "Go try it on."

Jova *did* love lingerie.

Davan did love *removing* her lingerie.

Fifteen minutes after her slipping into the exquisite gown, Davan tossed it on top of the mound of clothing piled at the foot of his bed. He didn't remove the nylons or garter until after Jova shuddered and screamed out his name.

"Happy birthday, Jova." He was on top of her, soaked with perspiration and trying to catch his breath.

"This is the best birthday I've ever had," Jova told him before drifting off to sleep.

Quiet, serene.

Gently lapping at her.

Riding the mild ripples of the ocean.

Pampering her with lazy strokes.

Tension building higher and higher, centering at the nucleus of her body.

Davan's fingers bit into her naked thighs. Sluggishly, Jova awoke, the pulsation between her thighs pulling her into reality. He was positioned between her legs. His tongue's caress startled her. She was fully awake now, using the light from the bathroom to watch his head bob . . . up and down, bringing her closer—

He had not done this before. She encouraged his intimate kiss by lifting her hips to meet his mouth.

Languorously circling her undulating nub, he instigated her pleasure.

With indecent desire she anticipated the crushing flood of her climax. *"Davan."*

He showed her no mercy, grasping her bottom and hoisting her upward for better positioning of his mouth. Her mind traveled in a thousand directions at once. He pushed her to a place sex had never taken her.

So much more than sex, she thought. His liquid kisses sealed a lifelong deal between them. She heaved her body upward, enjoying the final strokes. Drowning in raw carnal satisfaction, and sweet emotions.

Jova collapsed.

Davan was beside her in an instant, holding her through the tiny shivers moving through her body. Her skin pricked with blistering sensation. She could hardly stand for him to touch her. She would never stand for him letting her go.

He kissed her temple. "Happy birthday, Jova."

"Yo, Jova!" Davan shouted from the sofa. He could get used to this treatment, hanging out all day in his boxers watching basketball with Jova in the kitchen. Never once did she nag or complain. His reward for the talent he had displayed in handling her body the night before. "What are you doing in there?"

"Cooking your dinner, he-man." She switched her hips past him with a seductive flavor, handing off a beer as she went by. He snapped the cap on the long-neck bottle and watched her disappear, wearing his robe—and nothing else—into his bedroom. Before the commercial ended, she sauntered by again wearing the sheer gown he had given her the night before.

Domestic life with his ex-wife had been nothing like this. No cooking. Every meal came from a fast food restaurant. No quiet evenings at home. Too much arguing. Listening to Jova clank around in the kitchen, Davan wondered what life would be like with her as his wife. His wife? Yes, his wife.

The baby scare hadn't scared him as much as he led Jova to believe. He wanted children. He wanted a family. He wanted Jova.

She strolled out of the kitchen, her hourglass figure dripping with black lace, her full breasts barely concealed behind the lattice. Watching her made him hot.

She saddled his lap. "Taste." She blew the steam from the bowl into his face, seducing him with the spicy aroma. She placed the bowl on the sofa and used her fingers to scoop up rice, vegetables, and chicken. Her fingers lingered against his tongue. "Well?"

"Spicy."

"You like spicy."

She kissed him—hard. She teased, tracing the perimeter of his mouth, tugging at his bottom lip. He slipped his tongue inside her mouth. She nibbled and sucked, cradling his face in her hands.

"You like dirty," she said, grinding her pelvis into him, learning he was already aroused by her sensual play.

"I like to get you dirty."

She raised a perfect eyebrow and burned him with her big, brown eyes. She raked her nails down his chest, and pinched his nipples, sending him into an electric frenzy.

Davan remembered the day on her sofa—she liked this position. He liked her lust for him out of control. Her hands roamed over his chest. She mas-

saged his shoulders with her fingertips and then applied more pressure with the heels of her hands.
He throbbed, ready to throw her on the sofa and
take her. But he let Jova lead this dance.

She left him. She stood up, leaving him hot and
aching. Arousal to the maximum. She turned her
back to him, shimmered her hips, and slipped the
gown over her shoulders. She tossed a seductive
smile over her shoulder as she let the gown slide
down her body.

Davan reached for her. She stepped away, laughing seductively. He growled. His control slipped
with the first glance of her round bottom, and indentation of her hips. "You're killing me, Jova."

"Come here."

He followed her to the bedroom. The lights were
off. Her nylons and garter were draped over the
headboard where he'd left them.

Jova walked up to him, confident in her nakedness. Her small hands caressed his chest,
roughened his nipples, and moved over his back.
Down his back, touching his hips, into his shorts,
boldly grasping his rock-hard erection. "Ohh—"
Davan moaned. She gave him a squeeze. He
flinched, taking in a deep breath. She pulled the
boxers down his waist, kneeling to remove them
completely.

"On the bed." Jova took foreplay to a new level.

Davan complied. If he didn't take her soon he
would explode. She focused her attention on making him harder—hotter than he had ever been in
his life. She stroked, lifted, and caressed. She left
him for a bone-chilling minute to retrieve lubricant
from the bathroom. He watched as she warmed it
in her palms, and then wrapped her hands around
his towering erection. She varied the speed and

pressure, throwing him into a state of disorientated arousal. She kissed his groin and tickled his perineum.

"*Jova.*" His spine bowed uncontrollably.

She tortured him by slowly unrolling a condom the length of his shaft.

Davan rose up, grabbed Jova around the waist, and gently tossed her down on the bed. He entered her quickly, having crossed his limit of seductive teasing. She rubbed his back and stroked his spine, calming the force of his caress. Her lips found his neck, his mouth. He worshipped the prize. Jova had gift wrapped it and presented it to him. She'd offered food to a starving man, and he took his fill.

It wasn't Jova's seductive game that pushed Davan to the limit. She opened his heart and revved up his body—and she could do this just by coming into the room. No doubt he was sexually attracted to her, but there was so much more involved: emotions, dreams. His body unraveled, and his heart detonated.

"*Jova.*" He would cherish her forever. No, more than that. He couldn't label the emotions. He pulled her on top, and hugged her tightly.

He would never let her go.

Chapter 23

"Good morning." Davan's fingers glided through Jova's hair. He was dressed in clean overalls, ready to take on the automotive repair world.

She glanced at the clock. "You should have woken me earlier. I promised you breakfast. We could have eaten together."

"Relax. Although I like the idea of sharing my morning with you, you didn't need to wake up this early. I just want to kiss you before I leave." His mouth lingered over hers, gently caressing her lips. "You were something last night."

Her cheeks warmed.

"Why haven't you ever married?"

She held the sheet against her nakedness. "Deep conversation for six in the morning."

He waited, strumming her hair.

"I've told you about my disastrous dating history."

"What do you think about settling down and having a family?"

"Marriage is a major commitment. I'd have to be certain I was choosing the right man to spend the rest of my life with." She tugged one of his dreads. "What's this all about?"

"I'm trying to figure out where your head is at."

He kissed her forehead and rose from the bed. "Gotta get to work."

Jova dozed until late morning. Davan's *appetite* the night before had left her sated, but exhausted. She recalled their early morning conversation while dressing. *"Just trying to figure out where your head is at,"* he'd said. If she didn't know better, she'd think Davan was seeing visions of domestic bliss dancing in his head. She dared to assume his feelings for her might be as strong as her feelings for him.

Before going home to David's house, Jova went downtown to provide a handwriting sample to Mr. Hammermill's expert. Feeling enthusiastic about her case, she drove to northwest Detroit, parked her Mustang, and walked the Avenue of Fashion. She visited the salons along Livernois Avenue, inquiring about stylist positions. She left her business card at several locations, then headed back across town.

"Uncle David, are you still in bed?" Jova knocked on his bedroom door. Getting no answer, she pressed her ear to the wood. She could hear him moving around.

"You're back. Did my nephew show you a nice birthday?"

"The best."

He shuffled around her.

"Are you feeling okay today? You usually get dressed much earlier."

"A little tired."

Concern stirred in Jova. Dark circles marred the sacks beneath his eyes. He shuffled, hardly able to lift his feet. He looked frailer, fragile with his pajamas hanging off his spindly shoulders.

"Do you want lunch?" she asked through the closed bathroom door.

"No," came his muffled reply. "Upset stomach."

"I can make chicken noodle soup. It usually settles your stomach."

He didn't reply.

Jova put soup on to boil. She could hear the shower beating against the tiles as she tipped past the bathroom to his bedroom, on the pretense of changing his sheets before doing the wash. She checked David's medication bottles. She kept a loose pill count; everything seemed in order.

David joined her in the kitchen for lunch. Dressing had not made him look any less disheveled. He seemed older today. He carried ten extra years around his eyes. He was listless, his take-charge, glowing personality nowhere in sight.

"I'm going to work in my office," David said, pushing his half-eaten bowl of soup away.

"You're not upset with me, are you?"

"No." He pushed himself up from his chair with the aid of the table. "I have a lot on my mind." He clasped her shoulder as he passed.

Maybe Mr. Hammermill had called and the news wasn't good. David would tell her, wouldn't he? Not if he wanted to have Davan here when he did. She cleared the table, discounting the theory. David wouldn't withhold any information about the salon. It must be as he said, he had things on his mind.

The day passed quietly. Jova finished the wash, cleaned the house, and started dinner. Between dusting and vacuuming David emerged from his office. She clicked off the vacuum and removed her headphones.

"I'm going to take a nap until dinner."

"No energy today?"

He shook his head no.

"Should I move your appointment with Dr. Greenville up to one day this week?"

He waved her off. "No, that's not necessary. This indigestion kept me up all night, so I'm sleepy today."

"You weren't feeling well all night? Why didn't you call me at Davan's?"

"Davan went through a lot to plan your birthday celebration. Besides, you spend enough time putting around the house taking care of an old man." He turned, rubbing his belly. "Don't let me sleep too long."

"I'll check on you in a little while."

Davan called soon after Jova finished cleaning. "How's my baby?"

Jova dropped back in David's recliner. "I love it when you call me your baby."

"Are you purring? If you're purring I can be there in less than ten minutes."

She giggled, her cheeks warming. "I don't know if my body can handle any more of you, Mr. Underwood."

"Cut it out. Or I won't ever get off this phone. How's my uncle today?"

Jova gave him the highlights. "He's still sleeping. Am I worrying about nothing?"

"Uncle David has these spells where he gets really tired. Dr. Greenville says it's because of the anemia."

"I'm going to move his appointment up. He told me not to, but I'm going to anyway. He'll just have to be mad about it."

Davan laughed. "I see he's in the best hands, Nurse Ratchett."

"Ha, ha."

"Listen, I have to go. It turns out that Hank didn't have jury duty a few months back. He was being arraigned. He called this morning to tell me he'll be out until his trial is over. Maybe longer, who knows? One of the guys will take over driving the tow truck tomorrow, but today it's me. I wanted to check on you and Uncle David before I took off."

"Can you make it for dinner?"

"I'll try. I'll call if it gets too late. Gotta go, baby."

He could melt her over the phone lines. She hugged the phone to her chest before hanging up, reliving every kiss and caress from the night before. "Girl, get a grip!"

Once dinner was finished, Jova tossed her crocheting aside and went to check on David. What she saw frightened her. David's face was gray and pasty. His sunken eyes were rimmed in red. He shivered, huddled beneath the afghan she'd given him. The blast of the space heater hit her in the face, making her step falter.

"Are you cold, Uncle David? It has to be over a hundred degrees in here." She shut off the space heater and touched his forehead. Cold and clammy. "You don't look so good. I'm calling Dr. Greenville."

"No." His weak, raspy voice stopped her. He sucked in a breath between words. "Just . . . indigestion. Help me . . . to the . . . bathroom." He threw the blankets and afghan aside. He was slow to swing his legs out of bed.

"I'll help you to the bathroom, but then I'm calling Dr. Greenville."

David swung his arm around her shoulders and they made slow progress across the hall to the bathroom. She could feel his rib cage. Dressed in flannel pajamas, he wore a white T-shirt under-neath the top. How could he be cold with the pajamas, blankets, and space heater? She didn't like this. He was feeling much worse than he wanted to admit to. She made sure he was steady on his feet, and then left him to call Dr. Greenville.

"He's at the hospital performing surgery," the nurse informed her. "If Mr. Underwood is in dis-tress, call 911 for emergency assistance."

Jova needed more help than the nurse could offer. She would have to force David to go to the hospital. She needed confirmation it was the right thing to do.

Mild panic set in. She'd felt this way when her mother's breathing stopped and she ran out into the hospital corridor, screaming for help.

David opened the bathroom door. Jova was there before he could call for her.

"No. Help me . . . to my chair."

She helped him into the recliner. "Dr. Greenville's unavailable, but the nurse says I should call for an ambulance and take you to the hospital."

"Just . . . indigestion."

"I don't think so, Uncle David. Your skin is cold, and you're having a hard time catching your breath."

He inhaled deeply. "I have . . . bad days. You . . . haven't . . . seen me . . . like . . . this before."

"Still—"

"No hospital. . . . Need medicine."

Jova sprinted to his room and returned with a res-cue inhaler. At his request, she gave him an antacid. Soon the rate of his breathing slowed, but he still seemed to be struggling with deep, irregular breaths. David dozed off, and she eased away to call

Davan. He would tell her what to do. He would come home and handle everything.

"Has Davan returned to the garage?"

"He's been here once, but had to go out again," the man answered.

"When will he be back?"

"Not sure. You wanna leave a message?"

If she left a message, scared him half to death, and it turned out to be nothing—

"No. Have him call me when he comes back."

"I can call him on the Nextel, Jova."

She glanced into the living room. David's breathing seemed easier. He looked peaceful. She had panicked over nothing. "No. Ask him to call me, please. Thanks."

Jova sat at the kitchen table and pulled herself together. For one frightening moment she was back sitting next to her mother's hospital bed. Her mother's death had hit her hard, but they knew her prognosis and had time to prepare for the inevitable together. Jova had bounced back quicker because of it. She suffered, watching her mother waste away from the cancer, but she'd had the opportunity to say good-bye before her mother became too sick to hear her words.

David had stepped in, filling the paternal void for her. For the first time, she worried about losing him, too. A thick sadness assaulted her. She tucked away her premature grief and focused on the more important. Her priority had to be making David's life fuller and helping Davan through his impending loss.

A curdling moan permeated the small house.

On her feet in a flash, Jova ran into the living room, finding David on the floor at the foot of his recliner. He was doubled over in the fetal position, clasping his stomach. She fell down next to him. "What is it, Uncle David?"

"Pain . . . horrible . . . stomach pain."

"I'm calling for help." She maintained her hold on David while stretching to reach the telephone.

"Three minutes," the 911 operator promised.

David huddled on the floor in Jova's arms, moaning in pain. She juggled the telephone, not breaking the connection. The emergency operator kept saying, "Stay on the line with me. Tell me what's going on." Jova described David's cold and clammy skin, his erratic breathing, and the severity of his pain.

"Jova," David managed.

"Wait!" she yelled at the operator, dropping the phone to the floor. She cuddled David's head in her lap. "What is it, Uncle David?" she asked soothingly while stroking the wet hair matted to his head.

"I can tell . . . this is bad . . . call Davan . . . to be with you." A sharp pain caused him to jump, squeezing his fists against his stomach. "I'm so glad . . . you came . . ."

"I know, Uncle David. You shouldn't try to talk."

"Davan . . . loves you . . . . Take care . . . Davan."

She stroked his head, helping him through another pain. "I will. *We* will. The ambulance will be here in a minute. I need to pick up the phone."

The operator called her name. "The ambulance is pulling up now. Open the door, then disconnect with me."

Jova eased David's head onto a sofa pillow and ran for the door. She waved frantically at the emergency medical technicians.

"They're here," she informed the operator. "Thank you."

"Good luck." The operator disconnected. Jova

would never know who had helped her through
one of the most difficult times in her life.

The paramedics worked feverishly on David.
Feeling the panic creeping up on her again, she dialed Davan at the garage. He hadn't made it back.
"Call Davan on the Nextel. Tell him we're on the
way to the hospital."

Chapter 24

Never had she imagined it would be this way. She pictured a fancy dinner with soft candlelight. There would be romantic music, tender kisses, and sweet loving. Instead, he pried her legs apart, rammed into her, and rutted around until he collapsed in a drunken stupor on top of her.

Dawn pushed Herman's weight off her. She scrambled to the bathroom and showered away alcohol breath and gritty sweat.

Herman had never treated Jova this way. Dawn had witnessed flower deliveries and surprise gifts. He looked at Jova with pride; he looked at Dawn as if she were a piece of meat.

She had also witnessed his downfall. As he gambled everything away, his friends and family turned their backs on him. His laziness had prompted him to run away from the farm in Alabama, back into a life of gambling.

This wasn't right. The man of her dreams wouldn't come at her like a jackhammer in a cheap motel. Especially when he'd come into money. Dawn didn't know how much, but it was enough to pay of his street debts and buy his way into the largest poker game in town. To get through the door you had to show five thousand dollars, and the stakes skyrocketed from there.

Dawn found her discarded clothes. Herman never stirred. Her prize catch. What a mistake.

Now Davan would be an entirely different matter. During their brief encounters, he had remained a gentleman, moving slowly toward pursuing a relationship with her. Until Jova jumped into the middle of her mix and ruined it all.

But Jova had gotten what was coming to her. A cunning smile spread across Dawn's face when she remembered Jova's shock about her quitting. And rumor amongst the beauty salons was that Tresses & Locks had folded. The building had been sold, and Jova's employees were beating the pavement in search of work. Served Jova right. Served them all right.

"Where you going?" Herman rolled over, waking slowly.

"I have to get home."

"Stay with me. I don't want to be alone."

The last thing Dawn wanted was to have him abuse her body again. "I really have to go."

"But we haven't celebrated." He sat up against the headboard, not bothering to cover his nudity.

"Celebrate what?"

"I have plans for us. You bring me luck. I have money in my pockets, and stand to make a lot more as soon as I can get to the tables again. You have to stick around and help me spend it." He reached for her. "Been a long time since I've had a beautiful woman in my bed."

Maybe Herman could be salvaged. Dawn dropped her purse to the floor and took his hand.

"I'm going to multiply my money at the big poker game, and then you and me are going to see the world. Las Vegas, Atlantic City, the Mississippi game boats. We can run down to New Orleans. What you think about that?"

A smile spread across Dawn's face. This was the life she wanted: traveling and not needing to work. "You want me to leave town with you?"

"Hell, yes. We're going to stay at the best hotels, and eat at the most expensive restaurants. When we get tired of traveling, I'll let you pick out a little house for us to settle down in."

"A house?" Dawn moved into his arms.

"I should have been with you in the first place. Jova couldn't understand me. Her life was the salon. She couldn't see the big picture, but you know what life's about. What do you say? Are you going to stick with me? Bring me some more of that good luck?"

Stars danced in her eyes. "Yes, I'll go with you."

Herman would keep his promises. As long as Dawn brought him good luck.

Chapter 25

Jova saw Davan the moment he burst through the double doors. She ran across the emergency room lobby into his arms.

"What happened, Jova?"

She would not cry. She had to be strong for Davan. "David didn't look good. They took him back and called Dr. Greenville, but that's all I know. I'm not family so they won't tell me anything."

Davan pulled her through the lobby behind him. The authoritative tone of his voice brooked no argument as he questioned the receptionist. "Dr. Greenville is with him, Mr. Underwood. The nurses will move him to the intensive care unit as soon as the doctor finishes his exam. They said you should meet them in the ICU."

Davan never released Jova's hand as they hurried through the winding halls of the hospital up to the intensive care unit. They checked in with the waiting room receptionist and found a quiet corner to wait.

"Tell me everything that happened," Davan said. His face was hard, but worry lines creased his brow.

Jova gave him the details of the day. "I didn't know what to do."

He tightened his grip and she knew she'd done okay.

"There's Dr. Greenville." Davan pulled her out into the hallway where they watched a small army of people push David into the ICU. Six people, not counting the doctor, wheeled complicated machinery alongside the gurney. They rushed past, only giving them a glimpse of David's motionless body.

"I'll be right with you," Dr. Greenville said as he passed Davan, following the caravan.

The receptionist came forward and showed them into a private waiting room adjacent to the ICU.

Davan sat forward, his elbows braced on his knees. "Uncle David didn't look good."

Jova rubbed his back.

"Was he awake in the ambulance?"

She nodded.

Davan buried his face in his palms.

"They could have given David something to make him sleep. Let's wait until we talk to Dr. Greenville before we start worrying." But Jova had seen David's slack facial features and all the machinery. He was in serious trouble. If not trying to be strong for Davan, she would be in a full state of panic.

Davan paced the hallway in front of the ICU entrance twice before returning to the small waiting area. She'd allowed him time alone to gather his strength, and express his grief in private. He returned, haggard and irritated with the wait. "What's taking so long?"

"I don't know." Jova coaxed him to sit next to her. "If no one comes to talk to us in five minutes, I'll ask the receptionist to find out what's going on."

Dr. Greenville appeared before Jova had to speak with the receptionist. He greeted them briefly but politely before sharing David's condition. "The aneurysm has ruptured."

Davan went slack.

Jova placed a comforting hand on his shoulder. "How is he, Dr. Greenville?"

Davan pressed his face into his palms, gathering himself before facing the doctor.

"He's critical," Dr. Greenville answered. He went on to explain David's treatment, but Jova had to ask him to repeat it in terms they could understand. "Basically, either machines or medicines are doing everything for him. His heartbeat, breathing, blood pressure, kidney function—the medicine and machines are doing it all."

Davan broke away from Jova's touch and crossed the small room. He stood facing the wall when he asked the doctor, "Is he going to get better?"

The doctor hesitated and Jova could see him searching for the right words. "He might get better than he is at this moment, but he will not fully recover."

Davan braced his palms against the wall and hung his head.

After a long moment of thick silence, Jova asked, "What happens from here?"

"We continue to treat him and keep him comfortable."

"Is he awake? Can we see him?"

Dr. Greenville looked grim. "He's not awake, but you can visit with him."

They looked to Davan, who was frozen in his stance against the wall.

"Do you have any more questions, Mr. Underwood?"

Davan shook his head no.

"The nurse can reach me if you do." The doctor

moved to the door. He stopped with his hand on the knob and turned to Davan. "This is a difficult time for you and your family. I wish there were more I could do." His attention turned to Jova. "This course of events isn't unexpected—"

"Because my uncle wouldn't fight for his life," Davan interrupted angrily. He pushed away from the wall.

Dr. Greenville continued. "If you have any additional family that would like to see him, you should tell them to come quickly."

Davan cursed angrily, returning to his stance against the wall.

"We will," Jova said. "Thank you, Doctor."

"I'm very sorry." Dr. Greenville nodded and left the room.

Jova tentatively stepped up to Davan. He stood statue still. She placed a comforting touch on his shoulders, moved closer, and hugged him from behind. Davan was a proud man and would want to grieve in private.

"I'll be outside," Jova said softly before leaving the room. In the corridor, she slid down the wall, pulling her knees into her chest. She hid her face while she cried for Uncle David, and the pain Davan was feeling. She couldn't control her sadness as well as Davan, but she didn't want him to have to comfort her. Here, away from him for the moment, she would cry tears of regret for David, Davan, and the memory of her mother. When Davan exited the waiting room, she would be a stone pillar for him to lean on. She'd be strong, handle minute details, and take care of business, allowing him time to say good-bye to his uncle.

"Jova?" Davan's voice was soft, sad. "Let's go see Uncle David."

The intensive care unit was an ominous place. Dim lighting set a calm mood sharply contrasted by beeping machines. The staff was friendly and professional, balancing work obligations with concern for the patients and families. Being in the ICU reawakened memories of Jova's mother's death. She pushed them away and concentrated on David and Davan.

"Oh, God," Davan said, turning away from the bed. "This is not my uncle."

Extraordinary measures had been taken to save his life. The multitude of tubes puncturing his body was evidence of this. David's body was swollen, almost disfigured from water retention. The nurse stood at the bedside, explaining the purpose of the tubes and machinery. She left quickly, pulling the curtain around the bed to offer them a measure of privacy in the open unit.

Davan pulled a chair up to the bed and carefully held David's hand. Jova stepped back as far as the curtain would allow and still give them privacy. He reached for her, wrapping his arm around her waist. "Thank you for getting him here."

"He was worried about you."

"He was in pain and he's worrying about me?" Davan shook his head in disbelief. "My uncle tries to put up a hard front, but he's always been a kind man."

No argument from Jova. "Can you believe the way he stepped up and took me in?"

"Just like he took me in twenty years ago."

Charlene Underwood arrived the next morning with the assistance of an open airline ticket purchased the day David announced his illness. Jova didn't know what she'd expected, but Charlene wasn't it. In direct contrast to her older brother, David, Charlene's voluptuous figure had survived the aging process. Davan's dark skin and obsidian eyes had not been inherited from his mother. Charlene was much lighter with a bronze tan and light brown eyes.

She'd been crying, as evidenced by the streaks in her heavy foundation, but sometime during the flight she'd decided to put emotion away and don the hat of master-organizer. She eyed Jova suspiciously, but remained polite, directing the actions of everyone from the hospital staff to Jova.

Charlene grasped Jova's arm as they trooped into the ICU. "Maybe you can wait outside, dear," she whispered sweetly. "Let the *family* have a minute alone."

Jova stayed behind as Charlene followed Davan in to see David. If Davan had heard his mother's request, he would have insisted she be allowed to visit. This was not the time to ignite a family squabble. Charlene didn't know her from Adam and she wanted her brother, surrounded by family. Jova couldn't argue with the logic. But Charlene didn't understand her relationship with David, Uncle David. She didn't understand Jova's relationship with Davan. She didn't understand that seeing David unconscious was tearing her apart, too.

Jova sprang to her feet when Davan and Charlene came through the ICU doors followed by Dr. Greenville. "How is he?" she asked Davan.

He shook his head. "Not good. Dr. Greenville wants a family conference."

Jova stopped, lagging behind, hit with the memory of her mother's family conference. Dr. Greenville and Davan were already in the private conference room when she snapped out of it and sprinted to catch up.

Charlene wheeled around, impeding her process. "This is a *family conference,* dear." She stepped into the room and closed the door in Jova's face.

Jova leaned against the wall, watching the door to the conference room. She wrung her hands together, wondering what Dr. Greenville could be saying. She should be there. She had been a part of David's treatment plan for months, even more so since moving into his house.

Dr. Greenville came out, offering her a nod of encouragement. Ignoring Charlene, Jova entered the waiting room. She joined Davan on the sofa, wrapping her arm around his.

"Where were you?" Davan asked.

"Outside." She glanced at Charlene, who was huddled in the chair whimpering. "What did the doctor say?"

"There's nothing more he can do for Uncle David. He wants us to think about withdrawing treatment."

Jova tempered her reaction. "What are you going to do?"

Charlene jumped out of her chair as if she had been electrocuted. "We're not listening to that doctor's nonsense! If he can't save my brother we'll find a doctor who can."

"Dr. Greenville is a good doctor, Mom," Davan said, trying to calm her. "He knows Uncle David's history. We shouldn't change doctors now."

"He seems like a quack to me. David's been here one day and he wants us to give him permission to pull the plug."

"It's not like that." Davan looked, and sounded,

exhausted. "We need to consider what Dr. Greenville is telling us."

Jova caressed his back. "Uncle David wouldn't want to be kept alive on machines."

"*Uncle* David?" Charlene shouted. "*You* have absolutely no opinion in this."

"Mom!"

"What are you even doing here?" Charlene directed all her anger and frustration toward Jova. Davan tried to mediate and quiet his mother, but she couldn't be calmed. To keep the situation from escalating, Jova left the waiting room.

"Jova, wait." Davan jogged down the corridor. "My mother is not usually like this."

"My being here is upsetting her. I should go home."

"David would want you here."

"I know, but your mother needs time to accept me. Look, I'll visit with David and then go home. Promise you'll call and let me know what's going on."

Davan pulled her into his arms, kissing the top of her head. "See Uncle David first. I'll call." He released her and hurried back to his mother.

Davan and his mother argued for hours about how to treat David. Back at his apartment, the disagreement continued. Finally, Davan ended Charlene's rationalizations. "Mom, Uncle David gave me legal guardianship over his medical affairs if he should become incapacitated. I've listened to what you want. I understand how you feel, but you haven't been here."

Charlene watched Davan, realizing the man he had become.

"Believe me, I didn't agree with most of the decisions Uncle David made when it came to his health, but for the first time I understand they were his decisions to make. He was clear about how he wanted to die. He wouldn't want to be kept alive on machines when there's no chance of him recovering."

Charlene dabbed at her eyes.

"Uncle David was a proud man. I won't let him die like this. He deserves to have me protect his dignity." Davan turned away, but stopped before leaving the room. "There's something else, Mom."

"What? What else could you possibly want to do to the man?"

"This isn't about Uncle David. This is about Jova. I don't think you've been very nice to her."

Charlene made an exasperated sound. "This is a time for family. She shouldn't be sticking her nose in our affairs, but despite that, I've tolerated her."

"No, you have to do more than tolerate Jova. Jova has been taking good care of Uncle David, and Uncle David is crazy about her. I want you to treat her better, with respect. She's hurting too."

"Did she complain about the way I've been treating her? Excuse me, but I'm upset about my brother who's lying in the hospital dying."

"Jova would never come to me and complain about my mother. She would tolerate however you treat her to make things easier on me."

Charlene rolled her eyes and muttered something about Jova acting "snobbish."

"Listen, Mom, I love Jova. Don't take your anger or hurt out on her. I won't stand for it. This is a rough time. Let's try to get through it together, not fighting with each other. Understand?"

Thoroughly chastised, Charlene softened her haughty demeanor.

"Mom?"

"All right, all right."

"Once you give her a chance, you'll like her."

"I'll reserve my opinion until the rest of the family arrives."

Changing Charlene Underwood's viewpoint on anything was virtually impossible. Tomorrow the family from Utah would begin arriving, good-byes would be said, and then they would have to make the sensible, hard decision about David's treatment. Until then, Davan had given his mother enough to stew about.

He kissed his mother's cheek. "I'm going to check on Jova. Think about everything we've talked about, and we'll make a decision in the morning."

Visiting David's home with him not there seemed an invasion of his privacy, until Jova ran into his arms. She provided a soft place to fall. He could relax and drop all pretenses. He didn't have to pretend to know all the answers. She didn't judge him because he couldn't understand David's treatment decisions. She would support him, comfort him, and love him.

Jova fussed over him. How was he holding up? Did he have dinner yet? Could she make any calls for him? How could she help at the garage? Once he assured her everything was under control, he gave her an update.

"You're doing the right thing."

"I know, but it doesn't make me feel any better. Tomorrow, I have to tell Dr. Greenville to stop treating Uncle David. *I'm* ending my uncle's life."

"No. Don't see it that way. You're being too hard on yourself. Uncle David decided how he wanted to live and die a long time ago. You argued about it, but he stuck to his guns. He never wavered about what treatment he wanted. It would be wrong of you to disregard his wishes and keep him alive on machines because it makes you feel better."

Davan absorbed her kindness. "I don't know what I'd do without you."

"You look tired. Why don't you lie down?"

He stood, grasping her hand. "Come with me."

Jova cuddled up behind him in her bed and held him until he fell asleep.

Chapter 26

Twenty-five of David's extended family arrived the next day. Davan's second cousin Kay, and her husband, Hooper, would stay with Jova at David's house. The eldest, and most difficult, Underwood, Marie, would stay with Davan and Charlene. The rest of the family had rooms at a local hotel.

By early afternoon the family had all gathered at the hospital. Davan announced his decision to stop extraordinary treatment for David and institute comfort measures only. He'd already argued his point with Great-aunt Marie so there was no fuss.

The family paraded in to say good-bye to David before going home. There was a great deal of work to do. David's friends and acquaintances had to be notified of his dire condition. Two of Davan's cousins agreed to watch the garage until things settled down. A family dinner needed to be prepared at both David's and Davan's houses. The list became too long for Davan to handle. His favorite cousin, Kay, took over.

After the extended family left the hospital, Charlene and Marie stayed with David while Davan picked up Jova. He needed her with him. She held up well, but he knew this time would be difficult for her, too.

Dr. Greenville came early in the evening. He spoke kind words to Davan and his family before giving the order to stop the buzzing machines and potent medications. A single IV with pain medicine remained once the nurse completed her tasks. Davan and Jova, Charlene and Marie stayed at the bedside. Thirty minutes later, David died quietly.

Chapter 27

Jova played the perfect hostess to Davan's cousins Kay and Hooper. It was an easy thing to do with Kay being a delightful burst of energy. Her husband was much like Davan, quiet and supportive, but didn't let Kay get too far out of hand.

Davan's family and David's friends came and went late into the night, sharing condolences. The large number of people set the scene for a rotating family dinner. Jova didn't mind cooking for the group, it kept her occupied and too busy to feel the loss of David. Once the night ended, she and Kay cleaned the kitchen while Hooper handled the living room.

"Davan told me you took care of David the past few weeks," Kay said, handing Jova a dish to dry. Pudgy cheeks and a chunky middle hadn't stopped Kay from marrying one of the most handsome men Jova had ever seen. She had a perfect nose, which Kay confided had been surgically altered, and round brown eyes. Her outgoing personality and ability to command a crowd afforded her diva status within the Underwood family.

"You know how important independence was to David. It was more like he took care of me."

Kay laughed. "Sounds about right. David was always a hard worker. He didn't like anyone to do anything for him—not ever. I tell ya, it's a big job caring for the sick. Hooper's mother stayed with us when she became ill and it was hard on me."

Jova wondered what Hooper's role had been, but was too polite to ask.

"And what kind of hex did you put on my little cousin?"

Jova hadn't seen or talked with Davan since the hospital. She worried he was bombarded with caring for his family and didn't have time to deal with David's passing.

Kay prattled on. "Davan is *nuts* over you. I've never seen him so ga-ga over a woman. Not even his ex-wife. Isn't that right, Hooper?"

Hooper cut off the vacuum and joined them in the kitchen. "What?"

"Davan. Have you ever seen him so nuts over a woman?"

"Nope." Hooper shook his head. "Never seen it."

Jova's cheeks warmed. She remembered David telling her Davan loved her.

"So, how do you feel about my cousin?" Kay asked, not concerned with being intrusive.

Jova looked to Hooper for help.

He shrugged his shoulders. "I was wondering, too."

Trapped, Jova answered vaguely, but truthfully. "I feel the same way about him that he feels about me."

Hooper laughed.

"Cute." Kay thrust a bowl at her. She smiled. "You better not be messing around with my little cousin's feelings."

Hooper retreated to the living room. The vacuum whirled a second later.

"You don't have to worry."

Kay nudged Jova with her elbow. "So, will I be flying back to Detroit for a wedding any time soon?"

"Hey! I didn't say—"

"I know, I know. We haven't had a wedding in this family since Hooper and me jumped the broom. . . ." Kay's voice trailed off. "It would be nice."

Talking with Kay and Hooper was a welcome distraction, but once Jova went to bed, memories of David's kindness flooded her. She gave in to the tears, which were for her mother as much as for David. She would miss him, but felt assured he had lived out his life the way he wanted to. He'd expressed a few regrets, but all considered, Jova thought he'd been happy. She held on to that sentiment. David's life had been too short, but he'd been happy. Finally she found peace, and fell asleep.

Not an hour later, Davan's arms snaked around her waist. She woke with a start, but he calmed her by stroking her hair. He pushed her onto her back, and kneeled between her legs. The light edging into the room around the drapes revealed Davan's bloodshot eyes. He'd been crying. Jova wished she could have been there to comfort him and help him through his loss.

Davan watched her intensely as he pulled his sweater over his head. The muscles of his arms flexed and the ripples across his stomach quivered as he opened his belt. He blinked slowly, passion crossing his gaze as he unsnapped and unzipped his pants. When he worked the pants and boxers to his knees, Jova could see his need pulsing and ready to consume. With hands that slightly trembled, Davan pushed her gown up her thighs, over her head, and tossed it to the floor. His hand fum-

bled on the night stand for a condom. He used his
knees to push her thighs apart. He fell forward,
bracing his weight on his palms. He pressed his
forehead to hers, lowering his body.

Emotion in the room grew too thick for words.
But Jova had come to know Davan well enough to
read his thoughts clearly. He was grieving, in desperate need of a safe haven. His feelings for her
had somehow become entangled with the sorrow of
his uncle's death. He needed this closeness with
her to help separate the two. He needed to prove
the depth of his emotions by making love.

Jova felt the blunt tip of Davan nudge her mound
at the same time he kissed her. Tenderly, but with
great passion, he devoured her mouth. With one
deep flex of his hips, he entered her. He rocked
against her, slow and deep, while showering her
with kisses along her neck. She held him tightly,
comforting—loving him. He stroked her leisurely,
transferring his devotion with the sensitivity of his
caress.

"I love you, Jova," were the only words he said before exploding inside her.

"I need to show you something," Jova said.

Davan turned to her with questioning eyes. He
was sitting on the side of her bed tying his shoes.
He wanted to be with his mother when she woke
up.

Jova slipped from the bed and retrieved the white
commercial envelope from the top of her closet.
She handed it to Davan and watched him scan the
logo.

"David gave it to me. He made *preparations*."

"What kind of preparations?" His tone was sharper than usual.

"He said he didn't want you or your family to have to worry about making funeral arrangements once he was gone."

He glanced up at her before ripping into the envelope. A myriad of emotions crossed his face as he read the details. "You kept this from me?"

"I wasn't hiding it. It wasn't my place to discuss it with you if David hadn't."

"What other secrets did you have with my uncle David?"

"Davan, I—"

He unleashed his anger. "He was crazy if he thought I would go along with this. *Cremation?* I'm not having my uncle's body burned."

"Davan."

He threw the envelope across the floor and stormed out of the bedroom. Jova heard the front door slam before she could find her robe.

Later, Jova dressed with determination. David had entrusted this to her, and she would see to it his wishes were carried out. The thought of cremation made her uneasy, but who was she to judge him? David had done more for her than she could ever repay. No one, including Davan, would stop her honoring his wishes. She thought of Davan's stubbornness and understood David had given her this task for a reason. He knew she would fight for him. She'd fight his headstrong family, and she would fight Davan. He was probably watching the action unfold with a cunning smile, enjoying every minute of the impending clash of wills.

Jova made her way through Davan's crowded apartment, greeting everyone and introducing herself to the people she'd never met. Davan stood next to his mother, dressed in black slacks and a black sweater that hugged every muscle of his torso. She shook off the lust for his body and prepared for one hell of a fight.

"Davan, I need to talk with you."

He looked at the envelope tucked underneath her arm. "Not now, Jova."

"Now," she said firmly.

Charlene's head snapped around. "What's going on?"

"David made—"

Davan cut in. "I need to talk to Jova alone." He clasped his fingers around her upper arm and dragged her off to his bedroom. Anger was deeply etched in the crease of his brow.

Jova filleted any angry words Davan was going to say. "Davan, I love you."

He chest deflated with the easing of his tense stance.

"I love you, but I *will* go against you to see to it David gets what he wanted."

He watched her incredulously.

"I know I'm overstepping my bounds here, but I owe David. You're grieving, so I might be seeing things more clearly right now. You don't want to make a mistake you'll have to live with the rest of your life. David wanted to be cremated. How can we not do what he wanted? He made these arrangements, to make things easier for you and your family, not to start a war between us."

Gathering more courage, Jova took a deep breath and continued. "I'm prepared to discuss the arrangements with your mother. I'd like to have your support, but I will go ahead no matter what."

"You're going to talk to *my* mother in the same tone you're talking to me?"

Jova eased back. She didn't mean to come on too strong. She cleared her throat. "Well . . . yes."

"Good luck." He stepped aside, clearing her path to the door.

A moment of doubt made Jova hesitate. She pulled herself together, threw her head back, and stepped toward the door.

Davan caught her around the waist. "Wait a minute."

She turned to him, unmoving in her convictions.

"You'd really go out there and talk to my mother? Knowing she'll blow her top?"

Jova nodded once.

"She's going to faint."

She wrapped her arms over her chest.

He sighed.

"Are you going to support me? Fight for what David wanted?"

Davan ran his hands over a two-day old beard. "Uncle David wanted to be cremated? Did he tell you why?"

"No, and I didn't question him."

Davan contemplated his options. He gave in with a deep sigh. "I'll talk to my mother."

Great relief. "Thank you."

"Thank you for fighting for my uncle." He pulled her to him for a long hug. He palmed her chin and lifted her face for a kiss. "You had me on your side when you told me you loved me."

Chapter 28

Jova dressed in her Sunday-best kitten-gray, ankle-length wool skirt suit, black leather boots, and full-length white winter coat. She curled her hair into a conservative bob, wishing she had time to do something more elaborate. But when Kay roused her from bed saying Charlene expected her for breakfast in an hour, she didn't have time to dilly-dally.

Charlene opened the door to Davan's apartment, frowning. Great-aunt Marie stood welded to her shoulder wearing a similar frown. "Jezebel showed up," Marie said, and Jova knew she was in deep trouble.

Breakfast was being served in Davan's dining room. Home fries, eggs, bacon, and toast were waiting on fancy serving platters.

"You don't mind if we say grace first, do you, Jezebel?" Marie asked with a bite.

"I'd appreciate it if you called me by my name. Jova."

Marie turned up her nose. "Humph!"

Jova shook all the way down to her leather boots, but she would not cower to Charlene and Marie. Maybe it was a test to see if she was worthy of loving Davan. Maybe they truly hated her. Jova didn't know. All she knew was she would not let them see her quiver.

Charlene passed the home fries. "Jova, we might as well get right down to it. What's going on between you and Davan?"

"Have you asked Davan? If Davan hasn't discussed our relationship with you, I don't know if I should."

Marie shared an eye roll with Charlene.

"Where is Davan? He's not having breakfast with us?" Jova passed her the home fries and accepted the eggs from Charlene.

"I've talked with Davan," Charlene said. "But some things need to be discussed woman to woman."

Jova's hands shook when she took the platter of bacon from Charlene. She grabbed two slices, buying extra time before answering. "I don't feel comfortable discussing my relationship with Davan, but I will tell you how I feel about him. I understand you'd be concerned about your son." Two slices of toast, and then she passed the platter to Marie, whose lips were pursed together with unjustified anger.

"How do you feel about my son?" Charlene had the manner of a proper southern belle. She cut you to pieces with a sharp tongue, her smile never wavering.

"I love Davan. I love him very much. If you're worried I might hurt him, don't. I wouldn't."

Marie's fork clanged against the rim of her plate. "Forget this foolishness. I want to know what was going on between you and David."

"Me and David?" Jova hadn't expected this curve.

"What is a young woman doing living with a man old enough to be her father?"

"You've got this all wrong." Jova found herself in the precarious position of defending herself and her actions. "David treated me like a daughter. I don't have any family, since my mother died, and David started looking after me once Davan and I started dating."

Marie crossed her arms over her small bosom. "I think a Jezebel would try to get close to a dying old man so she could step in and take everything he's ever worked for when he dies. A Jezebel could love an old man long enough to rip him off."

Davan burst through the door of his apartment, a storm brewing in his eyes. He spoke through clenched teeth. "You sent me on a wild-goose chase." His glare darted between Charlene and Marie. "Jova, come here." He reached for her, shielding her behind his back as if she were in danger of being shot. He glanced over his shoulder. "Are you okay?"

"I'm fine."

"I can't believe you did this, Mom. I'm a grown man. All you need to know is that I choose Jova."

They've done this before, Jova thought. *Ambush and conquer.*

"As soon as Uncle David's will is read you should be heading back to Utah." He turned, dragging Jova out of the apartment.

No one could call Charlene Underwood a weak woman.

So she'd fainted. But only three times. The first during labor pains delivering her only child, Davan. He was a handful before he was even born. His rambunctious play and stubborn ways were what prompted Charlene to ask David to intervene.

Davan needed a strong male presence in his life and David had readily supplied it.

The second time she fainted was when Davan stalked into the room and announced David would be cremated. Blasphemy, but eventually—with much heated fighting—Charlene had gone along. The third time Charlene had been shocked into unconsciousness was when David's attorney read the part in the will declaring Jova Parker the legal owner of his home.

"Jezebel!" Marie shouted through the milieu. The extended family buzzed around Charlene offering cold towels, fanning her as if a drop in temperature would bring her to.

"Mom," Davan said. Did Jova hear a faint touch of annoyance in his voice? "Wake up, Mom."

She opened her eyes, one at a time, taking in the scene. "What happened?"

Davan pushed back the crowd and helped her into a chair.

Marie answered, "You fainted when you heard Jezebel had gotten David's house." She turned to Davan. "Where did you find her anyway?"

"Of course we'll contest it," Charlene announced matter-of-factly. A rumbling chorus from disgruntled family agreed.

"No, we will not." Davan stood over her, looking too much like his estranged father. "Jova has been living in the house. Uncle David left it to her in his will." He spoke sternly to the attorney. "No one in this family will protest a thing. Uncle David has been precise in everything concerning his death. We won't accept some of his wishes and fight others." He turned to his mother and a sea of onlookers. "It's time we stop trying to turn Uncle David's death into a circus."

Kay sided with her cousin. "Davan is right. What would any of you do with the house when you live all the way in Utah? Sell it? And then what? Kick Jova out of her home and fight over the money? I say David knew what he wanted. I say we honor his memory."

"Look, Mom," Davan said, addressing his mother, "believe me, I had a problem with some of the decisions Uncle David made. We argued, and no matter what I said, he stuck to his convictions. We'll probably never understand why he chose to do things the way he did, but we have to accept it now."

"No more fighting," Kay said.

Charlene and Marie were the joint matriarchs of the Underwood family. If they backed down, the family would back down. Davan and Kay stood against the extended family, a show of force strong enough to discourage any further arguments. Marie mumbled something about Jezebel. Charlene mumbled something in agreement.

"Well, Mom?"

Kay linked her arm through his, reinforcing their alliance.

"I guess we don't have much choice," Charlene conceded. "My brother deserves my respect."

Davan and Kay dropped Charlene and Marie at his apartment before returning to David's house. Jova and Hooper were anxiously waiting when they arrived.

"What happened?" Hooper asked, helping Kay off with her coat.

"David left the garage to Davan. No surprise there. He had insurance money he divided between Aunt Charlene and Davan. He divided the money from his investments fairly amongst the family, although Great-aunt Marie thought she was entitled to more."

"No surprise there either," Hooper said.

Kay dropped onto the sofa, releasing a weary sigh. "Sometimes, I'm ashamed of my own family. David wasn't a rich man. He was comfortable with his lifestyle, but not rich. These gold diggers acted like they planned to return to Utah rich."

Hooper gave her an I-don't-know-how-my-baby-survives look, draping his arm over her shoulders.

Davan sat in David's favorite recliner and pulled Jova into his lap, needing her warmth to ease the trials of another long day.

Kay brightened. "Davan really told Aunt Charlene. You should have been there."

"Really?" Hooper asked, hungry for details.

"What happened?" Jova asked.

"Uncle David left you the house."

"What?"

Davan held her in his lap by wrapping his strong arms around her waist. "Free and clear, the house is yours."

"I can't accept a *house*. It should stay in your family."

Kay waved away the reasoning. "Davan has fought Charlene for your right to keep this house—"

"With your support," Davan added.

"I only did what I believe is right."

"Davan." Jova wiggled around in his lap to face him. "I can't take this house."

"Why not?"

She paused, searching for a legitimate reason.

"You've been fighting to make sure David's wishes were kept, are you going to cross him now?"

"But what do I do with it?"

Hooper answered, "Live in it. Rent it out. Whatever you want. It's yours."

"You're okay with this?" Jova asked Davan. "Because if you're not okay, I won't accept it. I could sign the deed over to you or your mother."

Davan tucked a tendril of hair behind her ear. "I'm more than okay with it."

Jova looked askance at Kay and Hooper.

"It's a nice house," Hooper said.

"A good first house for a couple starting out," Kay added with a knowing smile.

A week later, Jova sat next to Charlene in the airport, awaiting the boarding call. Marie had dragged Davan to the sundries shop for magazines. Jova and Charlene had managed to remain civil through David's homegoing ceremony, but not much more. Jova put forth a good effort, ignoring the eye rolling and mumbled comments, attributing them to Charlene's grieving. She was glad to see the week end because she wasn't sure how much longer she could hold her tongue for Davan's sake. Now they sat in the airport obviously uncomfortable with each other, waiting for the airplane to start boarding.

"We need to come to some sort of understanding." Charlene clutched her carry-on bag, maintaining a cool exterior, but her knuckles were white. "It seems Davan is in love with you, and my brother cared enough about you to leave you his house. So, we should get along."

After a pause, where Jova felt Charlene wanted her to be gracious, Charlene continued. "I'm afraid this entire ordeal with my brother has made me a little crazy."

"I can understand."

"That's right." Charlene glanced at her. "You lost your mother not long ago." She squirmed. "You have my sympathies."

"Thank you." She should meet Charlene halfway. "I didn't mean to step in where I didn't belong. I spent a lot of time with David, and I felt I owed it to him to fight for what he wanted."

There was a long silence and Jova wished Davan would return.

"Davan told me you were with David when he—" She fought to contain her emotions. "Davan said you were there to call for help. And ride with him in the ambulance. You were the last to speak to him before he lost consciousness."

"It was hard, but he wasn't afraid."

Charlene smiled, thinking private thoughts. "Ever strong. David was always my rock."

"I'm sorry we had to meet this way. I hate that we got off on the wrong foot. I love Davan and I don't want there to be any conflict between us. I want Davan to be happy."

Charlene searched Jova's face for sincerity.

"Do you really believe I only came into his life to take advantage of your family's situation?" Jova asked.

Charlene hesitated, but answered honestly. "I don't know you well enough to make any judgments. And there's my mistake. I *don't* know you well, so I should rely on Davan—and David's judgment."

Davan and Marie approached as the first boarding call rang over the loudspeakers.

"The next time we meet, Jova," Charlene said, "I'll take time to get to know you."

Chapter 29

Jova stood in the middle of her new living room, taking in the ambience. The last of the Underwood family had returned to Utah two weeks ago. Davan went back to work at the garage a week ago. During that time, Jova had sought the peace and solitude she had come to associate with David's house. Standing in the middle of the living room, the house quiet and empty, she began to freak out.

David was gone.

Ownership of the salon was still in dispute.

Davan had become sulky and withdrawn, which was probably the most frightening occurrence of the past two weeks. She understood he was dealing with David's death in his own way, but she felt shut out of his life. After fighting his mother about them dating, he'd dismissed her the second Charlene took flight. *This is not about you,* Jova told herself. Davan would come around soon.

She pushed the questions away and concentrated on the aura of her home. Having a revelation, she changed into cutoff shorts and a T-shirt and began cleaning. She started in David's bedroom. She let the tears flow freely as she packed away his clothing. Personal mementos she boxed and set aside to give to Davan when he was ready to deal with them.

She packed David's office, labeling legal folders and putting those aside for Davan as well. Josh and two of his friends had volunteered—if she supplied pizza and beer—to help her switch David's furniture for what she had stored in the garage. Charity would take away David's clothing and furniture. The recliner would stay; she didn't have the heart to give it away.

Jova spent the balance of the day adding personal touches to make the house hers. She draped afghans over the sofa and recliner. She adorned the room more with her crocheted masterpieces. David's favorite afghan was draped over the guest bed. The house was now hers, but subtle reminders of David's life remained. And she wouldn't have it any other way.

Missing Davan, Jova stopped by the garage to bring him dinner. He sat preoccupied behind his desk as she described the changes to David's house.

His head snapped up. "I'm really busy here."

She felt as if she'd been slapped. "I didn't mean to interrupt."

He buried his head in his work, the dinner left untouched.

"Do you think you could stop by after work?"

Davan raised his head slowly. He looked thoroughly pestered. "I'm really busy here," he repeated, but this time he sounded as if he were conversing with a child.

"I didn't mean to bother you." Jova swung around and stomped out of his office. She muttered choice words on the way home. Her patience was slowly slipping away. Sulking, and being rude, would not bring David back. David wouldn't want anyone mourning this way over him, pushing away loved ones.

Most of Jova's anger was the result of missing Davan's kisses and the gentle way he stroked her hair. But she did want to help him through his grief, and he wouldn't let her.

When the phone rang later that evening, Jova rushed for it knowing it would be Davan calling to apologize.

"Jova? Lisa. You'll never guess why I'm calling."

"Why?"

"Herman Norman is trying to track you down. Somehow, he got hold of my home number and begged me to have you call him."

"Did he say what he wanted?"

He wouldn't give the information to Lisa. He needed money, Jova was certain. Probably, a bookie was threatening to break his legs again. He didn't know she suspected him in selling her salon. She could use this to her advantage and gather information to help her case. Maybe she could talk him into coming forward, admitting what he'd done.

Lisa was speaking rapidly into the phone, excited about Jova's potential vindication. "Do you know the motel? He gave me a return phone number, but he made no bones about wanting to talk to you in person."

"Give me the number."

"What are you going to do?" Lisa asked after giving her the number. "Don't go to his motel alone. If you really want to go, I can be at your place in thirty minutes."

"No. If I bring you along he won't give me any information I can use."

Lisa sucked in a shocked breath. "You *are* going to meet him! I wouldn't trust him, Jova."

"Herman is a lying, cheating dog, but he wouldn't hurt me."

* * *

He'd snapped at Jova for no good reason. Since David's death, Davan hadn't been himself. Grieving one minute, feeling guilty about the happiness he experienced with Jova the next, obsessed about the success of the garage. He was making a concerted effort to balance his emotions and return to his normal routine, but he needed more time.

Davan decided to go see Jova and apologize for the way he'd acted when she brought him dinner at the garage earlier. He saw her Mustang back out of the driveway. He could have flagged her down, but he didn't. He stayed two car lengths behind, careful not to let her see his truck. He couldn't explain what possessed him to follow her across town—other than jealousy. When she pulled into the hotel known for its one-hour rates, he thought his head would explode.

He fought a multitude of emotions, mostly jealousy, and watched as she hurried along, glancing between a piece of paper and the numbers on the hotel doors. She found the door she was looking for and knocked. The door opened quickly; she was expected. She disappeared inside.

Davan fumed in his truck for twenty minutes trying to decide what to do. He could wait it out, follow her home, and then confront her with what he'd witnessed. Wait for what? he asked himself. For them to *finish*? The thought pushed him to jump down from his truck and bolt across the gravel parking lot. He justified his rash actions; he was coming to Jova's rescue. After all, hadn't Herman robbed her of the salon?

"Can I help you?" The man from the salon—Herman—opened the door.

"What is it?" Herman's snotty attitude, like he'd been interrupted, pushed Davan over the edge. What had been about to happen in the cheap motel room? Davan hauled back and punched Herman dead in the face. They tussled, ending up on the bed, trading punches with Jova shouting for them to stop. After a few more punches, she jumped on Davan's back and placed a hammer hold around his neck. He released Herman, staggering across the room with her still on his back. Herman, the coward, ran out the door.

"What are you doing?" Jova shouted.

Heaving like a raging bull, he untangled her arms from his neck and stooped to lower her to the floor. "I followed you here. Why were you meeting Herman at a motel?"

"You followed me?"

"Hell, yes." He licked at the blood trickling from the corner of his mouth.

"Why?"

It had nothing to do with out-of-control jealousy. It couldn't be responsible for his following her like a PI, or starting a fight like a junior high school kid. He gestured wildly. "I pull up to your house and you're racing down the street. I wanted to know where you were going in such a big hurry."

Jova crossed her arms over her chest like *she* had the right to look indignant.

"What were you doing here with him?" Davan demanded.

"I'm not answering you when you're like this." She swiveled around and headed for the door.

Davan caught her arm. "What were you doing in a cheap motel with your ex?"

Jova yanked away. "Don't bully me. I don't like it when you use your size to bully me."

Davan took a carefully measured step back. Taking a minute to compose himself, he slowed his breathing and asked calmly, "Why were you here with Herman?"

"Herman called and asked me to meet him. I figured I could get something out of him about the sale of the salon. I might have been able to get him to come forward."

"Did he tell you anything?"

"You burst in and beat him up before I had a chance to ask."

Suddenly, he felt small. "I thought—"

Jova raised an eyebrow.

Davan rumbled with embarrassed laughter. "It's funny when you think about it."

"How so?" She placed her hands on her hips, waiting to hear the funny part.

"I haven't been in a fight since I was twelve."

She was softening. He could tell by her big, brown eyes.

"And the way you tackled me . . . pretty good."

She looked away to hide her smile.

"It's kinda funny, right?" He eased up to Jova, unfolding her arms and bringing her to him.

"Herman looked pretty surprised."

"God, I needed to work off that stress."

Jova pulled away. "I should be mad at you."

"I apologize."

"For what? You're just apologizing to end the argument." She tried to be mad at him, but couldn't. She wiped the blood from the corner of his mouth with her thumb.

His eyes blazed. "I'll apologize for anything . . . to get you to go home with me." He gave her a crooked grin. "Is the room paid for?"

She swatted him in the arm.

He captured her hand, pulling her behind him. "Let's go."

"I have my car—"

"Leave it."

Davan sprawled his nude, ready body across his bed after stripping Jova naked. He directed her to stand in the middle of the room while he folded his arms under his head and watched her.

"Is this how you apologize?" Jova feigned anger.

"Oh, no, dear. This is your *punishment*."

"Punishment for what?" Butterflies fluttered in anticipation of his answer as she wondered how far his punishment would go.

"Allowing another man near you." His eyes raked her body. "Boy, am I going to *punish* you!" His crooked grin slipped into place.

Jova backed to the door.

He heaved his body up on his elbows. "Where are you going?"

"How kinky do you think this is going to get?"

With hypnotizing calculation, his eyes roamed her naked body and his towering erection. "Very."

"Ah, the real Davan Underwood rears his ugly head."

He glanced at his eager erection. Jova swallowed—hard.

He moved to the edge of the bed, enjoying the power in projecting his sexual tension onto her. Her bottom lip protruded, pretending annoyance, but the glint in his obsidian eyes was enough to set her on fire.

"I like to *make love*. Kinky has no appeal to me."

"Really?" Davan asked, as if he could read the

truth by the quivering of her belly. Her nipples hardened in response to his arrogant smile.

"You should come over here with me." His deep voice rolled with the force of thunder.

"I don't like to be bullied."

"You can be on top." After a moment of electrified silence, he added, "I know you like it that way."

"I don't like it when you're arrogant either."

He defied gravity in the way he eased his taut, large body from the bed. "You don't like a lot of things." He took a menacing step toward her. "Bet I could find something you like."

He moved with the grace of a cougar, holding her captive with his gaze. His fingertips cascaded from her bare shoulders to her fingers, locking them together in his grasp. He coerced her into the middle of the room. "Stay here."

Jova watched as he sauntered over to the chest of drawers and pulled open the top drawer. He rummaged a bit, slinging two silk neckties over his shoulder. He glanced back at her, wearing nothing but a maddeningly arrogant smile. He showed her a red tie with a blue paisley design running through it. Holding it between his hands, he snapped it tightly, causing her to jump with nervous sexual energy. He looked deliciously dangerous, and temptingly edible at the same time.

Jova's nervous stomach hopped as he approached; a fleeting moment of panic. "Davan, the word games were fun, but—"

He snaked around to stand behind her. The steel edge of his erection grazed the small of her back.

"But—" Coherent thoughts evaporated with the brushing of his manhood.

"You'll like this." Davan reached around in front

of her, bringing the red and blue paisley tie up to
her eyes.

Jova stood limply, contemplating where they were
going, if she wanted to be dragged there, or go will-
ingly with a smile. She could feel the ripple of
Davan's muscular body as he moved. He was standing in front of her. She was usually comfortable
with her nakedness, but knowing he was examining
her with sexual intent made her cautious. Jova
could never claim herself sexually pious. She enjoyed good, hard, sweaty sex as well as
anyone—with the right person. But Davan was taking her to realms she had never seriously
considered.

Davan moved. "Concentrate on what you feel,"
he instructed. She felt the heat of his words on the
nape of her neck.

Concentrate on what you feel. The apartment was
warm and quiet. The heating kicked in and warm
air brushed her body from the vent above. A moment later, Davan's lips caressed the back of her
knee. She inhaled sharply, noticing the sandalwood
scent that clung to his body. His tongue lapped at
the back of her knee, the texture rough against her
baby-smooth skin. He moved away and she felt
bereft, chilly.

A faint ruffling across the carpet, made louder by
being submerged in total darkness.

Davan's slightly calloused palms grasped her ankles, shackling her. She jumped with the sudden
capture. He gave her a moment to recoup, and
then he was kissing her right—left—right ankle. He
lifted her foot. She balanced her weight on the
other.

Raw sensations, running amuck. *Concentrate on
what you feel.* Tiny, adoring kisses on the arch, each

toe, the heel. Now . . . he had her foot in his mouth. Warm, wet heat engulfed her big toe. Suction—too sweet—tantalizingly pulling at places very far away from the foot. She heard a faint moan, but didn't know if it came from her or Davan. His tongue glided over, under, around her toe. Never had she experienced this. Never would she have believed a man touching, worshipping her foot could be erogenous. Never would she go a day without a pedicure if it would entice Davan to do this again.

Davan placed her foot on the carpet and her knees buckled. He moved away. Again, she felt chilly. The heating cycle had ended. The only sound in the apartment was her rapid breathing.

Jova pictured what Davan saw, lying on the carpet staring up at her naked body. Her breasts bouncing with every heaving breath, puckered nipples tight and hard. A thin layer of perspiration coating her body—the result of his sexual play. Her belly quivering in anticipation of his next devastating move. The red and paisley tie obscuring her view of him.

And then she pictured what Davan's naked body must look like sprawled across the carpet. Back muscles rippling with the fluidity of a leopard as he crawled on hands and knees in a circle around her body. Erection jutting upward, bobbing with each move. The heaviness of his twin sacks taut with their need to release precious gems. Her knees buckled again. When he finished torturing her with amazing foreplay, he would bring her to climax before he pounded away seeking his own.

Davan's hands moved up and down her calves, his lips following a moment later. His knuckles kneaded her thighs. A hot puff of air tickled the hair of her mound, mixing with the moisture to give her an electrical shock.

He had to be on his knees now. His fingers passed her hips and cupped her bottom. He squeezed, placing a gentle kiss on her navel. His hands traveled upward, over her back, as his tongue loitered in her navel.

He was standing. His tip punched her belly. His desire made the air thick. His calloused fingertips crossed her shoulders, grasping her breasts and flicking her nipples. Pinching. Her head fell back. She moaned.

Davan left the tip of her nipple wet. He shifted position, pulling the other into his suckling, eager heat. While he lavished one breast with his tongue, he massaged the other. The sensations battled for dominance.

"Concentrate on what you feel," he whispered. His teeth nipped at one puckered tip, his fingers pinched the other.

Concentrate? Concentrate! She couldn't remember her name! He became master of her body, controlling her pleasure, and denying her nothing. The sensations made darker, sharper by her obscured view and his raw, erotic words.

"Davan!" She pushed him away in sexual frustration. One more stroke, or lick, and she would explode. And she didn't want that. Not until he was buried deep inside her. She went for the tie blindfolding her view of his beautiful body.

He pushed her hands away. "Not yet," he said.

"Now," she growled. *Growled?* Did he have the power to push her beyond her self-made boundaries?

They grappled with the tie. Davan cursed—she had almost gotten hold of it—and scooped her up into his arms. She felt the carpet fall away, her feet dangling in the air. He placed her gently on the bed and she went for the blindfold again. "Enough play," she scolded him.

"Not even close," he retorted, gathering her wrists. "Concentrate on what you feel. Let me run this show."

Jova settled instantly when she felt a silk knot slip around her right wrist, then her left. And now she was vulnerably open, in darkness. Her fingers wound around the bedposts.

Davan moved next to her ear. "Okay?" he whispered, asking multiple questions with one word.

Jova nodded, unsure, but curious. Unsure until he kissed her, lovingly, tenderly.

She heard the slide of the drawer in the bedside table. Paper ripping. A tiny snap of rubber. She tested the binds, and found them loose enough to slip her hands free. But she didn't remove them; she let her wrists go limp. The bed dipped and Davan kneed her thighs open. Her fingers grasped the bedposts, her wrists gliding against the silk ties.

The bed dipped on either side of her head. His thumbs grazed her cheeks. His heat radiated warmer—he was coming closer. His steel tip bumped her mound. His right hand moved away. Together: a surge, his moan. He charged forward, permeating all barriers.

Davan moved leisurely, rhythmically against her wild bucking. "I want you to enjoy this," he said, coaxing her to slow down.

Slowing down had stopped being an option when he lavished his hot kisses on her feet. It bothered Jova that he could exhibit such control when the world was toppling around her. She raised her hips from the bed, wrapping her legs around his waist and shimmying against him, repeating the erotic promises he had made minutes ago. She pushed him. She teased him. She brought him to the brink, fighting the sizzling heat of her rigid bud, until he was posed on the edge with her.

Jova demonstrated her control over his body, even while in the submissive position of being blindfolded and bound to the bedposts. The right words, mixed with the right move, imprisoned him in her seductive web.

"Jova!" he cried out, his body stiffening and fighting to maintain control.

She called out his name and gave him permission to come with her, exploding in a climax that rocked his world.

Chapter 30

She rocked his world. Davan smoothed Jova's hair between his fingers as she slept. She was intelligent and kind, independent and lovable; he'd never met a woman like her. He'd never been able to call a woman like her his own. Setting aside her own problems to help deal with his uncle's death, she exuded strength and loyalty. The *ex* still made him bristle, but what man could resist her? Of course Herman had realized his mistake in mistreating her and letting her go. But Herman was in for one hell of a fight if he thought he'd get Jova away from him.

Yeah, Jova had laid into him about following her to the motel and pummeling Herman. Not the thing for a trusting boyfriend, or a thirty-year-old businessman, to do. Try as he might, he couldn't feel any remorse for his actions. Herman had hurt his woman; it was his duty to retaliate—*umm*, protect her.

He snuggled up behind Jova. They fit perfectly, his hard body molded around her soft curves. She didn't flinch. Thoroughly sated after turning the tables on him, showing him who was boss in *his* bedroom. He smiled, laughter tumbling between his lips. The three silk neckties were draped over the headboard along with the black nylons and garters. Visual evidence of their sexual compatibility he would not hide, or apologize for. A healthy sexual appetite was essential to the survival of a relationship. He placed a gentle kiss on her cheek.

Watching Jova sleep, forced Davan to acknowledge crazy thoughts he'd been having lately. He'd alluded to it to his mother—and to Jova, if she'd been paying attention.

He wanted *more*.

Dating, bonding, and making amazing love to Jova weren't enough for Davan. He wanted more. He needed a secure future revolving around her. He imagined waking up, stroking her hair like this every night. He pictured coming home to a cozy house that smelled of good food with children laughing. Hell, driving a minivan to his kids' baseball game even made him smile.

After his first fiasco of a marriage, he'd never sought another wife, even though he hadn't ruled it out. He'd had many goals when he moved to Detroit, but he would never have guessed he'd meet the woman of his dreams within the first six months. If Uncle David had mentioned the beautiful woman who owned the salon across the street from the garage, Davan would have moved to Detroit much sooner. Now that he had her, he wouldn't let her go. Ever.

Jova had never hinted about kids or marriage, but what woman didn't want to get married and have a loving family? She shifted into his arms and his heart burst into fireworks. He saw their future so clearly. He'd do it right. Plan the most romantic evening . . .

* * *

"Tell me how to get in touch with him," Jova insisted. She'd just finished sharing the details of her last encounter with Herman.

"I don't know." Lisa hesitated.

"I need to talk to him. Just tell me where he's staying." Jova could just see Lisa sawing away at her nails, trying to decide. Five minutes later, Jova had weaseled a phone number out of Lisa.

Predictable Herman. Still staying at the cheap motel off the interstate. He'd shown up much better dressed than she'd seen him last, but dripping with desperation—no matter how he'd tried to hide it. Of course he wouldn't be far away. After promising Lisa she would be careful, Jova took off for the motel.

Herman looked as if he was expecting her when he answered her knock. He was clean, dressed in faded jeans and a T-shirt that looked too big for him. "You don't have the crazy man with you, do you?"

Jova ignored the sarcasm. "Why did you call me here the other day?"

"I could have told you if that guy didn't come storming in here trying to beat me to death. Who is he anyway? My replacement?"

"You could have told me what you wanted if you wouldn't have been trying to get me to sleep with you." She waved off his argument. "I'm here now. What do you want?"

As she suspected, Herman was out of money and running from a bookie. "This guy is out of New Orleans. They're an entirely different breed down there. He wants his money, *now*. If I don't pay him in full, including interest, by the end of next week he's going to kill me."

"I don't have any way of helping you." Clearly, she

stated she would not, could not help him pay his debt. Countering his desperate anger, she quickly changed the subject. "I lost Tresses & Locks."

Several expressions moved across Herman's face before he dug up a halfhearted sentiment. "I'm sorry."

"Seems someone sold it right up from under me . . . a real estate scam."

Herman dropped down on the bed.

"I think Dawn might have had something to do with it."

Herman was surprised.

"She couldn't have done it alone."

He jumped up, his feet leaving the floor. "I know you don't think I had something to do with you losing your shop."

Jova stared at him, askance.

"Is that why you agreed to meet me without any argument?"

"Settle down." Jova eased up to him. "If you did something because you were desperate, I can forgive you. Please," she implored, "if you have any way to help me get my shop back, tell me."

He looked as if he was considering her plea for a brief moment.

"You know I bought the salon with my mother's life insurance money. *You* helped me through one of the most difficult times of my life. How could you know anything about the bogus sale and not help me?"

He lifted a shaky hand, but stopped short of caressing her face.

"Herman?"

"They were going to kill me, Jova."

She suppressed her response for fear she'd scare

him off. "I understand you were in trouble," she
said carefully, "but that wasn't my fault."

"I know."

"It isn't my responsibility to sacrifice everything
to save you."

He glared at her. "Desperate times call for desperate measures."

Jova wanted to claw his eyes out, but she had not
completed her mission. "What's done is done, but
will you help me get my salon back?"

"How am I supposed to do that?"

"I hired a lawyer. Tell him—"

He pulled away.

"Herman, tell my lawyer what you did. He can
undo it and I can get my salon back."

"And I can go to prison. To prison, Jova. Do you
know what they'd do to a prison guard?" He shook
his head vehemently. "I'm sorry you lost your shop,
but better your shop than my life." He rushed out
the door, disappearing across the parking lot.

"Anything?" Jova pulled Lisa into the house.

"We're on the right track." She dropped her
purse on the sofa and peeled out of her jacket.
"Herman started flirting with Dawn right after he
lost the court case against you. She gave him
money, not a lot, a couple hundred here and there.
As soon as she quit Tresses & Locks, they became a
'couple.'"

Jova became weak from the betrayal. She sat in
the recliner, listening intently.

"Herman came into some money. Dawn doesn't
know how or where, but she did brag about showing the Right Way Realty people the salon while you
were away one day."

Jova muttered a few choice words.

"Exactly," Lisa agreed. "Anyway, when Herman came into the money, he whisked her off to Las Vegas, Atlantic City, and—"

"New Orleans."

"Yep, New Orleans. Herman was winning big time. They were even given comp suites in fancy hotels. Then he started losing. Word spread quickly and they were kicked out of the hotel in New Orleans. No one would give him credit."

Jova jumped in. She knew part of this story. "When Herman couldn't get credit, he started going to the street games."

Lisa nodded. "Herman lost a bundle, dumped Dawn, and disappeared owing a very bad man a ton of money. Dawn's back home. Working at the salon. Looking pitiful."

Jova contemplated it all, enough to boggle the mind. Her ex-boyfriend and her ex-friend conspired against her, and none of them had anything to show for it. "How did you get all this information?"

"Easy. Dawn was bragging at the salon. Some of the customers there get their manicures at the shop where I work." She shrugged. "Word spreads. Herman found out where I worked by asking around for you. He called the salon and asked me to get in touch with you for him."

The salon network. Better than AT & T.

"What are you going to do?" Lisa asked.

Jova's wary gaze swung to her. "I don't know."

"My mother asked about you," Davan said.

"Really?" Her fingers worked overtime with the crochet hook.

He watched her from Uncle David's recliner. Not the reaction he expected. "That doesn't surprise you?"

She nodded. She'd been preoccupied since he'd arrived with the rented movies.

"Jova?"

"Yeah?"

"Look at me, please."

She discarded the yarn and crochet hook on the sofa.

"What's wrong?" he asked softly.

She shook her head. "Nothing."

"Nothing? You look very sad."

"I have a lot on my mind."

"If something's bothering you, I can help. Talk to me."

She watched him for a long moment. She rubbed her eyes, shaking away whatever was on her mind. "I'm really tired. Can we call it a night?"

"Don't you want me to stay over?" He had planned on joining her in her bed, making love to her until he had to leave for the garage the next morning.

"Not tonight. I'm beat."

Davan stood on the front porch for a long time, debating whether or not to ring the bell and insist Jova let him stay. He wanted to force her to confide in him. He could help carry her burden. He stood on the porch, trying to uncover the reason for her strange behavior, when the living room light went out, leaving the house dark.

Chapter 31

Jova impatiently waited for Mr. Hammermill to finish his conference call and return to his office. She examined the family photos lining his credenza. Davan's office wasn't as aesthetic as Mr. Hammermill's, but there was plenty room for a set of family photos.

Mr. Hammermill entered, shattering her daydream. "Sorry to keep you waiting, Ms. Parker." He pulled up to his desk and leafed through a drawer, removing her file. "Were you able to get any information from Mr. Norman?"

Jova shook her head. "No. He definitely is responsible, but he wouldn't outright admit it."

"Couldn't get your hands on any tangible evidence? Bank statements, documents?"

"Nothing. He was living out of a cheap motel off the interstate. I went back yesterday and he had checked out. The desk clerk said he left without paying his bill."

"Probably won't be back." He took in a deep breath. "The handwriting test was only forty-nine percent conclusive. That's not enough to force legal action. Whoever did the forgery knew what he was doing."

"What about the attorney who claims to have power of attorney for me?"

Mr. Hammermill shook his head. "This guy is shady, but he handled the deal within the law. He claims he had no way of knowing the paperwork was forged, and we can't prove he did. Not without Mr. Norman to corroborate. The woman that came to his office posing as you had appropriate identification."

"The handwriting analysis won't help me. The shady lawyer can't be impeached. Where does that leave me?"

He shot her a dismal look, answering her question. "The judge lifted the injunction. The new owners can take possession of the property immediately."

Jova's mouth fell open. Shocked speechless, she hunted for an alternative they had not explored.

"I'm afraid we've exhausted all viable options. I could consult with another attorney outside this firm, but it would be a last-ditch effort to save the salon. A costly option that probably wouldn't do you any good." He raked his fingers through his hair. "I was on the phone just now trying to come to a solution with the real estate company. Sometimes you can work a deal in order to avoid bad publicity, but they have no legal responsibility for what happened. Like I've said, whoever put this deal together worked with a team of very good people."

Better than her team of lawyers. Better than the city and state laws.

"I've lost the salon."

"I could try—"

"But you don't think it would work."

Mr. Hammermill shook his head. "No. I don't think there's anything more you can do."

Davan's body was strung tighter than a bow. He had the attitude of a very mean ogre. He needed Jova. Thinking about her made his abdomen clench with sexual hunger. Not being able to see her was nothing short of mental torture.

She'd been avoiding him for the past week, and he had no idea why. He'd been dropping subtle hints about making a future together, preparing her for his proposal. No man wanted to propose if he didn't know where his girlfriend's head was at. Those surprise proposals in the chick flicks made good drama, but they left the possibility of being turned down. No, he'd been grooming Jova. Not that she'd noticed. She was growing more distant by the day, which brought him here, not having seen her, or kissed her, or made love to her in a week.

Davan dialed her number. No answer. He left a message. "Jova, I miss you. I want to stop by after I close the garage. Call me when you get this message."

He hung up with the menacing feeling she would not call.

He went home, but in the shower the nagging feeling Jova needed him would not allow him to relax. He wrangled with what to do. He was worried. True, she was an independent woman, and it was probably better to wait it out. But he couldn't, because he needed her.

An hour after his shower, Davan stood on Jova's doorstep ringing the bell with demanding urgency. The lights came on. She opened the door in a blue dorm shirt decorated with hundreds of tiny curling irons. She looked cute, innocent. But still the sadness hung on her.

Davan stepped inside before she could speak—or turn him away. Closing the door with his foot, he scooped her up into his arms and carried her into the bedroom. When she started to protest, he kissed her hungrily, with authority. He nibbled her neck, removing the tension flowing through her body.

Trapping her with his intense gaze, he pulled the dorm shirt over her head. The soft cotton glided easily over the dip of her valley and the mound of her breasts. When she was naked for him, he let his hands explore the curves of her hourglass body. He leaned down, kissing away her hesitations expertly.

He tested the weight of her breasts as he removed his own clothes. He pulled her nipple between his lips, licking and suckling. He worked the condom over his erection between each tantalizing bite. The tip of him nudged her sex while he sampled the underside of her breasts. Her body became pliant, accepting his touch.

His fingers probed her sex, testing for readiness. She whimpered. He used his middle finger to push deeper. He entered her body and her mind when he whispered, "I can make it better. If you talk to me, I can make it better."

Jova's arms tightened around his neck.

Davan separated her thighs. He fisted himself, guiding . . . guiding . . . penetration. She sighed heavily, closing her eyes and losing herself in the intensity of his stroke.

He loved her for a long time, fighting with sheer resolve when the surge of an orgasm approached. He fought physical pain to restrain himself, rocking into Jova with long, loving strokes. Meticulously, he proved his affection for her body was only a small part of the love he held for her.

Jova arched beneath him, her legs coming up around his waist, pulling him deeper. He felt the telltale tightening of her wet walls around him. He grasped her face, raining kisses on her, but steadying himself against her assault. She was not ready. No matter how much she begged, she was not ready for his loving to end.

"Jova." Davan held her face in his palm.

Through clenched teeth, she told him to stop talking and give her what she wanted. With raw words, he explained this was not about *that*, but about making love. He forced her, by withholding his full thrust, to play by his rules.

"Jova, you have to stop pushing me away," he said. She nodded.

He steadied her face, making her look into his eyes. "Stop pushing me away."

"I understand." She struggled through a particularly distracting round of intense stroking.

Davan pulled out to the tip and froze above her; torture for her, agonizing for him. "Whatever it is"—he was seized by the erotic pain shooting through his groin—"I can help. Let me help."

"Davan, I love you."

"I love you, Jova."

"Make love to me, now, and it'll be all right."

How could he deny Jova anything? And when she looked at him, clearly near toppling into ecstasy brought on by *him*, he would give her the world.

Anything, he thought, entering her to the hilt, slowly until she accommodated him with ease. He made slow love to her, and she fell into the rhythm when his kisses were applied to her neck. He kissed her feverishly until she tensed beneath him and plunged upward, taking all of him inside.

Jova shivered below him, watching him with intense eyes as he rocked deeply. He told her he loved her with every thrust. She grabbed his shoulders and brought him to her for a kiss that pushed him into the abyss.

Davan held her without words until she fell asleep. He dressed, whispered he loved her, and left as easily as he came.

Chapter 32

He'd run out of places to hide. Jova had turned him away. Again. Dawn became a traitor and wouldn't even consider hearing him out. His other friends had turned their backs a long time ago. The last family member he could ask for help had just slammed the door in his face.

Herman turned and descended the porch two steps at a time. The evening weather was warm and damp, but no jacket was needed. He wore a jacket because everything he owned he was wearing, and because he needed to conceal his identity. He didn't know the New Orleans people well. They could be sitting next to him in McDonald's and he wouldn't recognize them.

"Psst."

Herman whirled around. An unidentifiable figure stood a house length away, shielded in the darkness. Suspecting the worst, he turned and hurried down the block.

"Psst."

Herman ignored the man's hissing call and doubled his step.

The unmistakable sound of footfalls on cement splintered the darkness. Without looking back, Herman ran. He ran like his life depended on making it to the end of the block. He shot around the corner, jumped a fence, and crossed two backyards, detouring to avoid a vicious barking dog. The deviation led him into a dark alley.

Herman ran, the pursuing footfalls coming faster—doubling. He glanced over his shoulder to see that another man had joined the chase. Fear gripped his stomach. The men divided in their chase. He knew they would try to trap him in the alley. His only chance was to make it out of the alley before the second man could round the other side.

Herman saw the exit, illuminated by a distant porch light. His lungs burned. His legs ached. If only he could make it out of the alley—

A hulking figure jumped in front of him. "Going somewhere?" The distinctive New Orleans drawl cleared any question of who his pursuers were.

Herman bent over, bracing his hands on his knees, struggling to catch his breath. "I didn't know. . . . This is a bad neighborhood." He pulled himself upright and faked an easy laugh. "You're here about Ace's money."

The first man bumped his back. "Yep. Ace sent us to collect his money."

The hulk closed ranks. "Money is the only thing we can bring back to New Orleans. Excuses won't do."

"Hold on." Herman laughed again, vying for time to come up with compromise.

The first man pressed a gun into his back. "Money only. No more excuses."

"Hello?"

"Ms. Parker, this is Mr. Hammermill."

Did she dare hope he'd found a solution at the

last minute? She clutched the telephone to her ear. "Did you find something? Is there a way to save my salon?"

"Ms. Parker," he interrupted. "I'm calling because I wondered if you knew about Mr. Norman."

"Did Herman agree to help me? Has he contacted you?" Excitement made her fire the questions without giving him a chance to answer.

"No. Nothing along those lines." He paused. "I'm sorry to tell you this, but Mr. Norman was found in an alley three days ago. He's been shot to death."

The phone slipped from Jova's fingers.

Chapter 33

For three days, Davan's calls to Jova went unanswered. Finally, that morning, he'd spoken to her and made plans for the evening. The unexplained sadness still dogged her, but he knew how to chase her blues away. He countered her arguments, stubbornly insisting she come to his apartment for dinner.

Davan's original plan had been to recreate their first date. After taking a romantic walk to the waterfront at Hart Plaza, he would pick up a pizza from Greek Town and while they were eating on Belle Isle, he would pop the question. Sentimental and romantic, Jova would cry and wrap herself around him, answering him in the way she made love to him.

The plan fell through when Jova said she was too tired to go out.

Davan moved on to plan B. He'd make dinner at his place, set a romantic table, and ask her to marry him while her favorite Motown oldies played in the background. Still sentimental and romantic, Jova would make wild, passionate love to him when she accepted his proposal.

Davan dressed in his best black-on-black suit. Admiring himself in the mirror, he knew Uncle David would approve of his proposing to Jova. If his uncle were alive, he would have pushed Davan into asking her a long time ago.

He thought he would burst if Jova didn't arrive soon. He checked dinner and added finishing touches to the dining room table. He paced nervously when he realized she was fifteen minutes late. He called, but she had already left. He fought his nervous stomach, practicing the words he wanted to say.

Jova had been so preoccupied lately. David's death had hit her harder than she wanted him to know. The fight for Tresses & Locks was draining her. Davan also suspected not finding a position in another salon bothered her.

Tonight he would make her happy. Tonight he'd prove to her he was going to stand by her no matter what problems she faced.

He practically leapt in the air when Jova buzzed the intercom. His nervous stomach vanished when she stepped inside his apartment. He greeted her with a heated kiss.

"Nice to see you, too," she said.

"Dinner's ready." He directed her to the dining room table.

Jova lit the candles while Davan placed the serving dishes on the table. The conversation over salad and lasagna was cordial. She picked over dinner, saying her appetite hadn't been good lately. He wished he had selected a more romantic menu. Something he could feed her while she sat atop his lap. Her favorite Motown oldies floated from the stereo, but she never hummed along. She seemed distracted—and sad. He would not let his efforts go to waste. By the time the night ended, Jova would be very happy.

Davan took a deep breath and started his prepared speech, not wanting to miss a word. "Jova, I
know you've had a lot on your mind lately."

"I'm sorry. I haven't been myself."

The interruption temporarily derailed him, but
he recovered quickly. "I want to talk to you about
everything that has been going on—"

"I want to talk to you, too." She pushed her plate
away. With a pained expression, she continued. "I
was late tonight because I had a lot to think about
before I saw you. The past months have been hard
for me. My life is not where I want it to be right
now." Her eyes flickered to the right. "I'm not ready
to be in a relationship right now."

Davan felt Jova slipping away. He fought to stay
seated. He wanted to snatch her up and shake her.
This was not the romantic night he had planned.
"What? What did you say?"

"I need time alone to put my life back together.
Once I'm back on track, maybe—"

"*Maybe?*" A storm began to brew inside Davan.

"Once I'm back on track, if you haven't moved
on with your life, maybe we can start over."

"Start over?" he repeated, dumbfounded. How
had this gone from a marriage proposal to a
breakup?

"I'm sorry." Jova pushed away from the table and
started for the door.

"This isn't happening," he muttered. "Jova!" His
thunderous tone made her stop. "You're breaking
up with me because you're having a hard time? My
uncle died and you stuck with me. Why wouldn't I
stick with you? What kind of person do you think I
am?"

She didn't answer.

Davan rounded the table in three long strides.

"You can't just dance in here, break up with me, and leave."

"Davan, I was clear from the beginning. I told you I didn't want a relationship."

"Bull, Jova. We love each other. You can't walk away from me. I won't allow it."

"Don't bully me." She took a tentative step back.

Davan fought for calm. He rubbed his hand across his freshly shaven face and pushed away the toxic tone of his voice. He spoke slowly, tenderly. "Jova, I know you've been stressed lately, but this isn't the way to handle it. Ending us won't make anything better. I love you. I'll support you through whatever trouble you're having." He palmed her face and forced her to meet his eyes. "Talk to me, Jova."

As she studied him, tears gathered at the rim of her eyes. "Don't make this any harder."

"We can't break up. I'm going to tune up your Mustang tomorrow," he said, stupidly, not knowing how to argue his point because he didn't understand her reasoning.

She tried to step away, but he held her chin firmly. "Don't make this any harder on yourself," she said.

"Hard on myself? Jova, baby, I'm going to ask you to marry me tonight."

She gasped, her hands flying up to her mouth. She tried to move away. Not releasing her chin, he placed an unyielding hand in the small of her back. The tears sprang forth and ran down her cheeks between tiny hiccups.

"I want to marry you."

Jova shook her head frantically.

"I want to start a family with you."

She tore away from him. The tears weren't happy tears.

"What is it, baby?" He moved to take her into his arms. She pushed him away. "Jova? I love you."

She shook her head. "You don't know who I am."

"What? I know you better than you know yourself."

She muffled a cry.

"Why are we falling apart?" He could find no reason for it, other than her panic about the rawness of her feelings for him. "Whatever it is, I can fix it." He felt desperate. Their relationship was over and he didn't know why. He couldn't think past this moment.

"I have to get out of here." She jetted from the apartment, leaving the door open behind her. He went after her. He watched her push the elevator call button frantically. She turned, and ran for the fire door when she saw him coming.

He stood at the top of the stairs. "I can fix it, Jova," he yelled after her. "I promise you I'll fix it."

Chapter 34

Jova hated Davan. Hating him was the only way she could stick to her decision. Did he have to be perfect? Did he have to be understanding and supportive? Why couldn't he leave her alone? She wanted him to stop calling every day, leaving caring messages on her answering machine. She wanted him to stop coming by before and after work every day, ringing her doorbell. She wanted to stop finding notes, written in his slanted handwriting, tucked in the screen.

Most of all, Jova wanted the dreams to stop. Dreams or subconscious reenactments, she couldn't discern. They were too much. Every time she closed her eyes, Davan was there as handsome as ever, kissing and touching and stroking her. Nightly, she relived their first kiss, the first time he made love to her, and the early morning she awoke to find his head bobbing between her thighs. *Please*, she would cry when needing him became too much, *please make it stop*.

It would've been easy if Davan could see the truth about her. If he would stop looking at her like he had chosen the most perfect woman on earth to love. Why couldn't he see she was responsible for a man dying? Didn't he realize her insensitivity had caused her to lose Tresses & Locks? He was the only one who didn't understand she was a failure, having lost every cent of her mother's life insurance money.

Davan couldn't see these truths. Davan wanted to *marry* her. Marry her! Marry her? When had he gotten the notion in his head? And then to spring it on her the same day she'd decided to walk out of his life, to let him find someone worthy of him.

Jova pulled into her driveway. Sure enough, a note from Davan was tucked into the screen. She hurried inside, crumpling the letter and tossing into the grocery bag she carried.

Minutes later, she settled in front of the television with a chunk of German chocolate cake and a heaping bowl of ice cream. This had become her new Friday night routine. She needed to snap out of this funk and get her life back on track soon, but for the time being she needed to waddle in misery. Once she was cried out and empty of self-pity, she would pull herself up, formulate a plan, and try to salvage her life.

Davan would have someone new by that time. He wouldn't be single for long. He was too perfect: looks, sensitivity, and an entrepreneurial spirit. A gentleman and a sexual dynamo all rolled into one. What had he told her on their first date? *I have a big appetite.* The thought of him feeding from another woman made her hate him even more. Or love him no less.

If she picked up the phone . . . *just to make sure he's all right,* she argued with herself.

And when he answers, what?

"And when he answers, I'll break down into tears and beg him to forget every word I said."

The problem exactly.

"Exactly." She couldn't return his calls, answer the door, or read any more of his messages, because he would forgive her, and take her back into his life. She admitted the sad truth: Jova Parker was not good enough for Davan Underwood.

"Hey, Davan," one of the mechanics yelled.

He moved to the door of his office. A couple of the guys had abandoned the cars they were repairing and were gathered near the front windows of the garage.

"Someone's moving into Jova's shop," Davan was told when he joined the crowd. He watched a man and woman struggle with a key to open the iron-gated door. Three trucks pulled into the lot. A painting company, contractor, and supply outlet.

The men returned to repairing the cars, but Davan stood in the window for a long time. He lost track of how long he watched the Korean couple come and go. A moving truck with their personal items arrived and began unloading in the back. Before he could think it through, he crossed the street to meet the new owners.

A short while later, he had pieced together a section of the Jova puzzle. The Korean couple was moving into Jova's studio, and would be opening a shop for women to have manicures and pedicures—a nail salon—in a few short weeks. A very nice couple. Davan fought hard to keep his anger in check. He remained civil, welcoming them to the neighborhood, and left as quickly as he could.

Back in his office, he closed the door to contain the display of his anger in privacy. He cursed at Herman. He cursed at the new couple. He cursed at Jova for not telling him about this new development.

A man of action, Davan left the garage in the assistant manager's capable hands and drove downtown.

"Mr. Underwood, my condolences. I enjoyed meeting your uncle." Mr. Hammermill shook his hand before taking a seat behind his desk. "What can I do for you today?"

"I saw a couple moving into Jova's salon."

Mr. Hammermill threw up a hand, stopping him. "I can't discuss my client with you, Mr. Underwood. If Ms. Parker were here—"

Davan waved off the speech. "Is there anything you can tell me? If it's a matter of public record, you wouldn't violate confidentiality."

"I'm sorry. I don't feel comfortable having this meeting." When Davan didn't get up to leave, he tried to find a reasonable compromise. "I know you have a relationship with Ms. Parker, so I will help you, but please don't put me in this position again." He jotted down an address and handed it to Davan. "You're right, the sale of property is a matter of public record. If you visit the City County Building and ask for this young lady, she can help you find the records you need."

Davan stood, thanking Mr. Hammermill.

"Mr. Underwood," the attorney said as Davan reached the door. "While you're downtown, you might visit the public library and take a look at the newspapers dated on my note."

Davan examined the paper closely. He had assumed the date jotted there was the settlement date of Jova's claim. "Thank you," he said, closing the door behind him.

* * *

What the hell is Jova doing? Davan had never been madder in his entire life.

Had she broken up with him because she lost the salon? Would she be that shallow? Or think he was shallow?

He still didn't have any answers when he drove downtown to the main library. He found metered parking some blocks away and ran through sheets of rain and gusty winds to the library. He wandered through the museumlike building until he found assistance. Not much later, he was leafing through a stack of newspapers not yet transferred to microfiche.

It would have been much easier if he'd known what he was looking for. Davan finished scanning the newspapers matching the date Mr. Hammermill had given him. Nothing. He saw nothing related to the sale of Jova's shop. Rubbing his eyes, he turned to the first page, determined to go headline by headline until he found the answer to the Jova puzzle.

Nothing, only routine stories covering sports reports, weather, politics, and the economy. An unsolved murder grabbed his attention. *The victim's name is being withheld pending notification of his next of kin.* Davan read the story closely. He was grasping at straws, but nothing else in the paper was even remotely related.

He searched the stacks, finding the newspapers for the next seven days. Finding no mention of the murder again, he continued to search chronologically. There were too many unsolved murders of young black men in the city. Then he found an interview with the mayor about the recent string of murders in the city and their effect on tourism.

Tourism? What about the effect on the victims' families?

Davan read closely as the writer recapped the status of recently reported unsolved murders. The victim of multiple gunshot wounds found in an alley had been identified. *Herman Norman, 29, was one of the city's homeless. Will the police investigate this murder with the vigor used to find the assailant of other victims? At this time no motive has been named, and the police have no suspects. . . .*

Jova had lost the salon. Herman had been killed.

Davan's first thought: *She's alone in the world. I need to go to her.*

Jova didn't want him.

She'd made it clear. She made it clear every time she ignored his attempts to contact her.

Jova wore classic black dress slacks with a hipster jacket and a pearly white silk blouse. She sat in the middle of the second row, between Candi and Lisa.

"This is just pitiful," Candi said. "Three people showed up to pay respects to Herman? And I'm only here because I'm nosy. This guy must have been a real piece of work."

"That's one way of putting it," Lisa agreed.

Jova shushed them. "You're being disrespectful."

Candi clutched her purse to her side. "I think we've been more than respectful. I'm going to the ladies' room."

Lisa and Jova sat in silence. Jova stared at the casket, not much more than a pinewood box. The closed-casket ceremony had been necessary because of the amount of time between Herman's death and the identification of his body. Jova had stopped the caretaker from going into further detail about body decomposition.

"Why didn't Davan come with you?" Lisa asked, her tone solemn to match the occasion.

"We're not seeing each other anymore."

Shocked, Lisa wormed all the details from Jova. "I don't get it, Jova. You've had such bad luck with guys"—she rolled her eyes toward the casket—"it seems you would want to hold on to Davan."

Jova shifted her focus from the guilt she felt about Herman to the guilt she felt about Davan. "In the past, I've had a knack for picking the wrong men. It's always something—money, other women—something. When Herman died, I took a good look at my life. What if I've had it wrong all these years? What if *I'm* cancerous to relationships?" She dropped her head. "I couldn't take the chance of hurting Davan."

Lisa stared at Herman's casket, gathering her thoughts. "If that were true you'd be responsible for Herman wrecking your car, suing you, and stealing the salon. No way you made him do those things."

Jova understood her point, but she was the common denominator in all her failures.

"Davan can't agree with you."

She didn't try to justify her reasoning. It had been hard enough for her to make the sacrifice.

"You should rethink this before Davan gives up on you."

Candi ran around the corner, short of breath. "Come quick." Jova and Lisa stood up, but didn't move fast enough. Candi waved her arms like a windmill. "Hurry up! C'mon, c'mon, c'mon."

Jova followed on Lisa's heels. Candi pulled them

to the back door of the room. She peeped around the doorjamb into the room they had left.

"What's wrong with you?" Lisa asked, sounding as irritated as Jova felt.

Candi pressed a finger to her lips, signaling them to be quiet. A second later, she pulled Jova to the doorjamb.

"What is it?" Lisa asked.

"Dawn's here," Jova answered after peeping into the room.

The three women lined the doorjamb, watching Dawn. She was dressed in a tight black dress with matching pumps and a lace veil. She searched the front corridor, and then closed the door.

"What's she doing?" Lisa asked.

Candi shushed her.

They jumped back when Dawn turned in their direction. Mistakenly thinking no one would be hovering at the back entrance to the room, she went about her business. She lifted the lid of the coffin. Candi clamped a hand over her mouth. Lisa looked questioningly at Jova, who shrugged her shoulder. They watched as Dawn probed around inside the casket.

"Jewelry," Candi whispered her revelation. "She's looking to steal a dead man's jewelry."

Jova jumped into the room.

"What the hell are you doing?" Lisa caught the sleeve of her jacket, pulling her back.

She pulled away from Lisa's grip, stumbling into the room. Dawn swung around and the casket lid slammed shut. Startled, Dawn took a minute to recover and decide what persona she would use against Jova. "What the hell are you doing here?"

"You were rummaging through Herman's casket." Jova stepped briskly down the aisle until she came face-to-face with Dawn. "What were you trying to steal?"

"Not like it's any of your business, but I bought Herman a ring and I want it back."

Jova shook her head. "I'm ashamed I called you my friend. I really didn't know you at all. Were you messing around with Herman when we were together?"

Dawn crossed her arms over her chest. "Wouldn't you like to know? The answer will go to the grave with Herman, because I'm not telling you anything."

"You have no respect for the dead."

"You're right. I have no respect for Herman. He took my money, made me promises, and left me stranded in New Orleans. I'm not as self-righteous as you, Jova. He screwed me—in more ways than one—and I want what's mine."

"You screwed over me, and I'm not coming after you."

"Oh, get over it! Nobody wants to hear any more about you and that funky little salon. It's gone. Herman stole it, and I'm glad I helped him do it."

Jova shrank back as Dawn spat the venomous truth at her. Dawn went on a tirade, cursing her for everything she could think of. Unable to bear another minute without breaking into tears, Jova turned away.

Dawn grabbed her, spinning her around by the shoulder. "Can't take it, can you? Weak! I always knew you were weak. Herman steals everything you had, and what do you do? Nothing! He spit in your face, and he spit in your mama's face."

"What is wrong with you? Why do you hate me so much?"

"You think you're perfect. Herman and I showed you, didn't we?"

"Stay away from me." Jova turned again. She had to get out of the funeral home, away from Dawn before she lost it.

"I hate you!" Dawn screamed.

Jova turned around and Dawn's wild swing landed squarely in her face. "Why don't you climb inside the casket with Herman?"

Dawn swung again. Jova blocked it with her forearm, swinging with her other hand. Dawn pushed her. Jova grabbed a fistful of Dawn's dress, bringing her tumbling back with her. She landed against Herman's casket and the front end teetered off the stand. There was a loud crash. Jova ended up on the floor with Dawn splayed over her, and Herman's feet dangling over the side of the casket.

Lisa and Candi rushed into the room. They separated the wrestling women and escaped out the back entrance as the front door swung open.

"Oh, my God!" Candi laughed once inside the car.

"Did you see Dawn digging in the casket?" Lisa couldn't drive straight for laughing.

"Did you see them rolling around on the floor like a scene from *Sex in the City*?"

Candi and Lisa relived every second, crying through their laughter.

"Hey!" Jova broke in. "I just made a spectacle of myself. And you two have to take some of the blame because you should have come in sooner."

The laughter in the front seat died down to giggles.

Jova continued her lecture. "Dawn and I acted like wild animals. At a funeral! We'll probably go to hell."

Realizing how serious Jova was taking the catfight, Lisa and Candi sobered.

"I just want to know one thing from my two closest *friends*."

"We're sorry, Jova," Candi offered.

"What is it?" Lisa asked.

"Were my panties showing?"

The three women burst into raucous laughter.

Chapter 35

Where did Davan go from here? Uncle David was dead. Jova had left him. He tried to put it all into perspective. The garage was doing good business, and his finances were stable. He could not bring back Uncle David, or Jova. He had enjoyed his closeness with Jova. Just because she didn't want him didn't mean he couldn't have a relationship. There were plenty of beautiful, successful women in Detroit. Surely, he could find someone to replace Jova Parker.

Davan dressed casually for his date with Stevi. One of the guys in the garage had arranged Davan's blind date with the voluptuous diva. Their first date consisted of the traditional dinner and movie, but it went smoothly. They'd seen each other several times since. Davan found her no-pressure, easygoing attitude what he needed to help heal his broken heart. He'd initiated the discussion, and they'd agreed to test the waters and let the relationship develop slowly, without forcing the issue.

Tonight, they would spend a quiet evening at Stevi's place, watching movies and eating Chinese. Davan's stomach tightened into a knot the closer he came to her house. He couldn't shake the feeling he was cheating on Jova. But she had broken up with him. He had tried and tried to talk to her, but obviously when she ended things it included their friendship.

Stevi answered on his first knock. She was wrapped in strips of silk, her voluptuous figure tantalizingly ripe for Davan to pick and taste. "I feel like celebrating the end of my first semester in med school." She assumed a diva's pose, hands on hips, come-hither smile. "We can both benefit from the fruits of my labor."

What man could resist a beautiful woman who wanted to please him?

"Kay?" Jova curled up on the sofa with a bowl of popcorn.

Excited, Kay gushed her welcome over the phone line. After talking with Hooper and catching up on life since meeting two months ago, Jova trusted her instincts and disclosed her reason for calling. "Kay, I need to talk to you about Davan."

"What did he do? Let me tell you right up front, so you know going in, the Underwood men have a tendency to . . . well, they have an overactive sex drive, and—"

Hooper made a loud protesting noise in the background. "What about the Underwood women? Tell her about how you—"

The conversation became muffled. "All rumor." Kay laughed when she came back to the line. "I kicked Hooper out, so tell me what my cousin has done."

"You have the wrong idea." Jova hesitated, suddenly wondering if this had been such a good idea. She'd been drawn to Kay's open, hold-nothing-back attitude. Kay was big sister and mother rolled into one. In too deep, Jova decided to confide in her. "I broke it off with Davan."

Kay listened intently as she tried to justify her actions. Once she began, everything she'd been holding inside surfaced in one painful flood of emotions. Coming off her mother's death and her breakup with Herman, she wasn't emotionally ready to handle the occurrences of the past year. It all happened so fast, Herman suing her and bringing his troubles to her doorstep. Then she'd met Davan and fallen in love. She'd found and lost David, a father figure. That brought the Underwood family, and the turmoil with Charlene. She couldn't forget losing Tresses & Locks. And what about Herman's death?

"Jova," Kay said, "anyone would have a hard time dealing with all those things. I had no idea. . . . We dumped all our family problems on you." She exhaled loudly. "I'm glad you called, and no matter how things turn out between you and Davan, you call me any time you need to talk."

Jova would definitely take her up on the offer. "What do I do about Davan?"

"What do you want to do?"

"I love him, and I know I made a mistake pushing him away."

The answer came simply. "Go get him back."

It had never occurred to Jova it might be that simple.

"You said he's been trying to contact you. Answer the phone the next time he calls and explain everything. Either he'll accept your apology and help you through all this, or he won't. If he doesn't, do you really want that type of man in your life? But I wouldn't worry about that being the case. I saw you two together. Davan will be on your doorstep before you hang up the phone."

"I haven't heard from him in a while. He's probably given up on me."

"I don't think so. Aunt Charlene hasn't said anything about him calling and telling her it's over between you. She would ask, and he would tell her. I know my people. He's probably holding out hope."

Jova accepted Kay's reasoning, not necessarily because she believed it logical. She needed to believe there was a chance to correct her mistake.

"Are you going to listen to me?" Kay asked bluntly.

"I need to think about it, make sure I'm doing the right thing."

"Don't think too long. Davan is a good man, but his pride can get in the way. You know how men are about rebound relationships."

Hooper shouted words of protest in the background.

Jova decided to sleep on Kay's advice. The next morning, everything seemed crystal clear. Energized and ready to fight for Davan, she jumped out of bed. She needed a new outfit to help her win, one accentuating her figure while flattering her not-so-good areas. She would put her hair in an elaborate style. She wished she hadn't left the nylons and garters at Davan's apartment. She could wear them this evening, and let him peel them off. But they were slung over his headboard, along with the three neckties, readily available for use. Thinking of touching him again made her tingle all over. But she'd have to wait until tonight, and not then if she didn't get a move on. She tucked her hair

under a baseball cap, threw on jeans and an over-
sized sweatshirt, and headed to the mall.

Jova's search took her to Great Lakes Crossing.
She hadn't been there since her date with Davan.
She spent a leisurely day selecting the perfect dress,
a sexy midnight-blue number that clung to her
hips. Davan liked dark colors. Splurging—everything had to be just right—she purchased a pearl
necklace and earrings to complement the dress.
With a new dress and jewelry, she had to buy new
shoes. After a two-hour search she found a delicious pair of stilettos that would go great with the
garters.

And so Davan would know exactly what was on
her mind, she picked up three silk neckties. The
salesman in the men's store had looked at her
oddly, trying to figure out why she would buy three
matching neckties. She smiled and paid for her
purchase. After she apologized to Davan, she'd
demonstrate her surrender in the most provocative
way.

Jova checked the time, shocked at how long
she'd been at the gigantic mall. She decided to visit
the food court for quick takeout, then head home
to dress for her "date." She eyed the restaurant
menus as she moved through the busy area, opt-
ing for a burger and fries. Holding her bags,
reading the menu above her head, she heard his
laughter above the noise of the crowd. Her heart
fluttered, remembering the illicit actions usually
accompanying the sound. She panicked for a brief
moment; she didn't want him to see her until she
was all dolled up. Wearing faded jeans, a baggy
sweatshirt, and a baseball cap wasn't as effective as
the clingy dress. Hearing him laugh again, Jova

thought she'd burst if he didn't kiss her that second.

Boldly, she scanned the crowd, moving toward the laughter. It had been over a month since they'd seen each other. After a few steps she saw him. And her. Holding hands.

He must have been tuned to the shattering of her heart. Davan turned as if she'd called out his name. She was too close to run away. He hesitated, obviously deciding what to do. But Davan was a gentleman, what else would he do besides come over and say hello? She could take the high road, or she could be immature and run. Her eyes slipped to Davan's hand—his fingers were intertwined with the woman's—and a sharp pain pierced her heart. She turned to flee.

"Jova," he called.

She froze. Could she pretend she didn't hear him? See him?

"Jova." His heat pummeled her back.

She plastered a smile on her face and swung around. "Hi, Davan."

Damn. He looked good enough to eat. The silky dreads were gone, replaced by a close-cropped fade. His crooked smile and obsidian eyes taunted her. A network of protruding veins worked their way up his muscular arms, teasing Jova with memories of him holding her. The jeans were new, and so were the white Jordan sneakers. Her hero, the sexiest blue-collar worker in town, stood close enough to touch. But like a superhero, he was larger than life and bringing him down to the level of mere mortals was forbidden.

The woman with Davan stayed behind to pick up their order. Attractive, if you like women with pronounced cheekbones and full lips. She had a body rich in curves. She was much shorter than Davan; he'd have to stoop down to kiss her, which couldn't be all that great. The woman watched them warily through the breaks in the crowd—possessive, not becoming at all.

Davan grinned. "You look different dressed down." He playfully tugged the bill of her baseball cap.

Awkward silence.

"You'd better go," Jova said. The woman scowled at her.

He glanced over his shoulder. "I guess this is awkward."

"Very," Jova spat, mad at him for replacing her, and angry with herself for letting him go.

"This was not my idea."

"It sure as h—" She caught herself, backed down. "It wasn't mine."

"No?" He shoved his hands in the pockets of his jeans, bringing her attention to the bulge. "What did you think would happen?"

His question seemed to make the clingy dress heavier. She shifted the bags.

"You shut me out, stopped talking to me. I called. I came by. I left you notes."

Jova wanted to scream, *I know. I screwed up!* She never felt more embarrassed. She never felt more foolish. She tucked away her pride and pretended to smile. "Who is she?"

"Stevi. She's in her first year of medical school at Wayne State University." He sounded proud, maybe even a little smug.

Jova hated the woman a little more. Wayne State had one of the best medical schools in the country. Even Stevi's hair was great. "You went from a beautician to a doctor," she mumbled.

"What?" He bent slightly, placing his hand to his ear.

Her pride had suffered enough blows. "I have to go."

"I never judged you by what you had, or didn't have. *You* took our relationship and reduced it to that level."

Stunned, Jova didn't answer. It was almost as if he knew—

"I don't want to second-guess your decision." Davan's eyes moved intimately over her body. "How have you been?" Reading the store logos on her bags, he raised an eyebrow.

"Davan, honey?" Stevi's voice sliced into their conversation like a knife.

He turned and took the tray from Stevi. *Always a gentleman.* "Stevi, this is Jova."

"I've heard about you," Stevi said, not hiding her disdain. She gave Davan a smile, and Jova a scowl. "We should go."

Jova's throat constricted. Davan's new girlfriend was dismissing her. She wished David were alive so she could tell on Davan. *Childish,* she admonished herself, fighting back tears. "Bye," she muttered and hurried away.

Chapter 36

Nothing's changed, Jova coached herself. *The world continues to go around.*

And Davan will give her kisses to Stevi.

Only twenty-eight, she would make many more mistakes in her lifetime. She had to learn from them and keep moving forward.

Davan and Stevi will get married and have plenty of kids.

Maybe she could save enough to open another salon. She considered taking a loan against the house, but it seemed sacrilegious. Her mother had left life insurance money because she wanted Jova to venture out in the world, and to own a little piece of it. David had left her the house so she would be secure, and have a home to call her own. She couldn't use it as collateral.

Davan will sate his hunger using Stevi's body.

She had to let him go. She had to stop thinking about him all day. She couldn't dream about him anymore. She told herself to stop wondering what he was doing. No more sitting in her car, watching the garage. It had been her choice to end their relationship. She had to live with it.

The doorbell rang. Jova tossed aside her cro-

cheting and ran to the door, flinging it open, praying Davan had come to talk.

"Ms. Parker, I don't know if you remember me.
Patricia Hornsby from Right Way Realty."

How could she forget the woman who started the
avalanche that destroyed her life?

"Can we talk?"

Jova stepped aside. "I didn't mean to be rude."
Patricia hadn't stolen her salon. It wasn't fair to
blame her for Herman's actions.

They settled in the kitchen with two cups of tea.

Patricia expressed her sorrow over Jova losing the
salon. "If I had known, or even suspected, I never
would have closed the deal."

"You were a pawn."

They sipped tea while Patricia apologized pro-
fusely. "This has been eating at me for months. I
can't imagine . . ." Another sip of tea. "I wanted to
find a way to help you. My deposition didn't seem
to matter."

"I appreciate your honesty."

"It wasn't enough." She pushed the cup of tea
away. "I did a walk-through with the new owners
once you vacated the property. I found this." She
twisted in her chair to retrieve her bag. She pulled
out a delicately crocheted baby blanket Jova had
made for one of her customers. Woven with soft
pink and white yarn, it was to be a gift at her baby
shower.

"I hope you don't mind. I showed it to a friend.
We met when I sold her a gorgeous house in the
burbs. I told her all about the other fabulous pieces
I'd seen at your place." Patricia smiled broadly.
"She'd like to meet with you."

"I don't understand."

"My friend owns a shop. She sells baby clothes,

but only exclusive designs. Very upscale." Patricia added as an afterthought, "Actually, she owns several shops across the country. All the upscale malls, including Twelve Oaks and Birmingham. They both have a Baby Boutique."

"I've seen those stores."

Patricia dug into her purse, producing a business card. "My friend, Melissa Isenberg, would like to meet with you about selling your baby blankets in her store." She handed the card to Jova. "Melissa is very busy. It's hard to catch her in town. I hope you don't mind, but I took the liberty of making you an appointment."

Jova examined the card. "Monday? So soon?"

"She's very busy. I had to grab her when I could."

"I can't have a business plan together in one day."

"Business plan?" Patricia waved off the notion. "No, Jova. You aren't presenting a business proposal to a bank. You're thinking in the 'buying a salon' mode. No, no. We're working on the one-hand-washes-another principle here." She sipped from her tea. "Think of it as businessmen making a deal on the golf course."

"I'm not prepared for this."

"Do you have enough items to piece together a layette? Put together a layette, and bring a few other pieces. Your afghans are fabulous. You show up with the work, and I'll do the talking. Here's the plan. . . ."

"Davan, honey." Stevi pulled away from him. "Where are you?" She'd been trying to advance the kiss, but he offered her only quick pecks on the cheek.

"I'm watching the movie."

"You hate 'chick flicks.'" Stevi used the remote to turn off the television and VCR. "I think we need to talk."

With the apartment quiet, he could not distract the conversation.

"We've been seeing each other for weeks, and I know we promised each other space, but this is ridiculous. I spend all my free time with you—and you know I don't have much with school and all. I never turn you down when you ask to come by. We spend all this time together, but we aren't going anywhere."

"Neither of us wants a commitment."

Stevi shook her head. "I'm not asking for a commitment. You keep coming around, and I want you to be here when you're here. I could spend my time other places. With other people."

Davan felt the sting of her words, but remained quiet. No woman wanted to devote all her time and effort on a man who couldn't even carry on a decent conversation when they were together. He tried hard, but his mind kept comparing Stevi to Jova—and Stevi kept coming up short.

"I feel like I'm no more than a distraction for you. And it isn't hard to figure out from who."

"It's not like that," Davan defended.

"No? For the first couple of weeks all I heard about was how great Jova did this and that. She broke your heart, but hey, it's okay because Jova must have a good reason. I didn't say anything about the scene in the mall, but it irked me to watch you with her."

"I didn't mean to disrespect you."

"I know." Stevi rested her hand on his thigh. "I understand there may be lingering feelings. I'm not trying to press you into a relationship neither of us is ready for. What I'm saying is this. Medical school keeps me very busy. When I get time off, I like to unwind and have fun. I like doing that with you. You're easygoing and very good looking." She squeezed his thigh for emphasis. "But I don't want to devote all my time to you if you're going to zone out whenever we're together."

Davan turned to face her. "You're right. My mind has been elsewhere."

Stevi smiled. "A little more attention here then?"

He nodded. "More attention. Got it."

"Even though I'm not ready for a committed relationship, I still have . . . needs."

Davan laughed nervously. He hadn't prepared for this.

"We're both adults. We have no ties. I'm attracted to you." Stevi's hand crept up his thigh. "Are you attracted to me?"

"You're beautiful."

She moved boldly, cupping him with sure fingers. "Let's go to the bedroom."

Jova met with Melissa Isenberg at Twelve Oaks Mall. It went better than she'd hoped. She showed Melissa her best pieces. Melissa showered her with compliments. Patricia jumped in and helped negotiate terms they both were happy with.

How better to celebrate than shopping for new lingerie? Not that she would use it any time soon, but she missed the convenience of having lingerie at Tresses & Locks. She was coming out of Victoria's Secret when she heard her name called.

"Jova Parker?"

"Mario Ramphal?"

He tucked his cell phone into the inside pocket

of his suit. "It is you." He greeted her with a polite kiss on the cheek. "And you remember me. How long has it been? High school?"

Jova nodded. "High school."

"Whatcha been up to? Do you have time to grab a bite to eat?"

Knowing her plans to go home to an empty house, wishing she could share her good news with Davan, she accepted Mario's invitation. They took the escalator to the upper level of the mall and found a small pub. Mario requested a booth at the back of the intimately lighted restaurant. They ordered drinks while scanning the menu.

Mario's subtle flirting was not lost on Jova. He slipped seamlessly into the booth next to her. He leaned in close to discuss menu selections. In between sips of their predinner drinks, they caught up. He listened intently, ignoring the incessant ringing of his cell phone, as she told him about her life.

"Your phone is going crazy," Jova remarked.

"Comes with the job." He pulled the phone from his pocket. "If it bothers you, I'll turn it off." He replaced the phone and rested his arm behind Jova on the booth, leaning into her.

"Where are you working?"

"I'm a sports agent."

They shared a laugh, recalling the teasing he received in high school because of his obsession with sports. Their conversation was natural and easily transcended into mutual flirtation. Flirting with an old friend was safe, and just what Jova needed to regain her confidence after learning Davan had moved beyond her. At six feet and about one hundred and sixty pounds of tan, lean Italian muscle, Mario held an easy attraction. His dark curly hair and brown eyes made him resemble Benjamin Bratt. His genuine ivory smile gave him trustworthy, used car salesman appeal.

They finished dinner and Mario walked Jova out of the mall. By the time they reached her car, she knew his travel schedule for the next week and they had a dinner date set up when he returned.

"I'm so glad I ran into you," Mario said. He took her hands in his, rubbing his thumbs over her palms.

"It was fun."

"I'll see you next weekend, right?"

"Right." Her stomach made a nervous flutter as he leaned in and kissed her cheek, establishing boundaries already. Letting Jova know exactly what his intentions were. They may have been old friends catching up over lunch today, but this weekend would have a different theme.

Jova watched him walk off, weaving around the parked cars. No denying he looked good in the midnight-blue designer suit. He turned, walking backward, phone to his ear, watching her with a smile. She waved. Started her car. Thought of Davan. Wanted to call Mario and cancel the date. Thought of Davan and Stevi. She drove home not feeling so happy about the deal with Melissa anymore.

Chapter 37

Dating Mario became a convenient distraction. She made it clear, as she had done with Davan, she was not interested in anything serious. This fit the needs of a high-profile, jet-setting sports agent well. Their friendship remained casually comfortable. Mario mistakenly believed Jova's reluctance to advance beyond a hello kiss was due to her uneasiness with interracial dating. She let him believe this, not wanting to explain her heart still belonged to Davan and even the thought of kissing another man felt like a betrayal to her.

Being a very ambitious person, Mario renewed her entrepreneurial spirit. Not advancing fast enough with his previous employer, he had ventured out on his own. Now he boasted an impressive list of sports stars and had been approached by several in the entertainment business. He was considering expanding his clientele list, which accounted for the number of trips he took to New York and California.

Mario listened to Jova and Patricia over dinner at T.G.I. F. one evening and suggested they become partners. Patricia knew the right people. Better, she knew how to sell to the right people. By the end of the evening, Jova and Patricia were business partners, Mario had hired Patricia to manage a portion of his promotions, and Patricia quit her day job as a real estate agent.

Jova and Mario were having drinks at the pub in Twelve Oaks Mall when he suggested she expand her product line.

"How would I do it? I've been working double time to fill Melissa's orders. I'm fast, but crocheting still takes a great deal of time." She'd long given up on the idea of working as a stylist at someone else's shop.

"Work smarter, not harder, sweetie," Mario answered. He tossed back the remainder of his beer. "You have to find a way to mass-produce your product."

"My designs are unique, exclusive. I don't want an assembly line making products and slapping my name on the label."

Never deterred, Mario ate from the sample platter while he silently brainstormed other ideas. He'd taken several phone calls during the ride over, but the phone started buzzing again. Jova often thought their relationship would never advance— even if she did fall out of love with Davan—because of the incessant ringing of Mario's cell. How could he give her the attention she needed if his time was always divided between her and work? Davan never let running the garage interfere with their time together. He readily altered his schedule for her. When they curled up together on his sofa for a movie, the phone never rang. He didn't use phrases like "Hit me back" or "No deal, babe." He'd never told her no to anything she'd asked of him.

"I've thought of something," Mario announced, looking pleased with himself as he tucked away the phone. "The last time I visited New York, my client was being interviewed by a sportswriter. They're collaborating on a book about his life. Why don't you go that route?"

"I'm not a writer." Jova watched him intently. Mario's handsome Italian features became more pronounced when he formulated a successful marketing idea.

"You don't want to mass-produce your product, because it would lose its exclusivity. Exclusivity comes with a high price tag, which limits your customer base. If you want to be financially successful doing this, you need to make your craft available to the general public."

"Go on."

"Why don't you develop anyone-can-do-it designs? Start a buzz by packaging the patterns in a book. Once they take off, you can offer themed pamphlets. Set Patricia to work on a deal with a crochet needle company or a yarn manufacturer. Check out craft stores and offer them the rights to your patterns—like Martha Stewart with Kmart. Use your sales numbers from your work with Baby Boutique to support the idea. While Patricia's out doing her thing, you meet with the editors and find a publisher to help you pull it off."

Jova considered the idea, her smile beaming. "Sounds complicated." Her eyes widened at the thought of being able to do what she loved, turning a hobby into a lucrative business venture.

"Well?" Mario asked.

Jova threw her arms around his neck in a tight embrace. "I love it! It's a great idea." She rushed on. "It would take a lot of work. I'd have to talk to Patricia, see if she could sell the idea. I'd need to learn the publishing business. I don't know any editors or how to find one."

"I can help you with those details."

Jova's excitement drove her. "I'll need to talk to
an attorney who could handle the deal. And—"

Mario placed a finger over her mouth, quieting
her. Her arms were still locked around his neck. He
watched her with fierce fascination as he carefully
placed his hands on her waist. His touch was tentative, testing her reaction. When she didn't recoil, as
she had before, he leaned in and placed a tender
kiss on her lips. He pulled away, slowly removing his
hands from her waist.

"Mario . . ."

He placed his finger on her lips again. "I think
that went very well."

Jova submerged her longing for Davan's kisses in
the development of her how-to crochet book. She
spent weeks developing designs. She and Patricia
spent an afternoon selecting which patterns would
best represent the spirit of the first book. They soon
realized Jova had completed enough patterns for
the book and an introductory pamphlet.

While Patricia peddled the book to manufactur-
ers for their support, Jova worked closely with
Melissa. Upon hearing about Jova's expansion idea,
Melissa wanted legally exclusive rights to carry
Jova's creations. This prompted Jova to move forward with meeting with an attorney. The attorney
suggested an accountant. The accountant suggested a public relations firm.

One small kernel began growing by leaps and
bounds. Before Jova knew it, she was boarding a
plane with Mario to New York. He had arranged a
meeting between her and editors from two different publishing houses. He would be tied up with

his clients, but coached her until she was comfortable with the meeting.

Jova finished rehearsing her pitch for the last time.

"Great. You're ready," Mario said. They were sitting at the small table in his hotel room.

"I feel ready."

Mario watched her from across the table. He had let her know with subtle hints and discreet touches he was ready for their relationship to progress. To what level, Jova couldn't be certain, but it was obvious the level of affection would increase exponentially.

"It's getting late." Jova stretched her arms over her head. "I'm going to turn in."

The ever-present smile on Mario's face faded. His head turned toward the bed a few feet away. He turned back to Jova, sure she hadn't missed the gesture. "You can share my bed."

She laughed nervously, searching for a delicate way out of a messy situation.

"We're both in our prime, a serious relationship would ruin our friendship. When, and if, we're ready to slow down, we'll find each other." He kneeled in front of Jova, taking her hands in his. "There's nothing wrong with making each other feel good."

"You want to sleep together. No strings attached."

Mario nodded, holding her gaze. "What man wouldn't want to hear that a beautiful woman like you understands what he wants?"

Her words, back to haunt her.

Mario added, "Strings later—if we decide we want strings."

Looking down into Mario's handsome face, with his muscular physique flexing at her feet, she found the offer tempting. A forbidden encounter in a New York hotel with an exciting Italian was what the doctor ordered. Friendship, someone to bounce business ideas off of, a sex partner with no strings—Mario could be all those things. But he couldn't be Davan.

"No," Jova said with conviction, wanting to leave no room for doubt. He shouldn't try to seduce her or cajole her into changing her mind. "Your offer is very, very tempting."

"I hear a 'but' coming."

"You do. I'm not a casual sex kind of girl. I don't think I could separate the emotion of making love with the lack of emotion in just having sex."

Mario began to offer an argument.

Jova cut him off. "I don't want you to try to persuade me. We can have a friendship. We can continue to go out. We *can't* jump into bed and pretend like sleeping together doesn't mean anything."

He dropped his head in her lap. "How long are you going to love this guy?"

She stiffened. "What?"

"He's gone. I'm here. He left you bitter and never wanting another serious relationship. I'm into taking this as far as you want to take it. If you want serious, I'm in for serious. If you want to be friends, friends it is."

"You don't understand. Davan didn't . . ." *Do anything wrong*.

Mario jerked upright. "Davan is the guy you're in love with?"

She avoided being trapped by his eyes. "I don't want to talk about this anymore."

Mario returned his head to her lap. She sensed he was waiting for her to touch him intimately, giving him the signal he needed to move their relationship forward. Truthfully, she was tempted by the offer to expend her sexual energy with a man as dynamic and handsome as Mario, but as she'd said, she wasn't a casual sex woman. And he wasn't Davan.

Mario looked up at her with a wicked smile. "My offer doesn't expire. If you change your mind, all you have to do is call. You don't even have to say the words aloud. Just tell me you want to accept my offer. I'll come from wherever I am to make good on it."

She playfully pushed his head backward. "Such a romantic."

He captured her hand and held it to his cheek. "I like what we have. I don't want to mess it up." He paused, turning serious. "Strings with you wouldn't be so bad."

Jova peeked through the peephole and couldn't believe her eyes. Excited, she flung the door open.

Hooper stood on her stoop with suitcases in hand. Lots of suitcases. "This is all Kay's idea."

Jova pulled him inside, gave him a hug, and went to find Kay. She was in the driveway arguing with the driver of the airport transportation service.

"Why didn't you call?" Jova asked after the bill was settled.

"You don't alert someone when you're trying to surprise them."

The women settled in the kitchen while Hooper carried their bags into the bedroom. He joined them for cheesecake. "You don't mind us barging in on you, do you?"

Kay answered. "Of course she doesn't. She's practically family."

"I'm glad you're here. It's been too quiet without Uncle David around. What made you come out?"

"I wanted to see how things were going with you and my little cousin."

Jova delayed answering by eating a chunk of cake.

"Uh-oh. What's going on?"

Wisely, Hooper grabbed his cheesecake and headed for the television in the living room. Jova gave Kay the abbreviated version of why she hadn't told Davan she wanted him back.

"Do you think Davan really likes this Stevi?" Kay asked.

Jova shrugged. "They seemed comfortable."

"Comfortable? How good is a relationship based on 'comfortable'? A good relationship needs trust, love, passion. The things you and Davan had together."

"It's been so long . . . Davan's gotten on with his life."

"Is it your reason for giving up? There's all kinds of holes in that logic," Kay said casually. "Unless, of course, *you've* moved on."

Jova admitted she'd been spending time with Mario. She had reservations about telling Davan's cousin about her social life, but Kay was quickly becoming a good friend. She listened without passing judgment, asking the right questions at the right time to clarify in a delicate way if Jova was sleeping with Mario.

"Then there's still hope." Visible relief showed on Kay's face. "We have a lot of work to do here," Kay called to Hooper.

"I think we should stay out of it," he answered

back. "Not that you're going to listen to me. Good luck, Jova."

"I appreciate the sentiment, but I don't think you should place yourself in the middle, either. I don't want to get back together with Davan if he has to be pushed into it."

"Better to let it happen naturally," Hooper added from the living room.

Kay rolled her eyes.

"Does Davan know you're staying here?" Jova asked.

Kay shook her head. "Davan doesn't even know we're in town. We'll stop by his place this evening. Tell me what else has been going on. Catch me up on the fight for the salon."

Jova delighted in telling Kay and Hooper about her successes. Sales were up at the Baby Boutique. A publisher was considering the manuscript for her book. Her mind was flourishing with follow-up ideas.

The surprise visit revitalized Jova. She and Kay worked together to prepare dinner. Hooper joined them in the kitchen and they relived Uncle David's exploits. Kay told Jova how David developed his business, offering the story for inspiration.

Later that evening, Jova excused herself, leaving Kay and Hooper in the living room. She had to meet Patricia early the next morning.

"It's a shame." Kay snuggled into her husband's chest.

"What's a shame?"

"Davan and Jova made such a nice couple. He's good for her. Did you see the way he lit up when she came into the room? I know, I know. Don't interfere. I won't."

Hooper kissed the top of her head. "It'll all work out."

"I'm glad she overcame the whole salon mess."

"She still has some rebuilding to do."

Kay sat upright, excited. "We should celebrate. Let's give Jova a surprise party to congratulate her on what she's accomplishing."

"A surprise party? We don't know any of her friends. How would we pull something like that off?"

Kay crossed the room to the telephone table. She waved Jova's address book in the air. "Are you with me?"

Chapter 38

"Why'd you bring me here?" Hooper asked Davan. The bartender set two long-neck bottles in front of them. The bar was bursting with the Friday crowd.

"I wanted you to meet Stevi."

"Why didn't you want Kay here? The four of us could have gone out to dinner."

Davan sipped from his beer. He hardly ever drank beer, and Stevi never drank alcohol, so the bar seemed an unlikely place to meet.

Hooper nudged him. "Tell me what's up."

"She's nice, right?"

"Seemed so."

Davan twirled the bottle, lost in thought. "No matter how hard I try, I can't get into her." No matter how hard he tried, he couldn't make her Jova.

"Why do you have to 'get into her'?"

He stammered over his answer. At thirty, he should be settling down. Stevi was a good catch.

"All good reasons," Hooper said, nonjudgmentally. "But it seems to me you shouldn't have to *try* so hard to like a woman. If it's right, it's right."

They drank in silence, Hooper waiting for Davan to open up, and Davan contemplating his future with Stevi.

"Stevi knows it's not working."

"Really?" Hooper prodded.

"I'm going to have to break it off with her."

"Are you looking for my approval? You've never asked for anyone's approval for any decision you've made."

Davan propped his elbow up on the bar and leaned his chin into it. "You're staying at Jova's?"

Hooper told him how they'd showed up unannounced, with enough luggage to stay a month. "Jova never batted an eye. She's never asked how long we plan to stay. She just made us dinner and showed us where to sleep."

Davan smiled. "Yeah, she's great." After another swallow of beer, Davan said, "Has she asked about me?"

"I've heard your name tossed around between Kay and Jova."

Hope swelled in Davan's heart. She hadn't forgotten him. "Is she seeing anyone?"

Hooper threw him a look confirming he'd overstepped his bounds. His pride made him give up on phone calls, unannounced visits, and cute notes, but his heart wouldn't let go of the hope Jova would be in his life again someday.

Hooper cleared his throat. "A guy has come by the house a couple of times."

Davan's stomach tightened and he couldn't catch his breath. Obscene thoughts ran through his mind. Images of what the man would say and do to Jova. Through clenched teeth, he asked, "Serious?"

Hooper shook his head no. "They seem like friends."

Davan nodded his understanding. Friends today, but if the man had two good eyes he wouldn't wait long before making a move on Jova. She was the perfect woman.

"Does—"

Hooper cut him off. "It's not right for me to discuss Jova's private life with you. You want to know? Ask her yourself."

If only she would have taken his phone calls. Or answered the door. If she had trusted him enough to discuss her problems instead of shutting him out. He didn't care about the salon. Herman was inconsequential to their relationship. If she'd shared her fears he could have reassured her he loved her no matter what.

He'd had weeks to relive their chance meeting in the mall. If only he'd said this . . . If only he'd done that . . . Day after day, the scene tortured him. Dressed in jeans and a T-shirt with her hair stuffed into a baseball cap, she maintained her always-to-gether, nothing-ever-upsets-me attitude. He was dying inside and she was the same cool Jova, taking the world on alone. Seeing him with another woman hadn't flared the same jealous anger he felt when hearing about her new male "friend."

Hooper broke into his thoughts. "Kay's giving Jova a surprise party."

"A surprise party? Her birthday's in February."

Hooper told Davan about Jova's success with her crocheting.

"She deserves it," Davan said, feeling pride in her achievements.

"Kay said to invite you. Actually, she said to tell you you're coming to the party, no excuses. And if you object, I'm supposed to make it clear that I'll drag you hogtied to the party."

* * *

Jova discovered Mario's indiscretions by accident. They were at his town house. In between him taking phone calls, he was dressing for dinner. She'd met him at his place to save time between the commute from the airport and the restaurant. While he showered in the master bath, she used the guest bath to check her hair.

Mario had been in California the past three days and the cleaning service wasn't due until the end of the week. Jova noticed the stray hairs in the sink first. Long and straight, they didn't match Mario's short, dark curls. She allowed her curiosity to prod her into investigating further. Someone had left incriminating evidence in the cabinet beneath the sink. A woman felt very comfortable in Mario's town house. Or she wanted to discourage the competition.

Hearing Mario outside the door, Jova grabbed a box of the feminine products and joined him in the living room.

"Are you trying to tell me there will be no sex with you tonight?" Mario joked.

"I found this under the sink."

"I didn't give anyone permission to move into my town house, if that's what you're thinking."

Suddenly, Jova didn't know what she had hoped to gain by confronting him. She'd been the one who'd insisted on the platonic relationship. She had no right to question his sexual activities with other women.

"Are you rethinking the strings?"

Jova watched him, uncertain. She cared about Mario—as a friend. She couldn't deny his dark features were attractive. He was ambitious, and successful. He supported her in her efforts to build a career.

"Jova?" he pushed. She'd been quiet too long.

"This doesn't feel right. Who is she?"

He raised an eyebrow, clearly not wanting to give her the information.

"Is she your girlfriend? Is she in love with you?"

He laughed. "No. We have an *arrangement*."

"I wouldn't want to cause anyone to be hurt. If you have a chance at a future with her—"

"I don't want a future with her." He stepped closer, taking the box from her hands and tossing it onto the sofa. "I'm up front with everyone I date."

She knew this to be true by her own experience with him.

"Now, unless you want to discuss strings and the exchange of keys, let's go to dinner."

Davan sat behind his desk at the garage, struggling to concentrate on paperwork. After talking with Hooper and hearing about Jova's business ventures, he'd done some dreaming of his own. The books looked good. The garage was bursting with business. Uncle David had always wanted to expand and this seemed a good time to do it. This would make David proud. Davan had started scouting out locations and thought the northwest side of Detroit most viable.

A soft knock disturbed his mental planning. "Come in." He stood up and offered his chair to Stevi.

"We need to talk."

Dreaded but expected words. He leaned against the windowsill, his arms crossed over his chest.

"This isn't working."

"I didn't expect you to be so blunt."

"Do I ever bite my tongue?"

Davan smiled fondly. "No." It's how she'd battled stereotypes and other obstacles to make it into medical school.

"I've tried—"

"I know, Stevi. Don't apologize. My mind hasn't been straight."

She wrestled with her decision. Her eyes roamed his body freely, as if memorizing every muscle. "I know why your mind hasn't been straight, and I have to say I wished I had the same effect on you."

No sense denying the obvious truth. "Are you going to be okay? I never wanted to hurt you."

"I'll be fine. We both knew the rules going in."

He'd known the rules with Jova, too, but it hadn't stopped him from falling hopelessly in love with her.

Stevi stood and gave him a hug.

She stopped at the door. "I'd say something sappy like call me if you ever need a friend, but it wouldn't be a good idea."

Davan understood perfectly. They had crossed the line of casual friendship, but not progressed into a committed relationship. Calling or seeing each other would only keep unrealistic expectations alive. "You're a wonderful person, Stevi. I wish you all the best."

She smiled, turned, and closed the door behind her.

Chapter 39

Jova loved the weather this time of year in Michigan. By late April the constant rains had subsided and the mild temperatures allowed her to dress in a fantastic leather suit she'd been itching to wear. The cinnamon-colored dress not only complemented her skin tone, it hugged her curves, accentuating her best features. The hem of the dress stopped just above her knees. A fabulous pair of designer sling backs drew attention to her calves. The outfit was completed with a matching leather jacket.

Jova stood in the bathroom mirror flat-ironing her hair to hang bone-straight down to her shoulders. Kay helped select the perfect jewelry.

"What are you and Hooper going to do while I'm out?"

Kay shrugged, holding a pair of earrings up to Jova's earlobe. "We'll probably catch a movie."

"You're welcome to come with me and Mario. We go to these celebrity dinners all the time. Usually, I end up sitting with people I have nothing in common with while he tries to schmooze new clients."

Kay moved behind Jova and held a necklace to her chest. "Why do you even bother to go out with him? Anyone can see your heart's not in it."

"He's a good friend. The parties are bothersome, but he always introduces me to people who can help with my business venture." She nodded her agreement with the selection of the necklace. "Listen to me, 'my business venture.' My mother would be so proud of me."

"I'm sure she would. Hooper and I are proud of you, too. We consider you a part of our family."

"Thank you." Jova turned and they embraced.

"Okay, don't make me cry." Kay went back to searching for earrings.

Hooper crossed the doorway, giving a wolf whistle.

"Stop flirting with Jova!" Kay yelled.

"Jova? I'm flirting with my wife."

Davan shaved away the two-day stubble on his chin. A few inches had been trimmed from his Afro earlier. He stepped into the shower, bracing his hands against the cold tile while the hot water pummeled him. He wrestled with any doubt he had about showing up at Jova's surprise party. Both Kay and Hooper had assured him it would be okay. They also told him her male "friend" would probably be there. He lathered his hair, reminding himself to stay cool. He had no beef with this man. His mission was greater than an arbitrary male friend.

He planned his every move while he soaped his body. As he rinsed, he rehearsed his words. Everything had to be perfect. If it didn't go well tonight, he'd probably never have an opportunity to see Jova again.

When Hooper had first told him about the surprise party, he had absolutely no intentions of showing up. Let Kay kick and scream. Let her call his mother and complain. He was not going to Jova's party without her personal invitation.

But as the days rolled by, his need for Jova thickened until taking in a deep breath became a struggle. He still loved her. He couldn't deny it. There was no way to circumvent his feelings. His disastrous relationship with Stevi proved it, and he had the suspicion no woman would ever satisfy his needs.

Jova had stepped into his life and ruined him for anyone else. He remembered their meeting while he toweled himself. One look and he'd been thrown for a loop. And then he'd gotten to know her. He'd sampled her kindness, watching her with Uncle David. He'd been witness to her loyalty when she'd supported him through Uncle David's death. He'd also seen her at her most vulnerable. He didn't agree with her decision to leave him, but he admired her strength in fighting for her salon.

Davan's confidence built as he slipped into his suit. Kay had told him to come casually dressed, but he wanted to make a lasting impression on Jova. Right after the barbershop, he'd driven downtown and bought a new suit. Knowing Jova's appreciation of fashions, he'd asked the salesman for the best Italian suit in the store. It was black with faint pinstripes; he'd admired the sensuous feel of the fabric beneath his fingers. He'd added a white shirt. The salesman chose the perfect black tie. Davan had been wary of the conflicting design woven through the fabric, but as he tied it around his neck, he discovered the salesman knew his job.

He tucked a white handkerchief into the breast pocket and checked the hang of the suit once more before slipping into his shoes. The salesman couldn't believe he'd been in Detroit a year and didn't own a pair of "gators." After much debate, Davan agreed to pay the hefty price, but refused to consider any color other than black.

"Here we go." Davan grabbed his keys on the way out the door, ready to get his woman back.

Mario flipped his cell phone closed and shoved it into his pocket. "I don't know what happened. We were supposed to meet in the lobby. I checked with the front desk. They don't know anything."

"Maybe we should call it a night." Jova touched his arm fondly. "You'll reschedule."

"Yeah, but it's strange." He held the lobby door open while she passed. "We could grab dinner and go back to my place."

Jova wagged her finger at him. She'd made it clear she didn't want to hang out at his place with other women in the picture. "Why don't we go back to my house and order pizza? Kay and Hooper are at the movies."

"You don't have to worry about me getting along with them, you know. It was awkward at first, finding out they were your ex-boyfriend's family, but they've been friendly enough."

Jova wouldn't expect anything less from Kay and Hooper. It'd been bristly at first, but once she'd assured them she and Mario were only friends, they'd accepted him. Kay kept a close eye on him when he came around, as if guarding her only daughter's virginity, but she was always polite. Still, Jova considered Mario's feelings. "Are you sure? We could call it a night and plan something for later."

"No. Your place is fine."

Less than an hour later, they stood on Jova's front porch.

"What's wrong?" Mario asked.

"The screen door is locked. It must have caught when Kay and Hooper left."

"Use the back door."

"Can't. Dead bolt and chain. I'll have to go through the side door off the kitchen. I don't like to use it because it opens up into the basement."

Mario followed her around to the side of the house. "Don't tell me you're one of those people afraid of basements."

"Afraid, no. Do they creep me out? Absolutely." Jova searched for the correct key, angling her body to catch the overhead light. She tried two keys before the door swung open.

"Do you want me to go in first?"

"Chivalry? I'm a new millennium woman." She smiled. "Just stay close until I turn on the lights."

Jova stepped inside with Mario close behind. He had closed the door before she found the light switch. She flipped it with the blunt tip of her finger, illuminating the basement.

"Surprise!"

The basement was packed with Jova's friends, new business associates, and past customers of the salon. Mario had even invited several key contacts he wanted her to meet. Including the couple they were supposed to be having dinner with at the hotel. The crowd spilt upstairs to the living room.

The food was catered. A DJ played a mixture of old and new, heavy on the Motown oldies. Balloons and streamers hung from the ceiling. A personalized banner congratulated Jova on her recent success.

"Were you in on this?" Jova hugged Lisa close.

"Kay did most of the work, but I helped. Candi and Josh are here too." She glanced over Jova's shoulder. "Mario is *something*."

"He's a good friend."

"He should be more than someone's friend."

"Jova," Kay called, "up front."

Jova cried when Kay gave her congratulatory speech. Jova thanked everyone for their support through her tears. She greeted everyone near the buffet table, the best place to be sure she didn't miss anyone. Afterward, the lights were dimmed and the music started. A song with a medium tempo began, and Mario dragged Jova to the center of the crowd.

"I can't believe you were in on this."

"Hanging out in California has made me a pretty good actor." He placed his hands lightly on her waist, careful to respect her space. "You have great friends."

She glanced over at Kay and Hooper, locked together in a heated embrace, moving much too slow for the tempo of the music. It would be nice to have such closeness one day . . . with Davan.

The music changed—a Motown oldie—and Mario pulled her closer. She had to stop fantasizing about Davan. He was in another relationship. She had pushed him away. This was her life now. With these people surrounding her in their love and support. She needed to start viewing things differently. Beginning with her relationship with Mario. She felt comfortable in his arms. Maybe she could parlay the comfort into a committed relationship.

"Excuse me."

Jova and Mario both turned, looking into Davan's fierce eyes.

"Excuse me," Davan repeated, "I'd like to dance with Jova."

Mario silently sized him up. "When we're finished."

"I'd like to dance with her now."

Mario released Jova, ready to do battle. She stopped him by firmly grasping his arm. "It's okay. Why don't you get a drink? I'll find you in a minute."

Mario engaged in a stare-down with Davan.

Lisa made her way through the crowd. "Jova, do you mind if I dance with Mario?" A subtle lifting of her eyelids asked for more than a dance.

"Not at all." Jova gave permission for Lisa to proceed. Lisa was a good friend. Their personalities would work well together. She should have thought of introducing them a long time ago.

Mario looked as if he might protest until Lisa fit his arms around her waist. Quickly, his attention changed focus.

Jova expected Davan to take her tentatively in his arms. Instead he held her possessively close. The press of their bodies warmed her with inappropriate emotions. The crowd melted away until she was alone with Davan, the hardness of his body pressing into her belly.

The amount she missed him multiplied tenfold as she inhaled his cologne. Her fingers rested on his shoulders, the soft fabric encouraging her to run her hands across his body. She fought the urge, retaining her dignity.

"Congratulations on everything you've accomplished."

The heat of his words brushed her ear. She swallowed hard, clearing her throat before she could speak. "Thank you," she choked out.

The music changed, but Davan did not release his hold on her. "I don't think I've ever seen you looking more beautiful." He pulled back to see her face. "Are you happy?"

She couldn't hold his obsidian gaze. "Things are going well."

He pulled her closer. "That's not what I asked you."

The last note of the song prompted Mario to reclaim Jova. Without addressing Davan, he took her hand and led her away. She nodded politely, unable to stay focused, as he introduced her to his business acquaintances. Her attention trailed off and she found herself searching the crowd for Davan. She didn't see him. Had he left the party? Was he off somewhere with Stevi? Jova had only seen her once, she wasn't sure she'd recognize her again. The thought of them being squirreled away together in her house was too much to handle.

Mario was getting ready to drag her off to meet another businessman.

"I need a minute," Jova told him.

"Why? Is something wrong?"

"No. It's a little crowded down here. I'm going to go outside and get some air."

"I'll come with you."

"No. I need a minute alone." She smiled, telling him everything. "Lisa's watching you."

His head swiveled.

"Maybe you should go talk to her." Jova made her way through the crowd, stopping for polite but brief conversation. She stepped outside and took in a deep breath of fresh air. Wondering about Davan and Stevi had almost triggered an anxiety attack.

"You walked out on me because you weren't ready for a relationship."

Jova swung around, startled when Davan stepped out from the darkness.

He joined her in the beam cast by the overhead light. His dark eyes blazed with unrestrained anger. "When you felt you were ready to start dating again, you don't come back to me. You start going out with the Italian Stallion."

"Mario is a friend."

"He had his hands on your waist. Hell, he almost called in the Mafia when I asked you to dance. Slick, expensive clothes—you went out and found the exact opposite of me."

"What's with the prejudiced remarks? Are you upset because Mario is Italian? Is that why you're yelling at me?"

He rubbed his hand over his chin, fighting to calm down. "I shouldn't have made those cracks. I don't care if he's black, white, or Italian. He shouldn't *be* in your life." The anger bubbled again. "You were going to call me, when?"

"I should go back inside."

Davan grabbed her arm. "Don't even think you're going back in there until we settle this."

"Settle what?"

"Settle us. You ran out on me without any reason. You wouldn't even discuss it with me. I've played by your rules for months. Tonight you're going to explain everything to me, and we're going to work this out."

"I'm not ready for this. I have a houseful of people inside, here to spend time with me. I can't do this now."

"When?"

"I don't know when."

"Then I'll decide." He looked away, thinking. "I

think now would be a great time. You don't want to do it here, fine. We'll go to my place."

"I'm the guest of honor. I'm not leaving."

He still had hold of her arm. "We can do this any way you want, but you're not going back inside until we talk."

"I—"

"No, Jova. No more excuses. Don't ask me to understand. Don't ask me to give you any more space. Look what you having space has done to us."

"I'm on a date."

"I see you're choosing the hard way." He bent, tossed her over his shoulder, and made his way to his truck.

Chapter 40

Jova performed all the way to Davan's apartment. That's what his mother called it when he acted exceptionally bratty as a kid. She'd say, "Davan *per-formed* today at the mall." He'd learned exactly what she meant today, the hard way. Twice, he had to jump out of his truck and chase her. Each time he threw her over his shoulder and hauled her back. The last time he'd gotten smart and secured her in the seat belt. And then he twisted his seat belt through hers for extra measure.

Jova was in rare angry-black-woman form. He couldn't quite understand why she was so mad at him. They were in love, and she up and left. He needed an explanation. It was probably the demanding an explanation part that had her screaming at him.

Davan pulled over to the curb a few blocks from his house. He started loosening his tie.

"What are you doing?" Jova asked. "Why are you stopping here?"

"Because," he answered through clenched teeth, "I can't stand one more second of your yelling." He could see she remembered the erotic game he'd taught her with his silk ties.

"So what are you going to do?" She eyed him warily.

"I'm going to make a gag out of my tie."

"You're going to gag me?" she asked incredulously. She crossed her arms over her chest in a show of defiance.

"If I have to." He held the tie up to her chin. "Can you stop yelling at me?"

She engaged him in a staring contest he had no trouble winning. She fell back against the seat. "Fine."

She used the silent treatment against him the remainder of the drive. Davan didn't know which was worse.

He kept a firm grip on her upper arm until they were inside his apartment. He locked the door, using the chain. Something he hadn't done since he moved in.

"Jova, I want to do this the easy way." He sounded calm and in control, but actually his stomach was a mass of jumping nerves.

She stood in the middle of the room, seething. "What are you going to do now? Tie me to the chair?"

He hadn't thought of that. He discarded the idea. Better to save it until they were playing love games. "Let's both calm down and treat each other like we have a history."

She stood frozen, probably considering her options. He hoped he hadn't left her many. Eventually, she opened her fists and took a seat on the sofa.

Davan sat next to her. "Let me start by saying I'm sorry. I practiced what I would say to you all day. I never considered you might not want to come back here with me. I bullied you, and I know you hate that. I'm sorry."

The anger lines marring her beautiful face faded. "So, you'll take me back home if I ask?"

"Whenever you want."

She started to say something, but pressed her lips together instead.

"I hope I say the right thing here, because I don't want you to leave. Not yet."

They sat in silence, both pondering how they'd gotten to this point.

It was Davan's show, so he began. "Jova, please explain to me why we aren't together."

Clearly, she'd expected a verbal attack. She picked at the hem of her leather dress while softening her temperament and formulating an answer. "Everything went wrong."

"You said you had to get your life together. Why would you have to leave me to do that? Was I smothering you?"

"No."

"Bullying you into doing things you didn't want to?"

"No, of course not."

"What, Jova? You wouldn't take my calls. You wouldn't see me. You didn't answer my notes. You left without any explanation. Tell me why you walked out of my life."

She struggled. Davan watched as she fought to keep the tears at bay. She was reliving the past months, trying to make sense of it all. Confusion flashed across her face, followed by sorrow and sadness.

"Jova?" he prodded.

"It all made sense at the time. Everything fell apart. I lost the fight for the salon."

"I know. I don't care."

"Herman was killed—because of me."

He reached for her, but pulled back, not having permission to touch her. "How is it your fault? I read the papers."

A tear fell. Jova turned, and wiped it away. Once she had her emotions under control she explained. "Herman came to me and begged me to help him. I was cold. I accused him of stealing my salon. I pushed him to help me get it back. I told him I wouldn't help him."

"Help him do what?"

"Raise the money for the bookie."

"Jova." He inched closer, but still did not touch her. "You couldn't save Herman. What were you going to do? Rob a bank? He'd already stolen Tresses & Locks from you. How many times were you going to pay his debts?" His hands ached to push the waterfall of hair away from her face, tuck it behind her ear, and place a kiss on her temple. "Listen to me. You're not responsible for what happened to Herman."

"If I had tried to get the money—"

"He would have paid the bookie, gambled again, and stolen something else from you. You have to know this."

She wanted to believe him. She needed permission to throw away the guilt.

"It's not your fault," Davan whispered. He chanced reaching out to her. He let his fingers glide through her hair, pushing it behind her ear. His knuckles grazed her face, sending a thrill through his body. "You know I wouldn't lie to you. It's not your fault."

Jova's head dropped. He gave her a minute before he pressed on. "You left me because you lost the salon and Herman died. What did this have to do with us?"

She tossed back her hair, ready to take responsibility for her decision. "I didn't want to drag you down. Your uncle had just died. You were running the garage. I didn't have enough to offer you."

"What do you think I want from you?"

Stunned, she blinked several times before answering. "I don't know."

"I want you to love me." His fingers went through the silk sheet of her hair. "I didn't fall in love with you because you owned a beauty salon."

Silence settled around them.

Davan tentatively asked the question keeping him up at night. "Once you settled the salon and got past Herman's death, why didn't you come back to me?" *Why Mario?* he wondered.

"I wanted to."

"But you didn't." His passion spilled over into his words. He backed off, so as not to scare her away.

"I saw you with Stevi. The day I ran into you—the dress and shoes, I bought those to impress you."

"And then you saw me with Stevi and didn't go through with it."

"I couldn't. I walked out. I knew I had no right to interfere if you'd found someone else. I shouldn't be here now."

"That's why you put up such a fight in the truck."

"Yes! Why open up old wounds? I don't want to hurt anyone else."

Davan's heated gaze traveled her body. He wanted to turn the clock back and correct his mistakes before they could tear them apart. "Jova, Stevi and I aren't seeing each other anymore."

He'd managed to stun her into silence again.

"Stevi is a good woman. I tried to replace you

with her. It didn't fit. She knew it. I knew it. She had the courage to do something about it."

"You're not seeing her?"

He shook his head. He cupped her chin in his palm. "No one can replace you in my life. I tried to push you away as easily as you pushed me away, but I couldn't do it. I was always comparing her to you. It just didn't fit."

The obvious question flickered in her eyes.

"I never slept with her." He tried to hide the embarrassment caused by male pride. Deciding this was the time to come clean, or risk losing Jova, he confessed. "I couldn't—*respond*—to her. No matter what she did, my body understood I belong to you."

Wisely, Jova didn't question him further.

"You thought Stevi and I were together, so you started seeing Mario."

Jova nodded.

"How serious are you about him?" Davan braced himself for the truth.

"We're friends. Only friends."

He waited for her to answer the obvious question.

"I've never been intimate with him."

Relieved, Davan contemplated his next move. "Where do we go from here?"

She didn't answer.

"Jova, I love you. Do you still love me?"

Bravely, she tossed her hair back and answered. "I love you, but—"

"I want to show you something." Davan took her hand and led her to his bedroom. When he turned on the lights, Jova clamped her hands over her mouth. He moved around behind her.

"This is all I have to offer you." He remained silent while she surveyed the scene on his bed. The black negligee was spread out on the side of the bed where she usually slept. The nylons and garters were neatly hanging over the headboard. The three infamous silk ties were lined up on his pillow. Atop Jova's pillow was a blue velvet box.

Davan placed his lips next to her ear. "I knew you were high maintenance and I was blue collar from the beginning. I don't care about you losing the salon if you don't mind me working in the garage. I'm looking into opening another location. If you'll stick with me, I'll be able to give you the life you deserve."

Jova was still frozen with her hands over her mouth.

"I want more nights of you wearing that gown. I want to come home, peel away the garters, and make love to you. Think of what else we can do with those ties."

Davan peeled her fingers away from her mouth. His hands cascaded down her arms, drinking up the softness of her skin. He gave her a gentle nudge toward the blue velvet box. His tongue caressed a line across the nape of her neck. She took a tentative step forward. He kissed her cheek, pressing his arousal into her from behind. He matched her steps, pushing her to the bed.

Jova slowly lifted the lid of the box.

"I want you to have my babies." His fingers danced on the curve of her belly.

She shivered.

"I want you to be my wife." He held her around the waist from behind.

Jova stared at the diamond engagement ring.

"I wish I could have bought you the biggest stone in the store."

"This is beautiful."

Davan turned her in the circle of his arms, his

hands cupping her bottom. He kissed her jaw, working down to her chin. "I don't know why we had to go this roundabout way to find each other." His fingers gathered the hem of her dress. "We're back where we started, and I still want to marry you."

The box pressed into Davan's chest.

Jova's voice trembled. "I love you."

"Will you marry me?"

She looked down at the box, then back up at him.

"Will you?"

"After everything I did wrong, you'd not only take me back, you'd marry me?"

Davan answered with a passionate kiss. His hungry caress hurried to relearn her body. He pushed the leather jacket off her arms. He lowered the zipper of her dress, shoving it down over her curves, leaving it in a pool on the floor.

He kissed her again, his hands grazing her breasts, but capturing her mound and resting there. "Promise me you won't run from me when you get scared."

Jova took in a sharp breath as his fingers probed past the dainty underwear.

"Promise." He held her in a death grip around her waist while another finger surged into her heat.

"I promise." Her knees buckled.

Davan pushed her back onto the bed, kneeling between her thighs. "Do you think I can make you happy?" He kissed her inner thigh.

Jova nodded.

The lick of his tongue followed another kiss. "Will you marry me?"

"Kiss me."

Davan dipped his head, kissing the place he knew

would be swollen and throbbing for him. Jova shuddered, a giggle escaping her. She hadn't expected him to kiss her there.

"Come here, Davan." She held her arms open wide, still holding the blue velvet box.

She didn't have to ask twice. He wrapped her in his embrace, kissing her with all the pent-up passion he'd saved for her return. His body, so unresponsive to another woman, sensed her presence and raged to reclaim her.

Jova's eyes were closed, her lips parted when he pulled out of the kiss.

"Wow!" they said together.

"Make love to me," Jova said.

"Answer me first. Will you marry me?"

She made him wait an agonizingly long moment. "Yes."

About the Author

Kimberley White is the author of many sensuous romance novels. She is a registered nurse pursuing her masters degree. She enjoys teaching writing courses and speaking at conferences. Ms. White loves to hear from her readers.

Contact her at:

P.O. Box 672

Novi, MI 48376

kwhite_writer@hotmail.com